TiM Te MARO
AND THE
SUBTERRANEAN
HEARTSiCK
BLUES

TiM TE MARO

AND THE SUBTERRANEAN HEARTSICK BLUES

H.S. VALLEY

Hardie Grant

BOOKS

Tim Te Maro and the Subterranean Heartsick Blues
first published in 2021 by
Hardie Grant Children's Publishing
Wurundjeri Country
Ground Floor, Building 1, 658 Church Street
Richmond, Victoria 3121, Australia
www.hardiegrantchildrenspublishing.com

A catalogue record for this
book is available from the
National Library of Australia

Text copyright © 2021 H.S. Valley
Illustration and design copyright © 2021 Hardie Grant
Children's Publishing
Cover design and illustration by Julia Murray
Typeset in Sabon LT Pro 10.5/17pt by Cannon Typesetting

Hardie Grant acknowledges the Traditional Owners of the country on
which we work, the Wurundjeri people of the Kulin nation and the
Gadigal people of the Eora nation, and recognises their continuing
connection to the land, waters and culture. We pay our respects to
their Elders past, present and emerging.

Printed in Australia by Griffin Press, part of Ovato, an Accredited
ISO AS/NZS 14001 Environmental Management System printer.

1 3 5 7 9 10 8 6 4 2

The paper this book is printed on is certified
against the Forest Stewardship Council®
Standards. Griffin Press holds FSC® chain of
custody certification SGSHK-COC-005088.
FSC® promotes environmentally responsible,
socially beneficial and economically viable
management of the world's forests.

Dedicated to my wives,
Corie, Elise and Q

CHAPTER 1

SUPALONELY

You'd think a place like Fox Glacier High School for the Magically Adept – which has taught magic for decades – might've found a way to *heat* its super-secret underground compound, or at least the sick bay. Especially since it's under a river of ice. The ceilings are low, the walls are thick, and there's an air-circulation system anyway – it could surely have been a *warm* air-circulation system. If not with magic, then with a solar-powered something; the glacier is pretty reflective. And cold. The sick bay *shouldn't* be cold. It's unhealthy.

This wet mess the nurse has put on my head isn't helping. And it smells. She's gone off somewhere, maybe to make a note in her ledger about *what's happened this time,*

Mr Te Maro? I bet she has a tally. To be fair, us Defensives are probably winning for the highest number of avoidable injuries. At least they're usually only to ourselves, and not to others – unlike the Minders.

Theirs isn't a bad Specialty – the things they study do a lot towards mental health care and law and stuff – it just seems to have attracted shitty people in my year. And one group in particular has been making the whole lot look bad lately. Last time I was in here it was because one of them had decided it would be hilarious to make me hallucinate that my custard was full of spiders. I'd ended up with a broken dessert bowl, a five-centimetre cut on my shin and no more custard. Come to think of it, the time before was their fault as well, and I have a scar from that, too.

I'm still thinking about it when their poster boy, Elliott Parker, walks in; I'm pretty sure he was the one who found out I don't like spiders. I feel my shoulders bunch up – he doesn't look injured enough to be here legitimately. He's still in full uniform, even though it's after eight. He probably likes the way the blue stripe brings out his eyes or something. Or maybe the contrast of dark, scholarly grey and his floofy blond hair sparks joy. Who the hell knows with him.

He stares at me for a second as I lie on the only occupied bed, and I wonder if the nurse's proximity is enough to keep him from being a dickhead. Though, I *would* like to practise some of my new Advanced Defence magic on him. Disembowelling, perhaps. Maybe that's technically Advanced *Offensive* magic. Maybe I don't care.

'Te Maro,' he says.

'Dickhead,' I reply.

He's looking at me like my being here is suspicious, which is ridiculous since I'm obviously actually injured and he's just swanning around like he normally does. Plus, the other Tim got expelled last year so he could probably afford to use my first name now. Maybe he's still sulking over it. They were friends, or whatever passes for it when you're low-key evil.

'I see whoever did *that* didn't manage to knock some manners into you,' he says, eyes flicking up to my hairline.

'Would you prefer *Sir* Dickhead?'

The nurse comes out to find out what the noise is about. 'What brings you here, Mr Parker?'

He shoots me another look, wary this time. 'Things I'd rather remained private,' he says, and blushes, his pale skin giving him away. Mine never betrays me like that. Thanks for the melanin, Dad. Shame you buggered off somewhere and left me and Mum alone.

The nurse sighs and beckons Elliott into her office. I close my eyes and try out a hearing-enhancement spell, even though I don't have a mea to help me focus my magic. I stop breathing so I can hear better, but it doesn't seem to work; they're too quiet. I bet he's got an STI.

I compile a list of horrific things he might be infected with while I wait for whatever the nurse has put on my head to do its thing. It was a tiny cut, but apparently 'the real danger with exploding snow globes is the unsanitary water inside them' and she's worried about infection. Nobody sees the irony in my girlfriend (ex-girlfriend, now) owning a snowglobe when we live under a glacier. Or that it's *that* particular piece of crap which landed me here and not the river of actual ice a couple of metres above our heads. Or that it's her fault I'm here; she's a Healer and they're meant to be the good guys.

Elliott slinks out of the office a few minutes later, looking shifty. Maybe I was right. Maybe the imagined 'Parker's Pustules' are real and his crotch truly is encrusted with weeping purple sores. The nurse wanders off to rummage in a cabinet. Elliott comes closer and with the way he's looking at me, I wonder if the carving around my neck will be enough to protect me. Perhaps a full-body condom would be more appropriate, considering what might be wrong with him.

'So,' he says, and sits on the bed next to mine like we don't dislike each other all of a sudden.

'What do you want?' I reply, making sure to keep the hostility out of my voice lest he think I'm trying to start something when I'm actually just trying to stay still enough that the goop on my head doesn't slide into my eyes. It's been hard enough lying here with my hair in a bun, the hair tie's digging into my head and it hurts.

'I want to know if you're going to do anything about the situation we're in.'

I fight the urge to turn and get a better look at his expression. My eyes hurt from glaring sideways. 'What situation?'

He sighs. 'The one where my ex-friend has run off with your ex-girlfriend.'

I was under the impression she'd run off alone after I exploded a snow globe all over her homework, but hell, when is life ever simple or painless or not a complete and utter mess? 'Since when?'

'By the looks of your manuka poultice, about half an hour ago,' he says – accurately, which is a bit suspect. 'I must say, I didn't expect she'd have clobbered you.'

'She didn't.' I want to scowl at him, but I have to keep my eyebrows still. 'How do you know all this?'

'Blake – roommate, ex-friend – very kindly informed me that our own arrangement was at its natural end and he was taking up with your girlfriend.' He sighs again and, in the blur of my periphery, I see his gaze drop to his hands, clenched in his lap. 'Apparently they're in love.'

'They're in *love?*'

Thinking back, less than an hour ago, Lizzie *was* trying to explain something when I really wanted her to stop talking altogether – everything she said felt like another brick on my chest, and I lost control of my magic for a second. Picture frames rattled on the wall, a magazine shivered and slid off her bed and then one lone snow globe shattered outwards, glass flying and its tiny penguin inhabitant suddenly exposed for the first time in its life. It's been years since I lost my shit like that – I would've been a kid the last time, maybe twelve, my magic just starting to manifest. Now I guess the unbridled joy of Dad walking

5

out and my girlfriend leaving me is enough to render me a hazard.

'*Tim*,' Lizzie had said, her voice so concerned, so careful … I saw a thousand patronising words in her eyes. *Look at you, losing control. What's wrong with you? Get yourself together, Tim. Cheer up. Get a haircut.* What if what she really wanted to say was, *And by the way, I'm in love with Blake Hutton.*

'Apparently.'

I don't have enough faith in her right now to not believe Elliott, and my eyes start to prickle so I focus on him instead. It's better than crying. 'What arrangement?' I ask, even though I think I know what him and Blake might've been up to. Maybe marvelling at the fact we might have certain interests in common will distract me from my misery for a second. Then again, maybe I'm projecting.

'Have a little imagination, Te Maro, won't you?' he says with a tilt of his head and a smirk that's interrupted by the nurse. Right, not imagining that, then.

'You're lucky I found this, we were almost cleared out last month,' the nurse says, appearing at the foot of the bed with a tiny glass jar in her hand. 'After – well. You know.'

'Sadly, yes, I do know,' Elliott says with a pained look and I have a sneaking suspicion that my imaginings regarding his crotch problems might not be completely unfounded.

'How are you, there, Mr Te Maro? All absorbed?' she asks. I don't know how she expects me to know – I can't see it.

'I think he needs another minute, Ma'am. I'll stay with him,' Elliott says, and I twitch with the urge to gape openly at him. We've never been friendly, to put it mildly. To be less mild, I hate him and I'm a hundred per cent sure the feeling's mutual, so I don't know why he's offering to keep an eye on me.

But the nurse just says, 'Very well, give me a shout,' and disappears again into her office. Maybe she's adding to the Minder ledger this time: *another case of purple sex-boils, order more ointment.* I'm mildly horrified she's leaving me alone with him.

'So, Te Maro. My ex, your ex, both terrible people – what say we mess with them a bit?'

There it is. I could've guessed this would be a mostly selfish endeavour. Dick.

I wave my hand at the little jar in his hand and take a punt. 'Perhaps a bit less *messing around* with them would've done you some good?'

'Or in your case, perhaps a bit more?' He cocks his head to the side and I want to belt him, sod the bloody goop on my head. Let it fall in my eyes, I can fight blind.

'I hate you,' is all I say though, focusing on the low, grey concrete ceiling and the dusty metallic criss-cross of ducting.

'That's irrelevant and not remotely surprising,' he huffs. 'The question is, will you stand for your little girlfriend running off with a big, bad, nasty Minder?'

'That's stereotyping,' I say, even though I usually call

them something far worse. Usually when they're trying to practise on us without permission.

'Just because it's a stereotype, doesn't mean it's not true,' he says, pointedly adjusting the expensive-looking silver ring on his middle finger. 'He really is quite big.'

My mind goes places with that statement, and it takes me a second to realise Elliott might be causing it, trying to push my thoughts towards jealousy. I don't know who decided it was a good idea to teach a bunch of teenagers how to manipulate people's brains. I wish they hadn't. Even though I kind of want to be able to do it too. Becoming a Minder was, admittedly, my second choice, since it's the second most versatile Specialty, but I'd rather have quit school altogether than commit to hanging out with any of that lot on purpose. Elliott's not even the worst of them. At least there are three less Minders now after last year's fiasco and the Principal's zero-tolerance attitude towards people actively setting the school on fire. I like to think she doesn't like Minders either, anymore.

'I don't care,' I say, forcing my mind clear. 'You said you wanted to know if I was going to do anything about it – I'm not. What else do you want?'

'Well, you know ... proper central heating, not living underground for most of the year, a flat white that doesn't make me cry a little inside, an entire tray of apple crumble, maybe my parents sending me a postcard once in a while ...' His voice trails off like maybe he didn't mean to say that, and I wonder if he has anyone else to talk to. Only him and

Manaia are left from his little group of Aucklanders after last year, and I doubt the other Minders are any good to confide in. I wouldn't tell them shit. 'Anyway. I'll settle for petty revenge.'

'I'm not dating you to piss off Blake, if that's what you're getting at.'

'Interesting that's where your brain went.'

'Pretend that wasn't your aim.'

'My aim is to annoy him, not confuse him.'

'So what do you need me for?'

He huffs out a breath. 'I want you to help me come up with something so they *both* suffer, since if it wasn't for Elizabeth I'd still have a perfectly good *friend* with perfectly good *benefits*, and absolutely no need to talk to you.'

'Sucks to be you. Sadly, I don't feel super motivated to help you with anything, since I don't actually like you.'

'What do you want, then?' He tosses his hands up in the air. 'Do you want me to pay you?'

'I don't need your money, Elliott.'

'OK, one, from the state of that hoodie, I think you probably do. But, two, if you're this stubborn, then surely you at least want to get your own back on that heartless praying mantis of a woman who just left you for someone else? Apparently without even telling you that was the case.' He stands to leave. 'I'll think of something and let you know.'

'I wish you wouldn't.'

'And yet, I will. Spend a night alone with your thoughts

9

and see how you feel.' He comes to stand over me. It's unnerving; I still don't trust him.

'He looks about ready, Nurse Hiatt,' he calls out, then, 'ta-ta.'

'Whatever.'

Twat. Unimaginable, unspeakable twat. Who the hell says 'ta-ta'? Is he an eighty-year-old woman? Why would I ever help him? What could he ever do for me? And why, after four and a half years, can he not just leave me alone?

CHAPTER 2

SITTING INSIDE MY HEAD

A night alone with my thoughts is not what I need. Especially when some bastard has drawn attention to the fact that that's what I'm having. And that I'm no longer *having* anything else. Nothing even resembling sex, a sex dream, or even a spirited wank, since every time I think of getting myself off, I think one of two things: either Lizzie saying, 'It just wasn't very good for either of us, was it?' or Elliott saying, 'Interesting that's where your brain went.' The overwhelming curiosity about being with another guy – the itch that's been growing in the back of my throat for months now – is far too much to deal with this late at night. I'm going to look wrecked tomorrow and Lizzie will think I've been up all night crying over her.

I need to not be awake. I have some of Silvia's sleep drops in with my toiletries for emergencies. Is this an emergency? Trying not to look pathetic in front of your newly ex-girlfriend? Let's say it is. I fish them out, drop a half dose on my tongue and screw the lid back on. I can hear Sam in the back of my head saying it's a waste of resources, and Silv will probably give me a lecture tomorrow about overusing them, but I know she wouldn't have made them for me if they were actually dangerous. She knows me too well. That happens when you grow up with someone.

When my parents got jobs here – about a year after hers and Sam's – Silvia's mum was the Deputy Principal and Sam's dad was teaching English. It was the beginning of summer and I'd had to leave my old primary school in Wellington to move to a frozen nowhere with no friends. Except those two were here, and it ended up not being as bad as ten-year-old me expected. The images of those first months come back with the smell of hot apple and damp stone and the sense that time was completely irrelevant; a constant drifting cycle of food and books and board games. We were too young for proper classes but stuck here regardless, always together, exploring all the old tunnels and consuming our weight in Milo and scones in between random sessions of homeschooling. It feels so vivid I wonder if Silvia's potion is messing with me or if I'm getting extra nostalgic at the ripe old age of seventeen. I fall asleep and dream of being ten. I wake up feeling a hundred and drag myself through the cold concrete corridors to breakfast.

'Te Maro, you look like shit, don't you sleep?'

Elliott is looming over me, putting my Weet-Bix in shadow. It's gone from a boring, slightly sad bowl of mush to fully grim and depressing mush. I've barely sat down and he's in my face, ruining my breakfast. What a cock-widget.

'What do you want, Elliott?'

'Acquiescence. I have an idea, and it's excellent.' He grins, a hell of a difference from his usual smirk, and it's startlingly evil-seeming this early in the morning.

'Go on, then,' I sigh, since I expect telling him to piss off will be less effective than half-ignoring him.

'We're starting our new topic in Life Skills today.'

Ugh. Yes. Life Skills. Our collective punishment for surviving adolescence. A class dedicated to teaching us how to act like normal adults, supported by hundreds of painfully upbeat video presentations from the International Magical Education Council. They claim to promote 'cooperation and emotional wellbeing among the young magical adept in a potentially hostile outside world', but my being would be a lot weller without it. They've even managed to knit it together with the national curriculum so that we can't claim it's completely useless. The only helpful thing they've taught us all year, though, is how to deal with family and friends who didn't win the genetic lottery and end up with magic, and that wasn't even for credits. Currently, we're in the middle of 'Family, Relationships and Reproduction', so –

Shit. He's right. He's actually right.

I swear into my Weet-Bix, because it's not loud enough in my head.

'Yes,' he agrees, and I look up to glare at him just as Lizzie walks past in her prim little uniform and her too-short skirt which I used to love and now just wonder if it contributed to Blake taking a fancy and stealing my girlfriend. She gives me a weird look. Elliott doesn't notice. 'We're starting our new assignment today, Te Maro, for which you and I are currently partnered with our former significant others. But I have a plan.'

I can see where this is going. I don't like it. Swapping so I'm partnered with Elliott is only microscopically less bad than having to work with Liz.

'If I bring it up in class, it has the potential to pan out one of two ways,' he goes on. 'Either the exes try the old, "but can't we still be friends?" and persist in our current configuration, leading to horrifyingly awkward and painful bullshit, or Ms Fake Enthusiasm tries to exert dominance over the class again and, even if Blake and Elizabeth want to change partners as well, we won't be allowed.'

'Hang on,' I say, because that's not what I expected. 'If you think there's nothing we can do, why are you talking to me?' *Why must you make my life any less enjoyable than it already is? Oh right, because you're you, and you can't seem to help it.*

'Because I didn't say there was nothing we could do, I just don't think it'll work if *I* do it. It needs to come from you, since you're … you. Half the teachers' favourite student and so *perfect* you've probably never broken a rule before.' He huffs. 'And because your mum works here so they might listen to you.'

There it is. The blatant abuse of power. That said … if ever there was a time … 'So you want me to demand we swap partners, and you and I work together?'

'People don't say no to you, Te Maro,' he says. (Not true. I just got dumped. That's a resounding 'no' in all caps. With glitter.) 'They all know you, they all like you. You have that wholesome, do-good image that teachers favour, and that athletic, slightly dangerous edge that girls like, with your long hair and your school-sanctioned weapons training. You're the perfect, windswept, biracial poster child for international relations and the –'

'Do people ever get a *chance* to say no to you?' I interrupt because, honestly, I just want him to shut up.

'Constantly,' he sighs and, because my life only knows how to get worse, he sits down opposite me. 'Please don't be one of them. I have to share a room with the guy who just left me for a *girl*, and if you do nothing I also have to do this horrific assignment with him and I might actually die.'

This sounds a lot like begging. It also sounds like he thinks I'll give a shit if he dies. 'That would make breakfast a lot more peaceful.'

'I will buy you an actual unicorn, Te Maro. Please.'

'I don't think that would be remotely useful to me, being that I'm not a virgin or a girl.'

'A stylist, then? A haircut? A new wardrobe that's not

15

entirely from Kmart? One nice, possum-merino jumper that really brings out the flecks of hazel in your eyes? Maybe a handbag to carry around all your issues? A dog? Am I getting close?'

'You're getting annoying.'

'Look me in the eye and tell me you don't want to throw them in the deep end. That you don't want their new-found *love* tested to its absolute limits with this stupid assignment. This sort of thing ruins relationships, which we're obviously immune to, but *they* aren't. They will *suffer* for *four whole weeks* and *we* will have our revenge.'

He has a point.

'Fine, I'll do it. Now, piss off.' I turn away from his smug smile and go back to my sad mountain of Weet-Bix as he gets to his feet.

'You probably won't regret this,' he says.

'I am literally filled with confidence.' And what would almost pass as curiosity if it were any other person, but it's Elliott so it must be horror.

He walks away and I'm left alone to wonder what I've got myself in for. Can it be worse than doing the assignment with my ex-girlfriend at the same time that I'm trying to get over her? Maybe. But I have until first period to come up with a better idea and, if not … well. Microscopic improvements might be the best I can hope for.

The others all arrive then, but Silvia and Sam are late for reasons I expect are both highly frowned upon in a school setting and quite depressing for the freshly dumped. Silvia's glossy black bun looks a little worse for wear, and while Sam's number one never shows any signs of bedhead, there's a loose, lanky sort of swagger in his step that usually means one thing. They sit opposite me and the mischievous twinkle in Silvia's dark eyes is confirmation – worst best friends ever. Way to rub it in.

I lean across the table and quietly ask if they knew about the apparently sexual nature of Elliott and Blake's relationship, but it turns out they had no idea either.

'I can't imagine the two of them together at all,' Silvia says, her brow furrowing. 'Elliott is so … I don't know, fussy about everything? And Blake is an idiot. The other day he asked our Classics teacher if Ancient Greece is still a country.'

I'm not expecting her to say something funny and I choke on my last sip of tea. It goes up my nose and I splutter for a second before it dribbles down the back of my throat. Sam monitors whether I'm in any real danger of dying over breakfast and manages not to find my minor peril too amusing. Well, he doesn't laugh, anyway. The day might've started out badly, but at least I have my friends to support me in my time of need.

Kinda depressing, though, that my time of need is as dire as choking while simultaneously trying to figure out if I'd rather be shackled to my ex-girlfriend or a guy I really don't like. Even if he apparently likes guys too – which, to be honest, if it had been anyone else, might've made it a much easier choice. Sadly, he's a dick.

Sam, Silvia and I don't have much more of a chance to talk through my two equally crap options before the bell goes for Life Skills, so I get almost zero help trying to think of a better way to avoid my ex-girlfriend than by using Elliott Parker. I can't even beg them to get involved with the partner swapping because they don't think much of Lizzie now either, and they think even less of Elliott. (That's what happens when you get your entire year group banned from the squash courts in Year 9 – everyone hates you and your stupid friends. Forever.) Plus, Silvia and Sam are good together and I don't want to ruin it for them. Same goes for Matt and Ana, even if they're just mates, and I'm pretty sure Nikau likes Hana and I don't want to get in the way of that. He's a good guy and she seems like she'd appreciate him properly. And I only have six friends so there's no-one else to ask.

There's a weird hum of anticipation in the air once we get to class. No-one else seems to notice, so I guess Mum's extra lessons over our weekly cups of tea are helping my perception. She teaches Empathy as part of the Healing Specialty (as well as teaching Soft Materials Technology), so I can both sew on a button and be anxious for other people as well as myself. Mum showed me a lot of little things when I was a kid, so magic wasn't as much of a foreign concept to me as it was to some of the others. It's probably why Elliott thinks I'm everyone's favourite student – I'm just easier to teach because of her. Easier than him, anyway. Partly because he's a pain in the arse and partly because his family isn't from around here.

All the magic in New Zealand and the Pacific Islands is really similar – mostly it's to do with the relationship between people and nature and stuff – so school caters for that, even though some of us have inherited from other cultures as well. And since whatever European branch Elliott sprouted off was obviously going to be different, he was always doomed to struggle a bit. I mean, everyone struggled at first, but I'm also pretty sure his magic is inherited from his grandmother, so he didn't even grow up with it in the house. You can tell the people who haven't quite got their head around magic existing, even once they get here; it messes with their abilities. He's not bad at magic now, though, as far as I've seen. And he gets good marks in all the normal subjects, so hopefully he'll actually be useful for this stupid assignment.

Lizzie comes in and sits across from me; the table isn't nearly wide enough to keep her at a comfortable distance. She presumably sat there on purpose, expecting us to have to work together. I wonder if she considered that yesterday, when she told me we were 'probably better off' not trying to make it work?

Of course, Elliott decides to sit right next to me like the two of them are competing to see who can make me the most uncomfortable. On the upside, they both seem pretty unsettled as well; Lizzie gives Elliott a shitty look and he doesn't take his eyes off his phone to even acknowledge us. It's a nice change from him talking, I suppose.

Ms Van Mill clears her throat and takes the roll, and Elliott nudges me in the side. I'm almost brave enough to say something about swapping partners, except she immediately starts explaining actual important things, like how many credits the assignment's worth and how long we have to complete the theory work, and I have to wonder, again, if I'm making the right choice. It's four weeks of an already awkward topic and I'd have to spend a decent chunk of it engaging in fake family fun-time with Elliott as well. I see everyone's eyes rolling or glazing over as she segues into the beauty of procreation and emotional readiness and how this assignment will test our ability to work as a team. She ends on the value of knowing the responsibility of child-bearing as young adults, right as she waves her hand at the large, sealed wooden crate in front of her and there's a shriek of nails dragging themselves out of thick plywood.

I feel Elliott's elbow in my side again. It's now or never, I guess.

'Welcome to day one of your lives as temporary par–'

'Excuse me, Ms Van Mill?' I ask, trying to look like the wholesome suck-up Elliott thinks I am. 'I'd like to switch partners.'

Lizzie's head turns towards me so fast I half expect it to fall off; she's like a russet whirlwind. Down the table, Blake looks confused for a second, then hopeful, then annoyed. Probably because he doesn't know that his ex already agreed to this – instigated it, in fact. Blake can have my ex-girlfriend all to himself and see, right away, whether they've got what it takes as a couple. Trial by fire. Worse ... by *fake baby assignment*. My loathing of this ridiculous project wanes slightly. I almost smile as I imagine what he might be in for. Sleepless nights, nappy changes and feeding schedules. Suffer, dickwicket.

Van Mill steps over to our table, one hand coming to rest on her hip. 'Mr Te Maro, we allocated partners last week.'

I pitch my voice low and lean towards her like I'm sharing something personal. 'I feel really uncomfortable about having a fake baby with my ex-girlfriend, Miss. I'll happily do it with anyone in this room that isn't Lizzie.'

'I can see why it might not be ideal, but –' She pauses, probably working out how to convince me to shut up and not make her life difficult. I can't help feeling a little bit guilty, but seeing Lizzie again has made me desperate to avoid her.

'Please, Miss. Considering I now have to grow up without a father, and after being dumped last night, I just –' I blink a few times for effect, like I might cry in her classroom. 'I just don't think I'd cope, and I don't want to worry my mother.'

'Oh, well, I see,' she says. 'Well. It would depend on another pair being willing to swap with you ...'

'What d'you reckon, Elliott,' I say as I turn to him for the first time all lesson. 'Wanna have a fake baby with me?'

He smirks. Raises an eyebrow. Looks for a second like he's going to refuse, then says, 'Sounds brilliant, Te Maro. Blake, Elizabeth, is that OK with you?' His voice lowers, turning sharp. 'Do you want to raise a baby together?'

'Very funny,' Blake starts, his grin broad but unsure. 'But come on, I –'

'We'll do it,' Lizzie cuts him off, eyes blazing hazel fire. Her competitive edge comes in handy again. Shame it's against me this time. Kind of wonderful that Blake isn't enjoying himself, though. Dick.

'Very well,' Van Mill agrees, falsely chirpy and all business again. 'It seems we're all in agreement. Though do remember that the baby is designed to react to the emotional state of the parents, just like a normal human child. So negative emotions will have a detrimental effect.' She looks at each of us in turn, not sure what she's seeing unfold. 'Your grades will be determined partly by the theory work and partly by how happy your baby is at the end of each of the four weeks.'

I answer for all of us, but mostly for myself. 'Then avoiding exes is definitely a good move.'

CHAPTER 3

ANCHOR ME

I can't say I've spent the last four-and-a-half years making charitable judgements about Elliott, but even if I had, I wouldn't have expected him to be so nice to our fake child. Since the second Van Mill handed him a tiny blanket and placed the thing in his outstretched arms, which was about an hour ago, he's become a doting, affectionate and protective ... parent. To an *egg*.

'Is this fathering thing going to be difficult for you, considering your own dad abandoned you last year?' he asks. 'It's been, what, four months? Five?'

Of course, then he goes and says stuff like that.

'I wasn't *abandoned*,' I sigh. I wish we could've done this assignment without all the talking, but Elliott seems intent on ruining the low hum of nothingness in the corridors as we head to morning tea. Van Mill held us back, of course, to 'make sure we were making the right decision for the babies'. Not a minute had passed before Blake was arguing with Elliott and Lizzie was glaring daggers at me like this was all my fault. Like I broke up with myself. Van Mill got sick of it pretty quickly and shooed us out into the corridor. I don't know where Liz and Blake went and I don't care.

'Fine, you were intentionally *left*,' Elliott huffs. 'Let's call it neglected.' He's fussing with the baby blanket and his words come out strangely gentle.

'Bringing up your children to be completely unlikeable is also neglect,' I say, but not so loud that he'll hear me.

'What?'

'Nothing.'

He gives me a long look, arms wrapped around the soft bundle of our new charge: a rugby-ball-sized, blanky-swaddled golden egg. I'm pretty sure he's not going to punch me. That said, I'm pretty sure the egg is metal, so maybe he'll hit me with it and the assignment will be over before it's begun.

'We don't have time to work on your enunciation, Te Maro, but how about I let you name our baby and, with my help, you can at least break the cycle of neglect and be a good egg-daddy to your new daughter.'

'Sure,' I deadpan. 'Thanks.' I do end up smiling, completely against my will, because 'egg-daddy' sounds perverse and bloody bizarre in his wanky, uptight accent. 'You wanna do the middle name?'

'That's very decent of you,' he says.

This is how our daughter ends up being called Meggan Christobelle Parker-Te Maro. Her surname is hyphenated alphabetically, of course.

This is going to be ridiculous.

And, of course, I haven't even started to think about how I might tell Mum about it. When I get to her rooms that afternoon, she's already shucked off her work clothes in favour of trackpants and a woolly jumper that's so massive on her it must've been Dad's. She's standing at the kitchen counter next to two steaming mugs of tea, picking crostulas out of a Tupperware container that looks older than I am. I don't know what she's doing to get pastry snacks out of the Croatian lady in the office, but I'm not going to pry because they're delicious and I don't want them to stop. Mum can't bake for shit so I know they're not trading food. Maybe the office lady is really into Mum's quilted oven mitts.

She meets me in the middle of the small living area for a hug, and a discreet, motherly assessment of my physical wellbeing. I must pass muster because she releases me and sets about bringing the tea over to the couch. Either that or she's noticed my life is a catastrophic mess and the tea is suddenly an urgent necessity. I take a seat at one end of the couch and she settles at the other, mug in hand.

'Allie Van Mill says you're partnered with Elliott Parker

for the baby project.' She looks at me, eyebrows carefully level, expression diplomatically neutral. 'How'd that come about?'

Right, so she knows something's up.

'Lizzie and I broke up,' I say, and her neutrality goes out the window. Which, I suppose, is a weird metaphor to use when there are no windows down here, only endless grey walls.

'*Oh.*' She puts her tea down on the side table and scoots toward me, arms wrapping around my shoulders until my own tea is at risk of spilling. 'Mitten, baby, come here.'

'I'm here, Mum,' I say, and let her hug me.

'Why didn't you tell me?'

'It was only yesterday. I hadn't seen you. I'm fine.'

'What happened?'

'She –' I'm not going to tell my mum the real reason we broke up, no-one needs that much information about their own son's sex life, but I can't think of anything else she might believe. Lizzie and I were together for almost a year, Mum knew her, and she knows me, of course. Mostly. I grab onto the only truth that isn't about me. 'She left me for Blake Hutton. Apparently they're in love.'

'Blake's an idiot. Silly girl.' She releases me and runs a hand over my hair. 'You're more handsome than him, anyway. I bet their egg-baby isn't cute at all.'

I want to roll my eyes but it's actually pretty funny by Heather Te Maro standards, so I let myself smile. 'Thanks, Mum.'

'Do you need me to do anything? I know you and Elliott don't get on. If you don't want to work with him, I can talk to Allie.'

'No,' I shake my head. 'It's fine. He's been OK so far.'

'If you're sure.' She keeps staring at me, pale green eyes narrowed, like *she's* not sure. 'Would you rather have dinner here tonight? I can go get us a couple of plates, bring them back? We can watch X-*Files* or something?'

'Nah, I don't want to make a big deal of it. Thanks, though.'

Mum still lives in the same rooms I grew up in, that her and Dad used to share up until a few months ago, and that all of us shared until I moved into the student accommodation when I was thirteen. It's not a big suite or anything, but it's far nicer than the dorms or the dining hall. My parents brought a lot of what was in our old house with us, so it still felt like home – until Dad left. Mum always says they took jobs here because it was good for all of us as a family, but I have a sneaky feeling that I benefitted the most.

'You know you're always welcome back here. You still have a key?'

'Yeah.'

She gets up and goes into the kitchenette area, rummaging in the chaos drawer for a moment before getting sick of it and summoning whatever she's looking for straight into her hand. I can't wait to be good enough to use basic magic without a mea or verbal incantation.

She comes back with a key – a chunky school one with DO NOT COPY stamped on it and a small dolphin-shaped bottle opener on the ring. 'For your dad's rooms, if you need it.' She folds it into my palm. 'I haven't been in there since he left so I don't know what's still there, but if you need some time alone, the space is yours. I know you probably don't get much chance to be by yourself.'

I don't know what to say. I knew Dad had his separate rooms, obviously, but I didn't think about them still just … being there. Empty. Maybe I assumed the new History teacher had taken them over, maybe I just didn't want to think about him after he left us. It's probably good Mum didn't mention it until now, because four-and-a-half months ago, when he walked out, I'd probably have been mad enough at him to go in and trash the place. Now, it kinda just makes me sad. But if I'm sad anyway then going to visit what's left of him might not be too bad. Maybe if I focus on missing him, it'll fill up the empty space Lizzie's left behind. Remind me what my priorities are.

'Thanks,' I tell Mum, and open my hand. It's weird to think about how a two-dollar dolphin key ring can make my heart drop into my socks, but I guess that's the peril of loving people who leave you; you develop disproportionate responses to inanimate objects they once touched.

'Finish your tea,' she says. 'I'm going to make us a proper drink. I reckon you probably deserve it.' She's up again and into the cupboards, pulling out glasses and a can of –

'You have Coke?'

'I do,' she says, wrapping her hand around it to make it cold. Condensation appears and there's a slight crackle, and I once again lament how long it takes to get so good that it's effortless.

'Where did you get it?'

I came here looking for snacks a couple of days ago and found nothing but popcorn. Certainly not Coke – the school refuses to get a vending machine because they've decided it's unhealthy, so if I crave it during the week, I look for it here. And if she'd had it, I'd have found it.

'I went into town this morning,' she says. 'I needed to post something.'

'Town' is over-selling it. The minuscule micro-sub-hamlet of Fox Glacier isn't that much more than the Four Square, which, other than being a convenience store, is also a post office and lotto shop. Other than that, there's a pub, a couple of small hotels, a few cafes and a petrol station. Anything you need outside of the absolute basics means a two-and-a-half-hour trip into Greymouth, where there's at least The Warehouse. Still. It's a change from spending all day in a concrete box hidden underground and only being allowed out on weekends.

'You didn't take me.'

'You were in class. I had a free period and one of the cars was available.'

'Mean,' I pout, but she knows I'm kidding.

Despite the limited number of licensed drivers here, and the limited attractions of town, the booking sheet for the school's vehicles is usually full, and if it isn't, something's usually broken down to make up for it. If students want to go to the shops, we're at the mercy of Sam's grandad, Murray, to drive us along in the shuttle to the tunnel's pedestrian exit in the woods. Then we have to walk the rest of the way into town (and back again). There's an old-fashioned phone mounted to the concrete wall where he drops us so we can call him to pick us up after. There's no secret, magically hidden highway on-ramp for us unlicensed plebs, and no CCTV to keep an eye on comings and goings. There's only Murray and his shitty van and his eidetic memory of who's in and who's out. Sometimes I think it'd be nice if everyone knew about magic, and we could have a normal school with fields and trees and stuff. And I could walk to the shops and back in less than three hours without having to navigate secret tunnels or muddy tracks through the bush.

'Next time I'll pull you out of class, Mitten, I promise.' Mum hands me a glass of Coke with ... I sniff it ... rum. Nice. Not a lot of rum, but she's my mother – she's not meant to know what I can handle when it comes to alcohol. That was Dad's area.

I guess that makes two things she doesn't know: my patrilineal affection for spirits and what went wrong with Lizzie. Which is how it should be. We chat about safe topics while we sip and wait for dinner: school stuff, and uni applications, and who I might want to apprentice with in Wellington. She knows a few people but there'll be more at the hui in a couple of months, when we've got our exam results back. I bring up the fact that I could just go into the military and be put straight into the apprenticeship program there. She frowns at that and reminds me (again) of Uncle Taika getting left in the mountains on a training exercise, and all but forbids it. He's not even her brother, he's Dad's, but she acts like it's a personal affront and that the military are all horrible bastards. I'll probably end up going into the police – Dad used to be a cop, and Defence obviously suits it quite well – but I wouldn't mind something a bit more outdoorsy. Physical combat training and protective magic is cool, but a part of me wants to be dropped in the bush and left to fend for myself. It'd be nice and quiet.

Mum and I walk to dinner together, shoulder to shoulder, and our conversation drifts back to the egg-babies. She tells me stories about when I was born and her and Dad had no idea what they were doing with me, but they managed because they worked as a team. I get the feeling she's worried that I'll fail my Life Skills assignment because Elliott and I don't like each other and maybe I won't be sensible enough to just deal with it.

I also get the feeling she hasn't forgotten the time Elliott glued a picture of Nicholas Cage to the ceiling when she was first teaching us levitation in Year 9. He and I had a bit of a fight about it, because Mum had been really pleased with how she'd decorated the classroom, and he'd ruined it, so I'd felt the need to punch him. We both ended up with detention and Nicholas Cage ended up staying exactly where he was as a reminder for me to stay calm and let her deal with things. I expect she's worried we'll regress and start acting like thirteen-year-olds again, like the situation had been about me and Elliott specifically and not the fact I was awash with fighty hormones and a bit of a mummy's boy. So it's kind of excellent when Elliott meets us at the door of the dining hall and completely proves her wrong. He gives Mum a polite hello, and then gives me a quick and strangely thorough rundown of his last hour alone with our new egg-child. When he's done, he passes Meggan to me, supporting her underneath like we were taught, before rushing off to the loo. I hold her close and she burbles contentedly.

'He seems to have matured slightly,' Mum says.

'Perhaps we both have,' I say, and look pointedly at her as I rearrange Meggan's blanky. 'I'm eighteen in a few months.'

'Don't, Mitten, you're making me feel old. Go get your dinner.' She ruffles my bun and nudges me towards the doors. 'And we need to get your hair cut. Weekend.'

'No,' I say, for what might be the hundredth time. She never lets up.

'Yes, I'll drive you.'

'No, you won't.' I head for my table, and call back over my shoulder, 'Love you.'

She makes a scissor motion with her fingers and carries on to the staff tables in the corner.

'Your mum trying to make you cut off your man-bun again?' Silvia asks. 'Can I do it?'

'No,' I give her a look; they're as bad as each other, her and Mum. I'm surrounded by women trying to ruin my life (or at least my hair).

Sam senses the argument and heads us off with a comment about how we're being graded on the egg-babies. It gets involved enough that other people join in, and my personal grooming is forgotten. The conversation dies off when the servery opens, but by the time we're heading back to the senior student lounge it's picked up again. Silvia decides the whole school should be updated every morning over the tannoy and Matt is making a predictions spreadsheet on his phone. I reckon we're about five minutes away from an illegal betting ring that uses Skittles for currency, which sounds about right for our friends. At least it's safer than the last one we did – no-one has to run full tilt into a pitch-black tunnel this time, so we might manage to stay out of the sick bay. Like I said, Defensives and avoidable injuries. Silvia, as an Alchemist, was obviously too smart to join in. Sam's a Philosopher, but he has the heart of a Defensive, and Matt's just a liability in all regards. The tunnel runs had been fun despite the bruising.

Lorraine, the senior-dorm supervisor, suggests a family movie to fill up the hours before bed and a large group of us pile in front of the TV to watch *Charlie and the Chocolate Factory*, since it's the only movie anyone can think of with eggs in it and someone decided our children needed to be exposed to positive representation in media. It's odd, people mostly stick to their own small groups in the evenings, but most of the Year 13s are together tonight. I get wedged between Sam and Elliott on a two-seater, and while it's not weird to be squashed up next to Sam, it's definitely far closer than I ever expected to be to Elliott without punching him again. This assignment is already changing things, and I don't know how I feel about it.

CHAPTER 4

EVERYTHING IS GOOD FOR YOU IF IT DOESN'T KILL YOU

The first 'night's watch' is decided by coin toss and I lose. Fortunately, so does Sam, so we'll be together in our hapless attempts to settle our new egg-daughters. Mine and Elliott's is back to making her weirdly authentic burbling sound and I'm super glad it's the only realistic thing about her. She seems like a weird mixture of mechanical and magical and about what you'd expect from something designed in Norway. I'm glad they went for something whimsical instead of fully anthropomorphic; I was dreading nappies.

Silvia has lectured us on a bunch of baby stuff but she still looks worried. She almost follows us as we pad away from the student lounge and off down the boys' corridor to our shared room, warm bundles of fake egg-daughter clutched to our chests. Elliott looks dubious rather than worried, but he can shove it up his arse, because it's a magic egg, not his heir.

Mine and Sam's room is the same as all the other senior doubles, hidden away in the southern corner of the school's west wing, far from the junior dorms and the weird smell of socks, body spray, and new magic. We have the middle room along the corridor, so we're the same distance from the shared bathroom at one end and the modestly sized, drably decorated student lounge at the other. They're weird bedrooms though, wide from left to right but sort of ... shallow. Either side of the door is exactly the right size to fit a queen-sized bed pushed into the corner, which is a nice nod to our senior status, but there's not much remaining floorspace because of that. There aren't even bedside tables – not that we need anywhere to put lamps or alarm clocks, since everyone can conjure their own light and phones are a thing, even if cell reception down here isn't. At least the wi-fi is good.

Other than the beds, there's a large, shared wardrobe, a set of drawers, and one small table that serves as a desk. (There used to be a chair, but then they taught us how to superheat things, so now there's not.) It's like the rooms were built for one-and-a-half people. And also weirdos who don't mind having the head of their bed right by the door. I lasted two nights before I picked up all my bedding and started sleeping with my head at the foot. Sam didn't even last one. He's more superstitious than I am.

When we walk in, we see that two tiny purple cots have appeared, one by each bed, just the right height to be level with the mattresses. It's impossible not to notice, because the already-narrow space between the beds is now only *half* the size of the doorway and even less user-friendly than before. There's a soft cushion in each cot, but it's not shaped to the curve of an egg and I immediately worry that Meggan's gonna roll off onto the floor and die if I forget to latch the gate thingies. I don't need our chances of doing well in the assignment to be ruined before even one day has passed. I roll up a couple of clean T-shirts and wedge the egg in place. Safe. She makes a soft cooing sound. Sam's one farts. We laugh as silently as we can and fall into bed feeling pretty smug, relaxed, and with no idea we're going to be awake again in two hours.

'Rough night, Te Maro?' Elliott asks as he walks in late for breakfast. 'Was our daughter too much for you to handle?' He smirks as he slides easily into the seat opposite me at my usual table and holds out his arms, expectant.

I hand the egg over, gladly, and finally get to pour myself a drink now that I don't have to be worried about spilling it on her head.

'It's loud,' I say. 'It's loud a lot. Approximately every two to three hours.'

I take a sip of my tea and it's lukewarm. Yuck. I pull my pencil case out of my bag, then the pouch that has all my mea in it, looking for something that reminds me of heat. I skip over a blue marble that's good for water but not right for tea, and a charred piece of what used to be our desk chair – it's obviously good for fire, but impractical if I don't want to accidentally set the table alight.

'Maybe your company isn't very relaxing,' Elliott says, poking shamelessly at the pouch, his manicured fingernails and shiny silver-and-onyx ring making my cheap little trinkets look a bit sad.

Everyone's mea are different, usually, with some obvious overlaps, and they can say a lot about you. Sam's are mostly hand-me-downs from his dad and granddad – cool old bits of machinery and polished carvings. Ana's are weird; a lot of them are scraps of paper with book quotes on them. I bet Elliott's are all expensive tat – he's probably above the standard aluminium can tab people use for cooling things down.

'I look forward to hearing about how relaxing Meggan finds your company tomorrow morning,' I say, and glare at him for a second before I realise how much extra effort that takes. I need caffeine.

I find my melted Lego brick tucked in the corner of the pouch and hold it in my left hand, wrapping my right around the cup. I close my eyes to focus, since Elliott is bouncing Meggan on his knee and it's distracting. I whisper the incantation and push my magic into the tea, willing it to be warmer. The cup tingles and starts to feel hot under my fingers and I pull my magic back before it boils over.

'We'll be fine, won't we, Meggan?' Elliott says to the egg, and his unabashed dedication to acting like it's a real child surprises me.

He got in trouble a fair bit when he got here; he and his little troupe of self-important city kids seemed hellbent on making sure everyone knew they considered this place below them. Understandably, their passive-aggressive dramatics about the cold and the decor and the lack of frappes and phone signal didn't win them any popularity contests. In hindsight I guess he's always been a theatrical shit and it's a shame he put all that effort into making people hate him.

'Do you want anything to eat?' I ask, because I've handed the egg-baby over before he could fix himself anything and I definitely don't want her back for at least an hour. I run a trained eye over what's left on the table between us. 'Bacon and egg roll?'

'OK.' He gives me a weird look. 'Thank you.'

It's at some point while trying to decide if Elliott's the sort of person who prefers moist, juicy bacon or dry, crispy bacon that I realise I'm making one of my childhood nemeses a sandwich and I marvel at the unending weirdness of my life. 'Sauce?' I ask, sighing.

'Aioli, if you don't mind.'

'Not tomato?'

'Tomato sauce is for children and truck drivers,' he says. Twat.

'I've seen you eat lasagne,' I counter. 'That has tomato sauce in it.'

'That's – Te Maro, really, were you born on a public bus? Do you have no idea about anything?'

'I know what tomatoes are.'

'The sauce in lasagne is called *Napoletana*. Not "tomato sauce". Should you be touching my breakfast if you don't know anything about food?'

'I know what Napoletana *is*, I just didn't know it had a wanky Italian name. And I can make a rather good one, if the need arises. Luckily your breakfast doesn't need it, since I'd be inclined to give it to you dry.'

'You'd give it to me dry?' He raises his eyebrow with a smirk, and in my slow and unslept state I can't figure out why, and I don't care. If he's trying to make a joke, then I'll take some pleasure in not reacting to it.

'I hate you,' I say instead, but without the venom it needs to mean anything. It comes out sounding as though I'm completely OK with it, and maybe I am. I guess, if I think about it, it's simmered down to a nice easy sort of dislike this year, now that his dear friends Tim Holt (who ruined my name), Cooper (who ruined my school jumper in Year 10), and Kane (who ruined everything in a one-metre radius) have all been expelled.

'Not in front of our daughter, Te Maro, she'll be scarred for life if she has to listen to her fathers fight,' he scolds as I

40

go to the next table to get the aioli. He's still frowning at me when I hand him his roll a minute later. Doesn't say thank you. Dick. Dunno what I expected.

'We need to fill out the parenting diary Van Mill gave us.' I take a sip of my tea. It's the perfect temperature. 'Should we do it now?'

'I'm *eating*. We've got Stats first; we can do it in class. Mr Russell won't mind so long as we get his work done first.'

I moan in utter horror. I wish it were possible to do four classes a day of just magic stuff. Unfortunately, for some reason the school expects us to get a normal education as well, so we have to simultaneously work towards our International Certificate of Magical Proficiency *and* National Certificate of Educational Achievement. 'Did you have to remind me? How has magic not found a way to do maths for us yet?' I take a large, reckless bite of my roll.

'They have. It's called a calculator, Te Maro; this is what I mean by *neglected*. You don't have basic things.' He smiles at me when I glare at him. 'Fortunately, you seem to have some natural ability with making me breakfast; you've got the meat to bun to condiment ratio nearly perfect.'

Meggan makes a gurgly sound and Elliott bounces her a little on his knee again, smiling serenely down at her golden dome where it pokes out of the blanket. If I didn't know better – that he's still a selfish, spoilt wanker – I'd swear he was enjoying this whole parenting thing.

'I'm so glad I could serve you to your liking.'

'I said *nearly* perfect, you could still do with some practice.'

'Get bent.'

'Already am,' he says, like it's no big deal, and the cold self-doubt that lives in my gut does its little dance of *Tim, you're a coward.* 'Well, half-bent. As is Blake, obviously, if you're into that. Maybe you could steal him off your girlfriend and exact your revenge that way?'

I won't let him bait me so easily into revealing anything unnecessarily. Not because he's going to judge, just because I don't have the spoons to even think about *all that* right now. However, I still, completely accidentally, picture myself successfully seducing Blake, even though I'd rather punch him. He's tall, and annoyingly good-looking, and if he'd never stolen my girlfriend I might've even forgiven him for being a Minder. I've seen him shirtless once, and if I hadn't already had a strong feeling I was not entirely straight, that would've been all the evidence I needed.

'No thanks,' I deadpan. 'He's not really my type.'

'Lucky you,' Elliott says, and that's it – he just sits there talking to the egg and eating his breakfast while I spiral into my thoughts.

Thoughts about Blake, and Lizzie, and then the familiar list of all the people I thought I just really liked as friends, until everything clicked into place last year. I don't know how long Elliott's known he was into guys, or what form his self-discovery took, but he's making it look easy when it really isn't. Or it hasn't been, for me.

Which seems really quite unfair. But hey, maybe this assignment won't be completely useless. Maybe I'll find out whatever Elliott's secret is and at least one part of my life will start to make sense.

CHAPTER 5

PACIFIER

That night, my head barely touches the pillow and I'm asleep. The day dissolves into memory and my subconscious plays with the remains. I dream, and Sam is there, somewhere in the background, laughing and patting me on the back. Playing a saxophone. Play-fighting. Shoving me. Shaking me awake.

'Tim, th'f'ck,' he moans, too close, above me in the dark. 'Dickhead's here. Tell him to bugger off, w' you?'

'Who?' I ask, too soon, as Elliott's voice comes through the door, a wailing egg-baby quickly drowning him out. 'Oh,' I say.

'Hurry up and get rid of him,' Sam grumbles, falling back into bed and wrapping himself in his blankets again.

I find my piece of smoky quartz and fill the room with

dim silver light. The floor is like ice. My pyjamas are old and a bit ratty and the button's missing on the fly. *Ugh.* I want a jumper, but I want Elliott gone more.

The handle squeaks as it turns. 'What?' I hiss at him through the gap, reluctant to open the door fully.

'She won't stop crying and I've tried everything,' he hisses back. 'What did you do last night?' He says it like I'm hiding some sort of secret from him, like there's a fake-egg-baby conspiracy and he's at the losing end of it. He looks tired and harassed and, worse, determined. I let him in. Sam's going to kill me.

The second they're inside, though, the wailing stops. The egg coos, then burbles. We stand there, frozen, waiting. The chill is creeping up my ankles.

'Well. I guess that did it,' Elliott whispers. He looks awkward and relieved, and he nods a thank you and turns to go. By the time he's touching the doorknob, she's started to grizzle. The door opens and she lets out a *wahh* and he closes it again. She coos.

I curse internally; despite the lack of sleep and the slow brain activity, her preferences are clear. Fine. I'll be night-dad and he can be day-dad. He can get one of those front-pack baby carrier things to cart her around in and I'll get a new best friend, because Sam might really, actually kill me. Or move out, or possibly both.

Elliott pads back across the floor towards me and I notice that he's barefoot and unjumpered as well. He must be freezing. Desperate.

'Leave her with me,' I say, trying to sound like I'm OK with it. Like it's not a giant pain in the arse. Like he doesn't owe me *so much*.

He doesn't even say anything, just nods dumbly and places her in the little purple crib. 'I like what you did there, with the cushioning stuff. It's good.' He nods again. 'Right,' he says, and turns, padding back across the floor.

He has his hand on the door again when she squawks, cries, then whimpers, and I hope like hell he's not just going to leave me like this as she winds up for a big one.

He doesn't, and once he's back beside me, she falls silent again. And my brain is like peanut butter and I'm confused and I'm cold and I'm tired and as the seconds tick by and she still doesn't cry, I manage to think about what that means. And then the real dread sets in.

'She hates us,' I say.

'She hates us individually. Apparently standing next to each other in the freezing darkness of your shitty bedroom, she's OK with us.'

'Our baby is a sadist,' I agree.

'All babies are sadists,' comes a muffled voice from Sam's bed, filtered through layers of down and wool. 'Get over it.'

It's too cold. I pull the covers back and get into bed again, leaving Elliott standing in the middle of the room. I fluff my pillows and avoid looking at him. Maybe if I draw it out long enough, Meggan will fall asleep and he'll never have to get between my sheets.

'What are you doing?' he hisses at me eventually. Apparently he hasn't caught on.

'I'm going back to sleep,' I whisper. 'What are you doing? You can't stand there all night.' I punctuate my words with a hopefully-not-too-inviting sweep of the covers on the other side of the bed, next to the wall. I need him to stay if she's going to sleep. If *I'm* going to sleep. I suddenly feel very thankful for whoever decided the seniors deserved bigger beds. If we were still in singles I don't think I'd have it in me to share with anyone, let alone him.

'You want me to get in your bed?'

'I want her to not cry and for all of us to be asleep. I don't mind if you'd rather share with Sam.'

A muffled expletive and a middle finger emerges from the pile on the other side of the room.

'Looks like that's not an option. Get in.'

'Te Maro ...'

'Just –' I sigh. I'm too tired for this. 'Please, Elliott, don't make this harder than it needs to be.'

I feel the bed dip, down by my knee, and the rustle of fabric. 'Heaven forbid getting in bed with you makes things hard,' he whispers. A shift of weight to the other side and the bounce of a body settling. The covers twitch away from me as he wriggles under them.

'Don't make it weird,' I tell him, and roll away towards Meggan's cot and my best friend and the part of my life that isn't entirely mental.

I breathe deep and focus on happy memories like the

school counsellor taught me, replaying summers with my cousins in Wellington: driving aimlessly around the city, a few beers, movies, games around the kitchen table. Christmases with Nana, pudding and custard, cups of tea at just the right temperature … I'm almost calm when he moves behind me and something brushes my arse and my happy thoughts go elsewhere.

Excellent. Now I want to have a wank and I can't because Elliott's in my bed. Thinking about it too hard doesn't help, because it reminds me of the last time I was in a bed with someone, and then I'm sad because it was Lizzie and she's left me.

That said, if she ever found out I was sharing a bed with someone else so soon, even innocently, it'd probably wipe that fake sympathy off her face. Maybe this wasn't the worst idea. Maybe I should Instagram it. Ha.

I go back to thoughts of food and family and presents and summer and ignore the boy in my bed. Nothing else touches me 'til morning.

'You three look a little worse for wear,' Silvia says at breakfast, connections sparking behind her eyes as she ponders how we've all managed to appear in the dining hall at exactly the same time. Three men and an egg-baby. Definitely a situation, definitely not comedy.

'Someone brought us a baby in the middle of the night and then decided to sleep over,' Sam grumbles.

'Elliott, presumably?'

'No, it was someone else that neither of us have a baby with, a very strange man,' I say, and I know I'm being that sarcastic, dickish version of myself but I can't bring myself to give even half a shit because I just spent the night in bed with my nemesis and it's a genuine surprise I didn't wake up with daggers in my back. 'Elliott is merely a coincidence.'

'Pardon me, I'm *merely* nothing.'

'Sorry, my bad, Elliott is nothing.'

He takes a breath to mansplain himself, catches the fact (admirably) that I'm taking the piss and sits down instead, holding his hands out for the devil-egg. I hand it over and start making us a breakfast we can't spill on a baby, because that's apparently what I do now.

Silvia hands their egg over to Sam and watches me out of the corner of her eye while she explains what she's decided to name it. Something about a swan and Greek mythology that I absolutely cannot follow this early in the morning. Sam nods distractedly at her as the rest of our friends drift in. They're just as quiet and tired-looking as I am, and equally puzzled at Elliott's appearance at our table. No-one says anything, though, which is a relief. Meggan and 'Leda' and the other eggs burble happily at each other, all their families together, sharing breakfast. A week ago I would've declared Elliott sitting with us to be a weird nightmare – cheese-induced, crazy even to think about it. Now I have to live with the fact that the first time I shared a bed with a half-decent-looking guy it was him, Sam was there as well, and I didn't even get off. And tonight, that damn egg is hideously likely to perform the same cursed charade. Which means sharing a bed with Elliott is something I'll just have to get used to. And the worst thing is, it doesn't bother me nearly as much as it should.

CHAPTER 6

JESUS I WAS EVIL

The next morning isn't much different. I wake again to a sense of being cheated by life and the dubious pleasure of seeing Elliott lying on his back, tenting my winter-weight duvet. It's almost impressive, but only if I think about it, and I'm not going to do that before coffee. Tea isn't going to cut it anymore.

Sam disappeared sometime in the night when Leda wouldn't settle, and I can take a guess he and Silvia dealt with that together. I've no idea how he circumvented the cameras in the girls' corridor, but it's not like I have a girlfriend to visit anymore, so who cares?

He and Silvia show up to breakfast hand-in-hand looking slightly more in love than normal, which suggests more than just baby care. If their shameless PDA wasn't enough to confirm it, Silvia's roommate looking positively livid certainly does. Manaia's a friend of Elliott's, and is sitting over at his usual table, intermittently glaring at Silvia and reading the paper. I wonder if any of that glaring is for Elliott and the fact he's abandoned her for Meggan. I look away before she catches me and focus on our breakfast.

Elliott holds the baby, I wrap sausages in a soft bread roll, adding, apparently, 'just the right amount of mustard', and we go through the whole thing again: taking the baby to classes, juggling her and my bag, books and laptop. Ruling a straight line becomes impossible. We pass her back and forth so much she grizzles all the way through Food Tech. It gets to the point where I start designing makeshift papooses in my head, while Elliott takes over chopping all of the vegetables under the dubious eye of an apparently baby-phobic Mrs Graham. She disapproves of 'such an interfering sort of assignment' that 'distracts you from the importance of your academic studies'. I act extra-parental to rile her up because it's not like we had a choice about whether to do the damn thing or not. It's care for the egg or miss out on four whole NCEA credits, and no-one wants the shame of failing Life Skills, even if it does mean writing a daily journal about a fake egg. It's better than answering endless workbook questions about actual human babies.

Elliott gives me a weird look when I mention acting enthusiastically parental, looking up from the wok with his eyebrow cocked and an air of mild disgust. I'm leaning next to him with my back against the bench to shield Meggan from any potential splattering. He's already insisted it isn't necessary because he 'doesn't splatter, thank you very much', but I don't want to be the reason we don't 'demonstrate daily care routines for a vulnerable individual', because I have a feeling he'd never let it go. I step in closer as he tosses the cup of frozen corn kernels in, so that we're side to side, touching. I whisper how maybe talking about playdates with Leda or something might piss Graham off a bit, if he fancies having some fun at her expense? It's not something I'd normally want to do; maybe Mum was right and he brings out the worst in me.

'How is having to look after your friends' egg as well as Meggan,' he hisses in my ear, 'going to inconvenience our Food Tech teacher?'

'We don't have to *do it* –' I take a breath, pretending I didn't phrase it like that when I'm pressed up against his side. He's warm and he smells like expensive cologne and I'm an *idiot*, obviously, but at least that's a nice, normal feeling I can use to ground myself. 'It's just that she's being a bit of a dick about the eggs, and it's unfair. If anyone was going to be a dickhead about this whole thing, I would've thought it would be you.'

He stops stirring and gapes at me. 'When have I ever been a dickhead to you specifically? Name one time.'

One time? Really?

'You guys were all shits from the day you arrived. You got us banned from the squash courts in the first month and then spent every weekend after that complaining there was nothing to do.'

'That was *not* my fault.' He scowls at me.

'You seemed to think it was pretty funny at the time.'

'I was thirteen, it was the first time I'd been away from home, and I didn't know anyone. Manaia was the first person to talk to me, so I stuck with her.' He throws in our sliced courgette and gives the wok a particularly violent flick to mix it in. 'Cooper, Kane and Tim were a bit much sometimes, but at least they didn't treat me like I should be ashamed of being from Auckland. You guys have no idea how insular you are.'

'How could we have been insular when no-one else knew anyone either?'

Elliott looks to the ceiling like I'm being unbelievably dense, which is something Lizzie used to do when I was about to get something explained to me in great detail.

'Every time someone asked where I was from,' he starts, 'and I said Auckland, they made this *face*. Like "oh, one of you lot". We didn't get included in anything social and people laughed at us when we got homesick or cold or confused about something. Like our feelings were less valid because we'd grown up in a big city. Like we weren't real New Zealanders.' He looks at me like I might have been one of those people, and honestly, I might've been and just never considered it a sin.

I don't even remember talking to him directly back then – there's just a vague, nebulous feeling of hostility. It's not a great feeling, knowing he remembers it vividly and I don't. It's making me question all of my own thirteen-year-old-boy behaviour, which is surprisingly uncomfortable. Especially considering he's probably right – he was someone I hadn't really thought of as a whole person at the time. A caricature of perceived evil, and evil didn't have feelings. The rivalry of Auckland vs. Everyone Else is ingrained, I guess. Doesn't mean it's right, though, and it's starting to sound pretty one-sided, the more he goes on.

'And it's ridiculous to blame a child for where they grew up or what their parents are like, or what bloody continent their magic came from, because they don't exactly get a *choice* in that. Just like I didn't get a choice in whether I came to this bloody school after the International Magical Education Council showed up at my door and told my parents I'd be in terrible danger if I didn't fulfill my *legacy*. So, yes, when I had to decide between one bunch of people who were fun and liked me, and a horde of other kids who hated me for no good reason, it wasn't much of a choice.'

I shift my weight, but the discomfort stays. 'That's fair enough.'

'How very gracious of you,' he says, and gives the wok another hard flick.

'I'm sorry people were mean,' I say, and it sounds so weird I almost wonder if he's using his Minder powers to make me feel sorry for him. I have the presence of mind not to mention it, though; there's no harm in making peace with him, even if I'm being manipulated into it. 'I concede you had valid reasons for being a dickhead.'

He sighs. 'I'll have you know, I wasn't a dick to everyone.'

'Well,' I say, trying to think of a way to lighten the mood. 'Apparently that's all you were to Blake.'

Elliott smirks at my innuendo – against his will, if the twisted resolution to his expression is anything to go by.

'So kind of you to draw attention to my failed relationship, Te Maro, when I've so generously refrained from mentioning your own. Why did Lizzie decide to dump you, do you know?'

Because I couldn't keep her happy? Because I'm undergoing some sort of uncontrollable fascination with dick? Because I'm bored of girls in general? Because there's this whole other part of me I know about but haven't had a chance to explore? Yeah, nah. That can stay a secret.

'Well, Blake's better-looking than me,' I say. 'Probably smarter, richer and, if your whining and constant bitterness about losing him is anything to go by, he's obviously good at *other things* as well.' Other things that I'm definitely not thinking about.

'You're right,' Elliott says. 'He is better-looking than you, and he has money, but he is *definitely* not smarter. And I dare say I would have to do more research before confirming whether he was better than you at *other things*.' He raises an eyebrow at me and his gaze skitters down my front as he looks away again.

'What?' I ask, feeling like I've lost control of the

conversation. He tosses a handful of cashews into the wok like he didn't just blatantly check me out.

'I might know Blake,' he says, 'but I don't know you. Assumption of your skill level would be pointless. And if I'm honest, probably not very flattering.'

'You probably assume I'm crap at stuff all the time. Have you ever been right?'

'Touché,' he says, and lowers his eyes to the flame, adjusting it slightly. 'From now on I will assume you to be utterly marvellous in bed and thereabouts, so long as you have your two best friends to explain what goes where. Apparently you had some trouble with that. And apparently they don't.'

One: I'm going to kill Lizzie for whatever she's been saying. Two: 'I'll be honest, neither of them have been nearly as helpful as Silvia's brother. He really knew where to put it.'

Elliott drops the spatula. I keep my eyes on Meggan, the peak of her dome shining among the folds of woollen blanket. We're near enough that I feel him turn away to pick the spatula up off the floor and throw it in the sink. Then he's close in my periphery, breath on my neck. I can't look at him.

Why on Earth did I bring up Mareko now? Is it so important that I defend my honour, that I tell Elliott that yes, I might have let this one girl down, but maybe it was because she was a girl at a time when I wanted a boy, and not because I'm useless to everyone? There's no need for him to know that we share certain ... interests. Telling him seems

57

a bit blunt, suggestive. And I'm not suggesting anything. Just because we shared a bed for the last couple of nights, and he just looked at me like *that*.

Unless … What if he's annoyed that I didn't tell him and still let him share my bed? Is that not cool? Does he feel violated? He was straight up about his own feelings towards guys, and probably assumed I was only into girls and was, therefore, safe. But now what? Is he going to think I lured him there, lied to him, took advantage of him while he slept?

But all he says is, 'Do you mean the former head boy? The one who got Dux Litterarum *and* Dux Artium in the same year?'

'Yeah.' I keep my eyes on Meggan.

'Well. You don't do things by halves, do you, Te Maro?'

Elliott sounds almost awed and it comes as such a surprise that I make the mistake of turning my head, and we're suddenly only a hand's-breadth apart and my eyes are already devouring him, ready as they were to decode his expression so I could make sense of his words. His grey eyes look almost blue in this light and I can feel him – heat and breath and the soft prickle of his magic touching me. He's … not unattractive.

The rest of the lesson is slightly awkward, heavy, and we forget all about provoking Graham in an effort to get our meal plated, photographed, eaten and evaluated. It obviously still weirds her out, though, that Elliott and I have partnered up for the egg-baby assignment, and swapped partners to work together in her class as well. She used to be really nice to me, but she's been shooting us odd looks all lesson. Maybe she's a massive homophobe. Maybe we have an even better reason to mess with her than just her disapproval of the assignment. I make a mental note to mention it to Elliott later, and do my share of the cleaning up while Meggan's other fake dad bounces her 'til she giggles.

He doesn't look at me again.

CHAPTER 7

MISTY FREQUENCIES

That night, over dinner, Silvia asks me if 'the whole family' is going to be in my room again, presumably meaning Elliott, Meggan and I. She sounds wistful, and Sam, on her other side, stops moving to listen, gravy jug poised over his potatoes. He's almost a foot taller than her, so his curious expression is in full view.

'I don't know. Maybe not, if she's happy with just one of us. Why?'

'I was just thinking it's kinda nice, you three being together as a unit,' Silvia says. 'You know. Practising. For, like, life. Sharing the work equally, letting Meggan know she has two parents who are there for her ...'

'Yeah, it's a shame they didn't have us share a room

with our assignment partners,' I say with a smirk, because I'm pretty sure that's what she's angling for. She just has to convince Sam to break the school rules. 'Would've been more realistic.'

'I agree.' She nods sagely. 'I mean, taking turns having the baby overnight is completely idealistic. More likely, you'd both be up in the night and both end up sleep-deprived, which would obviously affect your schoolwork. What do you think, Sam?'

'It's not exactly scientific,' he says, 'or helpful, you know – sociopolitically.'

Sam was raised by his dad and grandpa, so he's already noted that girls are being given the brunt of the care work, and a lot of the guys are coasting on their goodwill. He's also a Philosopher, which means he's been overthinking it since he noticed. I didn't have the marks for Philosophy, but it's too booky and boring and I didn't want to do it anyway. Sam revels in it. He likes psychology and sociology and the winding history of how magic came to be, and then came to be so rare. (He thinks it was fifty-fifty on colonisation leading to diluted bloodlines and then atrophy from hiding it for so long.) He's not afraid of having an opinion. He goes off now, lamenting the inequity of labour and how the egg assignment, in its current incarnation, is reaffirming archaic gender roles.

Silvia helpfully points out that the only girl in the class who isn't overworked is Manaia, who 'accidentally' dropped her egg-daughter (Ebony Dark'ness Dementia

Ravenway III) on the concrete floor this morning and is declaring it a feminist action, since she, Manaia, deserves to sleep.

'She probably won't want you and Leda in with her tonight then, will she?' Sam says. 'Come stay with us. Tim won't mind.'

I *don't* mind, but only because I'd much prefer I wasn't the only one with a bed-guest, and if both me and Elliott are there, there's no chance they'll be getting up to something I don't want to see. Or there better not be. When Sam and Silvia got together, we agreed on some ground rules, all of which basically equate to 'don't make Tim regret giving you his blessing'.

'Sure, we can have a playdate after dinner,' I say, my eyes flicking over to the staff tables to see Graham stuffing her face with potato, gravy dripping onto her chin. Gross.

Silvia starts planning a tactical evasion of the school rules with Sam, her brown eyes all wide and excited, and I make a mental note that she owes me one. Big time.

Over at the Minders' table, Elliott is doing his best to eat thick slices of roast beef with just his fork, Meggan on his lap. I look down at my almost empty plate. Should I go over there and help him cut his meat? Is that weird? I make a list in my head of reasons I shouldn't do it, not least of which is the fact it'll look super weird and I'm entirely not ready to deal with the scrutiny that will come with that just for the sake of being helpful. I try not to watch him struggle as I finish my own food, unfettered by the need to hold Meggan as well as hold cutlery. Maybe I could just go over there and take her, give him some time to eat properly. That's less weird. I'll do that. I stand up.

'Where're you going? There's apple crumble tonight.' Silvia sounds aghast at the thought I might miss out.

'My turn with Meggan,' I say, and try to walk casually, like Elliott and I had planned this.

I've never gone over to him before, he's always come to us, and I'm not convinced I'll be welcome. At least his other Minder friends probably know I'm partnered with him for this assignment; we made enough of a spectacle of ourselves in class. Maybe they've forgotten, though. Maybe it'll look like I've come to start a fight. I should've worn my tinfoil hat.

Manaia is sitting opposite Elliott at one end of the table; a group of guys are sitting at the other end. There's a subtle divide between them, a matter of only a few inches and some body language. I wouldn't have noticed from the other side of the room, or before our conversation in Food Tech. I guess he really does only have one friend left. The thought makes me feel sad for him, and it's ... weird. I imagine having only Silvia and, as much as I adore her, I'd miss the boys and the banter and the comforting solidarity of a pack. I wonder what Manaia is like, how close they are, whether her and Elliott ever had a similar relationship to him and Blake. They don't look like a couple, but I've heard rumours. Does he even like girls? Does she? Neither of them have openly dated anyone at school.

Manaia's pretty solidly built, bigger than him but shorter, with long, wavy dark hair pulled up into a thick, messy bun. She has freckles, which are pretty cute, but I feel like if I said that to her she might punch me and call me a misogynist. Silvia has a decent respect for her. They've only been roomed together this year, but there's been no whinging about mess, or snoring, or weird smells like there was last year. As far as I know, Manaia is tidy, sanitary and unobtrusive. And she once lent Silvia a book, so I know she can read. She's also, famously, now egg-child-free, so I know she's willing to kill something that annoys her.

She's also very much watching my approach.

She acknowledges me with only a nod, and Elliott turns to find out what she's been diverted by. He smiles when he sees it's me and I feel considerably less like an endangered animal. When I hold my arms out for the baby, his expression turns soft for a second.

'Oh,' he says, like he's surprised. 'Decent of you, Te Maro.'

'Always that tone of surprise,' I say as I bundle Meggan close.

'Have a seat.' Manaia indicates the empty chair at the head of the table and Elliott turns, throwing her a sharp look that seems sort of unwelcoming.

I can take a hint. 'Oh, no, I don't want to impose.'

'We insist,' she says. 'Sit.'

I feel disinclined to disobey, and Elliott must feel the same.

'Of course.' He recovers some sort of smile, but I don't trust it, and it's with a decent amount of reluctance that I actually sit down. 'Dessert should be out soon,' he says.

'Yeah,' I say, trying to be gracious about this new and uncomfortable version of hospitality. 'Crumble tonight, apparently.'

'Elliott's favourite,' Manaia says, smirking. I can't think why that deserves a smirk – it's only a dessert.

'More of a trifle man, myself,' I say, for the sake of saying something.

'Yes, well, everyone has different tastes. I'm all about the classic banana split.' Somehow she makes it sound dirty. 'Though Elliott's been known to enjoy that, too.'

'Silvia's mum makes a good pineapple pie,' I say, without considering that she's the principal and probably doesn't want to be regarded merely as a maker of pie, but I'm desperate for it not to go awkwardly silent.

'Great at expelling people, too,' Elliott says, and half a second later there's a scuffle under the table and he's wincing while Manaia glares bloody murder at him. I'm not sure what's happening. 'As she should've,' he amends. 'It was a well-deserved punishment.'

'Yes,' Manaia says. 'Safety first.'

Oh, look. It got awkward anyway. I say the first witty thing that pops into my head. 'If only their parents had had the same attitude towards contraceptives.'

Manaia lets out a surprised laugh, a loud *haa!* that leaves her looking delighted and impressed with me. I might not die tonight. Elliott, when I sneak a glance at him, looks ... conflicted. Which is probably better than flat-out angry, considering.

'Touché, Te Maro.'

'Always with the French,' I say, and bounce Meggan a bit on my knee. 'Your other daddy is a bit pretentious, isn't he?' I say to her. 'Lord knows what I was thinking when I agreed to this.'

'I was wondering the same thing about Elliott,' Manaia says. 'But he explained it very articulately and, let it be said, I totally get it.'

'Yeah, Blake is a bit of a dick.'

'Who?' Manaia says, and I wonder if I've got the wrong end of the stick. Except the stick is Elliott, so who could tell? Maybe both ends are wrong. But also – she *one hundred per cent* knows who Blake is; this school is the size of a suburban cul-de-sac.

There's another scuffling sound from under the table and it's Manaia's turn to look pained. It's weird, I don't really know what's going on and Elliott will barely even look at me. It seems he's fine with turning up in my bedroom in the middle of the night being needy, but I can't turn up and be helpful at a nice, normal time of day.

'Right,' I say, and stand, Meggan bundled in my arms. 'See you later, then.'

'Bye, Other Tim, nice to chat,' Manaia calls out, reminding me that I'm only a visitor in their lives. Even in exile, their Tim is the important one.

Elliott says nothing to suggest he feels differently, and when I look back, he's attacking his roast beef with something like anger and Manaia looks like she's just had a dangerous amount of fun at our expense. And I can't even tell how.

Later that night, Sam and I are rolling squash balls back and forth across the hearth rug, our eggs – propped up in our outstretched legs – acting as goalies. It's good Kinetics practice, pushing and pulling objects, and, in this case, altering their trajectory so they tap against our goalies and not our gonads. After a little while I manage to stop instinctively trying to use my hands and really lean into it, actually rely on the magic. The whole thing is surprisingly fun and we end up making far too much noise.

The senior student lounge isn't very big. It's a square room with two walls of bookshelves, a large TV, a gas fireplace and a tea station, and it's all very … grey. The rugs are grey, the couches and chairs and study tables are grey. The pinboards, even, are grey under the brightly coloured notices pinned there. The 'art' barely helps liven the place up since it's mostly charcoal sketches and ancient lithographs.

Silvia is presiding over us, curled in a grey armchair, intermittently sipping chamomile tea from a grey cup and reading excerpts from *What To Expect When You're Expecting*, its bright cover in wild contrast with the ceiling, also grey. I wish we could get some colour down here, but clearly it's either too much effort, or coloured paint costs too much money. And, unfortunately, even though we've learnt to affect organic pigments using magic, they haven't taught us how to colour anything synthetic. Apparently they've had problems with it before. Mum refuses to tell me what happened in case it gives me 'ideas'.

The squash balls are rubber, though, which is organic; I wonder if I could turn them the same colour as the carpet and get them past Sam that way? So far, neither he nor I have received a ball to the balls and we have our increasingly passable reflexes and our brilliant egg-daughters to thank for it. Until Elliott appears, distracting me for a second, and one slips past my thigh to tap against my right nut. It doesn't hurt, but it's weird and unwelcome and I'm probably making a face when he asks a question I don't really hear.

'Meggan,' I lament in an undertone, 'where were you when Dad needed you?'

Sam cracks up laughing and I want to throw the ball right at his crotch, but I know what'll happen. All-out war, with Silvia (and probably Elliott) telling us off for playing rough with the children. Instead, I just ask Elliott to repeat his question.

'I said,' he huffs, 'when are we all going to bed?'

'Might wanna take us on a date first, Elliott, jeez.' Silvia grins at her own joke, but at least she's joking and not scowling.

'You're a bit keen,' I say. 'It's only seven-thirty.'

'I'm only asking because I have some homework to do and I don't want to inconvenience you by being up too late,' he snaps. 'I expect we're all tired.'

'That's very considerate, Elliott, thank you,' Sam says. 'Is eight-thirty reasonable? And do you mind if Silvia stays in the room tonight as well?'

'Perfectly fine, it's your room,' he says.

'Do we have homework?' Silvia hisses at me.

'No, it's for Physics,' Elliott cuts in. 'Have you done yours?' he asks Sam.

'Of course,' he says. 'Let me know if you need any help with question eight – it's worded very ambiguously.'

'Typical Bloomfield.' Elliott sighs. 'Syntax like a sphinx.'

'She's a difficult woman to endure, isn't she? Rather flighty considering her field of expertise is meant to be based in fact. She acts like an art teacher. It's disgusting.'

'Maybe she's been living with one …' Elliott lifts a suggestive eyebrow.

Silvia looks freshly scandalised. 'Ohhh … That makes so much sense. I *knew* Ms Christiansen was dressing differently.'

'I can't take credit for noticing,' Elliott admits. 'Manaia pointed it out. I never would've picked either of them as the type.'

'Ha. How very heteronormative of you.' Silvia's voice is light, teasing, and I wonder what she's up to – she knows Elliott's not straight.

'Not something I get accused of often, by those who know me.' He returns her look.

'Really?'

'I would've thought you knew, considering the company you keep?'

'I did.' She smiles. 'I just didn't expect you to tell me.'

'I aim to exceed expectations.'

'I aim for the nose.'

'I won't forget that,' he says, and huffs out a laugh.

'Best you don't, considering the company you keep. Lately.'

'Noted.'

'Good.' Silvia's attention falls back to her book. 'See you later.'

'What was that about?' Sam asks as Elliott walks away.

Theoretical magical entropy he can manage, but some things don't quite click for him. After years of trying to date under my parents' watchful eyes, though, I've come to recognise an over-protective shovel talk when I hear one. I don't want to think too hard about Silvia thinking it was necessary, though, let alone explain it. It'd open it up for discussion, and denying what's going on in my head would feel too much like lying, so I plead ignorance instead.

'Not a bloody clue.'

CHAPTER 8

ALL FAKE EVERYTHING

Everything's fine until about half-past eleven. We all fell asleep pretty swiftly, egg-babies included, but I feel like I've had half as much rest as I need when something wakes me and I hear the door handle squeak and a baby cry. There's a whisper and a grumble and the swish of dressing gowns and then the decisive *doof* of the door closing.

'Wha' happened?' I ask the room, wondering who's gone and who's still here, if anyone.

'Your friends had to leave,' Elliott whispers from behind me.

'Why?' I reach under my pillow for my piece of smoky quartz, utter the incantation and push a little power into it, just enough so it throws out a bit of light.

'Apparently we were being too noisy.' Elliott's profile glows in the dimness.

'I was asleep.'

'I was not. And neither were they. And they were … you know.' He pauses, uncomfortable. 'Doing things. Things it's impolite to do in company. Even in a boarding school.'

I sigh. 'They said they wouldn't.'

'They lied.'

I don't know what's worse – the fact that Silvia and Sam were getting off a couple metres away, or the fact I slept through it. What if it's happened before? What if it's a thing they do? *Hey, Sam, I'm gonna sneak into your room tonight and we can hook up right next to Tim again, the thrill of getting caught really gets me going …*

Though …

'Hang on,' I say, rolling to face him and pushing my hair out of my face. 'Why did they leave if they were the ones … you know, making noises?'

Elliott looks up at the ceiling, avoiding my eyes. 'I may have made some of my own. To prove a point.'

'Elliott,' I say, suddenly feeling much more awake. 'Did you make pretend sex noises to scare them off?'

'No.'

'Did you make *real* sex noises to scare them off?' *Ugh*, what if they were all going at it while I was sleeping?

'No … I made fake noises so they'd stop making real noises, but they didn't. They acted all outraged and Silvia had a small fit, and Sam decided they should go. I imagine

Manaia's going to have to deal with them and their ... illicit tomfoolery.'

His word choice is ninety-nine per cent normal and one per cent Victorian spinster. 'Do my two best friends think I was a part of this?'

'Maybe.' He shrugs. 'Now you don't need to come out to them, at least. I helped.'

'They already knew, you cockwomble. I didn't need your "help".' I give up on propping myself upright and flop back on my pillow. 'Just because I'm not out yet, doesn't mean *no-one* knows I'm bi.'

'You're serious, then? The thing you said about Silvia's brother wasn't just you taking the piss?'

'Yes, I'm serious. And bi. Card-carrying member, thank you. All done. Hello, I'm Tim Te Maro and I'm bisexual, et cetera. Not that it's any of your business.'

He's quiet for a moment. 'We are sharing a bed; it's sort of my business.'

'Then sleep over there.' I point at Sam's vacated bed.

'In their fluids?' he scoffs. 'No thanks.'

'Fine, then, I will,' I say, and throw the covers right off, just to annoy him, letting all the cold air in as I get out ...

... just as a whimper comes from the bedside and we both freeze.

'*No, no, no,*' I breathe, realising too late that we've got a bit loud and annoyed and that I had definitely forgotten about Meggan even existing. Somehow the presence of

Elliott in my bed wasn't enough for me to remember that one small detail.

'I'll settle her, you go to sleep.' He sighs and wriggles over to my side of the bed.

It's the least he can do. Dickhead. I take two steps across the gap and lift Sam's duvet, take a deep, calming breath ... and immediately throw the covers back down. Cock-bollocking-arse-buckets. I turn back to my own bed and clamber over Elliott with no consideration for where my knees are. They can all bugger off. All the people. I get under the covers on his side, turn, and face the wall.

'Ow. What now?'

'Nothing,' I snap. 'I'm fine.'

'Clearly that's a lie, if the pain in my shin is anything to go by.'

My god, he's so annoying. 'Fine. I'm tired. That bed smells of sex. Everyone is getting laid but me, including my ex-girlfriend, and now my two best friends think I'm sleeping with you, and on top of that –' I realise I'm on a roll and just let it all out. 'I'm failing our Environmental Change assignment in Practical Magic and I miss my dad.'

He chooses, of course, to focus on the bit about him. 'You wish you were sleeping with me.'

I don't know where he gets his confidence. Well. Maybe I do. 'Not even slightly.'

'You could be doing a lot worse.'

'I'm sure that's what Blake thought before he left you.'

There's an outraged squeak from behind me, where he's

still settling Meggan, and this can't be helping but I don't care. It feels a lot like it's his fault that we're all awake and upset.

And then he has the gall to ask me, 'Are you ever not horrible?'

I squawk, 'Me?!' without thinking of volume; I'm too enraged at the hypocrisy. I spin around in a flurry of covers and tangled hair and he's sitting up scowling at me, and we have one whole second to seethe at each other before it all goes to hell. Meggan is fully awake and screaming before we have a chance to realise what we're doing, how much emotion is in the room, thick and regrettable and intoxicating nonetheless. I want to punch him and smother him and yell at him over the screams of our fake child.

'Could you maybe calm down?' he says as he scoots his arse up the bed (on *my* side) and lifts Meggan out of her little purple cot. 'Shhh, Petal, it's OK.' He holds her close and puts his mouth to her dome, whispering, his lips only just touching the golden surface.

'Sorry,' I say, and lean back against the wall, pulling the covers over my legs. What a night. I want a drink – a real one, or, failing that, a cup of tea. 'Got any alcohol?' I ask him.

I expect him to shoot me a pompous glare, but he laughs dryly and nods. 'I do, actually, but you might not want it.'

'I assure you, I do.' Meggan is still crying, but she's losing steam now that she's being held, and coddled, and nasty-dad-Tim isn't shouting at her other dad anymore. 'Is it in your bag?' I nod at the leather duffel he brought with him this time. The bag from which he'd pulled those black silk pyjamas and fluffy woollen socks, and a fat, fancy-looking pillow. Rich bastard. Weirdly sweet, too well-dressed, and cutely socked as he is.

'It is,' he says, and passes Meggan over to me. 'Here. Apologise to your daughter.' He leans out of bed to pull his bag closer. His pyjama shirt rides up a little.

The wall is cold and it's seeping through my pyjamas, so I grab one of my crap pillows out from under his fancy one and shove it behind my back. Something else slides out with it. The shape is extremely familiar, which is good because otherwise I would've assumed it was a wētā or something equally bitey and leggy and horribly unwelcome in my bed. I pick it up. Yep. It's definitely a sachet of lube. Kudos to the New Zealand sex-education system, but also, *shit*. I've just unearthed one of my own health class freebies from lord knows when and now I'm sitting here staring at it like a muppet. Worse, I'm doing it in front of a guy I admitted earlier today to finding mildly physically attractive. Who is also one of the small number of guys in this school who's also into guys. I wonder if I should be trying to hook up with him. Maybe I should make an effort to get this curiosity out of my system. It's ruined one relationship already; I'd be doing future-Tim a favour. I'm feeling strangely bold. Sleep deprivation and all that.

Elliott wriggles back onto the bed with a bottle in his hands. 'Right, Te Maro, get ready to drink your personal problems.'

'Care to explain this?' I ask, holding up the sachet.

He looks up and his expression flicks from confusion to disgust to mild outrage. 'That's *not* mine.'

'Of course not. Must be a coincidence I found it just after you moved in, under *your* pillow.'

'It's *your* bed.'

'Yeah, and I don't recall storing lube in it,' I lie. I've actually just remembered exactly when I stashed it there. The sheets have been changed a bunch of times since, though. Housekeeping must have replaced it every time, exactly where they found it. Somewhere in the school there's a colleague of my mother's who has too much insight into my sex life. Brilliant. Easier to ignore that, though, and pretend it isn't mine. 'Must be someone else's.'

'Sure,' he says, layered with sarcasm. 'That seems fair. Can't imagine why a healthy, single, seventeen-year-old guy might have a convenient stash of ...' He cocks his head to the side, squints. 'Sylk Natural Personal Lubricant.' He sounds like he, rightfully, doesn't believe a word of it.

Maybe I can blame the sleep deprivation again as I ignore his insinuation completely and decide to make things extremely awkward instead. '*Recently* single. There are plenty of reasons a healthy, consenting couple might use lube. It reduces the risk of condoms breaking, which reduces the risk of pregnancy and STIs –'

'I know that, Te Maro, I don't need a TED Talk from you about contraceptives.'

'It can make things more comfortable, especially if –'

'Oh my god, shut up.'

'You're trying something a bit adventurous, or one of you has an unreasonably large dick.'

'Are you trying to tell me you've got a big dick, Te Maro? Really?' I take note of the slight twitch of his mouth, and the fact he won't look at me.

'No, I already said it wasn't my lube.'

'So, what, are you telling me *I've* got an unreasonably large dick?

'No, you said it wasn't yours either.'

'So … a ghost hid lube in your bed,' he says. 'A ghost with an unreasonably large dick?'

'Could've been.'

'Oh my god, Te Maro, desist.'

'People have seen stuff down here. Heard things. It's old. The deepest tunnels aren't even concreted, they're just empty holes in the rock. No-one knows what they were used for. Endless darkness. Could be anything out there.'

'I'll accept ghosts exist, but not that they have any interest in giving you lube.'

'They might be voyeurists.'

'I think you mean *voyeurs*.' He twitches his eyebrow at me. 'Do you really think someone's soul is going to avoid crossing over so they can watch you wank? I don't think you're *quite* hot enough to keep spirits on a physical plane.'

'I meant *they* were wanking, not me.' I can't help picturing it. 'I wonder if that's what the cold, creepy feeling you get on the back of your neck is – ghost jizz.'

He snorts, completely against his will, by the looks of it. 'You have no respect for the dead, do you?'

'Not if they're wanking on me. I mean … it would explain that sound of rattling chains if they're – you know.' I make a hand gesture to sell my point and he rolls his eyes at me.

'You're a walking travesty. Could you –' He stops mid-sentence and closes his eyes, cheeks twitching.

'What?'

'It –' his mouth quirks into a smile. 'It would also explain all the moaning, wouldn't it?'

It's in a fit of giggles, half-exhausted and clutching a sachet of ghost lube and our egg-baby, that I realise we might actually be friends now. As we settle down, I pass Meggan over. She's grizzling a bit, but not crying now that we're not angry, and he hands me the bottle of illegal booze that he's pulled out of his bag. It's definitely not what it says on the label; I'm a hundred per cent sure that no flavour of Powerade is the colour of dried blood.

'What is this?'

'It's port.'

'Port? *Honestly?*' I ask him, withering. 'Are you ninety?'

'I wasn't anticipating sharing it with you, sorry.'

'It couldn't have been rum or something normal?'

'Blake drank the rest of my Mount Gay, said it was his right as part of the queer community to imbibe the blood of Gay Christ or something. To be honest, I often didn't listen when he talked.'

'Oh?'

'He's really not very smart, Te Maro. *Really*. I'm amazed your girlfriend didn't pick that up before it was too late.'

'Maybe she wasn't very smart, either.'

'Well, she did break up with a guy whose dick inspires ghost wanking.'

'Let's just have a drink and stop talking about my dick, please.'

'*Dick, please,* indeed,' he says, popping the sipper top open, his ring glinting silver in the low light. 'I swear I've never been this sexually bereft in my life.'

I can't believe we're having this conversation. Plus, now my room smells like an old lady's knicker drawer, which is something I never wanted for myself. Fruit and rot and a hint of nail polish remover.

'Have you got any glasses?' he asks. 'Tumblers? Paper cups?'

'You didn't bring any with you?'

'I wasn't planning on sharing my forbidden cache,' he says. 'For all I knew you might dob me in as soon as you knew I had it.'

'Fine,' I say. 'I'll go find something to drink the devil juice from.'

I crawl over him again, carefully this time, and tiptoe to the lounge, wondering if I'll ever have a weirder Thursday.

CHAPTER 9

LIKE SHE SAID

Within a minute I find myself back in bed with an egg-baby in one hand, an ungentlemanly amount of port in a shitty grey mug in the other, and my former-nemesis-turned-tentative-friend right there with me. It's nearly midnight. We should be asleep.

'How many days has it been for you?' Elliott asks out of nowhere. He's reclined now, on my pillow, on my side of the bed, and I bet it'll smell of him. Whatever that scent is that's slightly like myrrh and slightly lemony. He's produced a silicon bendy straw in my absence and he looks like a whimsical alcoholic.

'Since what?' I sip my port and it's horrible.

'Sex, Te Maro, keep up,' he says. Which, I guess, proves Thursday can indeed get weirder.

'Um. About three weeks.'

He makes a sympathetic noise. 'Almost one week for me. The morning before the night we all broke up.' His hand lifts off his chest and waves around like a sea anemone. 'Though, that depends on your definition. Maybe it was as long as three or four weeks before that. He got less … reciprocal, at some point.' He goes quiet and I don't think there's anything to be said to that. 'I wonder when they decided to leave us?' he says. 'When did they talk about it? What made it easy to decide on that one day, among all the other days?'

'I think that seed was also planted about three weeks ago, and I can take a very good guess at what triggered it.' I haven't told anyone any of the details yet. I had no intention of doing so, but it doesn't seem so weird now. 'Despite a valiant effort at indulging me, Lizzie had some very conventional heterosexual preferences and I did not. We ended up liking different things and what she liked didn't interest me enough to, um … make it possible to do them. And what I liked she found distasteful. Which makes it extra shitty she's left me for Blake, since he's obviously not straight either and probably likes the same things.'

'Shit.' He looks sympathetic, like he's sorry he even asked, but honestly it's a relief to just tell someone. 'If it helps, Blake's a total muppet. He was a tolerable roommate

82

once he started making himself useful, but I would never have called him a friend.' He snorts, a quiet laugh about something happening in his head. 'Manaia can't stand him.'

Another surprise. I'd assumed they were all birds of a feather, Elliott's group and the other Minders. It's something of a comfort to hear that even people who aren't my friends still think Blake's an absolute walnut. Another point to Manaia.

'She seems interesting. A bit scary.'

'She's my favourite person in the world, including my actual family, and you should, one hundred per cent, be afraid of her.'

'Good to know.' I remember a passing thought from earlier. 'Is she gay?'

'You should ask her, not me,' he says, and that's as good as a yes.

Meggan is quiet in my arms now and I think about putting her back in her cot, but it's a comfort to have something to hold on to. I don't miss the sex with Liz, but I do miss her hugs. She made me feel significantly less … messed up. Of course, thinking of her now has the opposite effect. I tip back my mug and get rid of the contents in the most efficient way possible – quickly and without caring how horrid it tastes.

'Another?' I suggest.

'Sure, let me put Meggsy back in her cot,' he says, and nestles his mug between the pillows before he reaches out and takes her from my lap. She makes a sleepy burble and then is silent. I don't really want to let her go. 'For goodness sake, Te Maro, stop moping. I can't have you all cuddly and drunk while holding the baby. It's not safe.'

'I'm not drunk yet,' I protest, and it's true. I've been practising my drinking and this is far, far from drunk.

'Just cuddly, then?'

'I … miss the closeness,' I say, and it's hard and horrible to squeeze the words out, but I hope I'll feel lighter afterwards. Confession is meant to do that. At least, that's what the school counsellor, Dr Peters, says. He's been right about other things.

Elliott sighs at me, though. Maybe he's about to tell me to *stop being so maudlin, Te Maro,* or maybe just to shut up with my stupid first-world problems. Instead, he says, 'I miss not being judged for my upbringing. Not just where I'm from. The money too.'

Now it's my turn to sigh. We are maudlin. 'If it helps, I decided a few minutes ago that we're probably friends.'

'Probably?'

'It seemed hasty to decide without your input.'

'I'm OK with it,' he says, and downs his second port in one wet mouthful. 'Shall we hug on it?' When I look at him he's smirking, teasing me. Meggan is safely tucked up in her bed and he's lying on his side, facing me, propped up on his elbow. He's very long. 'Since you miss the closeness.'

'I'm not going to spoon you,' I say.

'Funny that's where your head went,' he says. 'Prude.'

'Perv.'

'I could say the same about you.' He gives me a look. 'You've obviously been present for more than one of their amorous interludes and slept right through it.' He gestures to the other bed. 'Or pretended to.'

'I really bloody hope not.'

'I was making an awful lot of very explicit noises and you were right next to me, asleep. Oblivious.'

'I'm tired.'

'I literally moaned your name, loudly, repeatedly, and with an enthusiasm befitting the most devious acts.' He pops the sipper top of the bottle with his teeth and pours us both another port. 'I was half afraid you'd wake up and think I was very vividly dreaming about you.'

'Well.' I take a fortifying sip, knowing the exact liquid in *my* mouth has just passed though a piece of plastic he's had *his* mouth on. There's probably microscopic pieces of him in it and I'm drinking it. 'I'm flattered you faked enjoying it, considering I'd have no idea what I was doing.'

'What?' He looks across at me. 'Your mentor didn't give you a proper run-through? Or are you just a bit slow on the uptake?'

I sigh. As much as I might want to talk about Mareko right now, it's still hard to say the words out loud. Especially when Elliott's lying there, looking like my mortal enemy, but in silk pyjamas and with his hair mussed. 'We kissed. Once. A lot, but –' I squirm. 'Technically, just on the one occasion.'

'That's it? That's what confirmed your bisexual meanderings?'

How do I explain the fact that I pretty much already knew? That, looking back, there was no way on this Earth I was straight and that the second Liz asked if I was attracted to guys as well, it was immediately the most sense my life had ever made. That I probably didn't need to kiss Mareko at all, but that there was also no way I'd pass that up. Not right then, with the need to experiment lighting a fire in my pants and whole-hearted permission from my actual girlfriend.

I think she was hoping it was a phase, something I could get out of my system. And when Mareko came to visit over the holidays, she saw a chance and took it. I think she thought that him being Silvia's brother would somehow put me off and the awkwardness she anticipated would throw an unflattering light on men in general. Because he was like family, because I'd grown up with him on the periphery, and because she thought he was a nerd. But Mareko was a gift. A hot, heavy, teasing gift. And I was a seventeen-year-old boy with cock on the brain and he was a swarthy sex-god who could lift me with one arm while discussing the nuances of magic under a full moon. He was something I didn't fully recover from and very definitely one of the reasons Liz and I broke up.

'There was some light ... I dunno ...' I don't want to use the word *humping*. 'Rubbing? I suppose? How strong is this port?'

86

'Don't change the subject. Tell me about this alleged rubbing.'

'Uh, no.'

'I can tell you the pathetic details of my own self-discovery, if it eases your mind?' he offers. 'I know you Defensives like things to be fair. Reciprocal and all that.'

'Yes, apparently you haven't had enough reciprocity lately.' I do not need him telling me stories of getting off with anyone else I know and can vividly picture. Though it is comforting to know it wasn't as easy as he's making it look.

'Te Maro, stop flirting with these big words and tell me about the time you frotted the former head boy.'

'There's nothing to tell. It was … enough to know.' Tiny bit of a lie. I may have made a spectacular mess in my pants.

'You tiny, innocent flower petal.'

I can let him believe that. 'Shut up.'

'Be nice, I'm sure no-one else wants to talk to you about this. Silvia surely wouldn't want to know a single deviant thing about your dalliances with her brother. She'd get her moral knickers in a twist even knowing it happened, wouldn't she?'

'Probably.' He's right, of course. 'But it – it wasn't as bad as it sounds. Lizzie knew, so it wasn't particularly immoral in that sense.'

'She *knew*? That you were kissing your best friend's brother? Did she know he was humping your leg?'

'He didn't –' Another lie, he totally did. 'And yes, she knew. She – We'd been having some problems and she asked if maybe there was something to it and suggested that maybe I made sure I didn't completely prefer guys.'

'That's such a cliché,' he says. 'You don't want to sleep with her so you must obviously be gay. What is it with straight people?' He sounds a little bitter.

'She wasn't entirely wrong, to be fair.' I shrug. 'And some things bear testing.'

'You barely tested anything, by the sounds of it.' He takes a sip of his drink, his lips loose around the pink straw. 'I can't see why Mareko bothered.'

'It was enough,' I say. 'And he was very supportive.'

'I bet you aren't even bi.'

What?

'I am – How can –'

'Come over here and prove it.'

Oh.

'I'm not going to kiss you to prove how gay I am.'

'Then do it to prove how gay *I* am.'

Wow.

'I'm not *questioning* that.'

'Neither am I, but I'm bored and soaked in port, Te Maro, and woefully single, and you're just sitting there talking about how you made out with a guy who literally came top in every interesting subject this school offers, and it's more than a little ... inspiring.'

'Then go have a cold shower. We're barely even friends, we can't just –'

Can we? Is that a thing we can do? Just ... hook up?

The tiny part of me that was curious about Elliott is swiftly shrivelling into its raisin form – a weird, wrinkled little thing, desiccated by anxiety.

'I assure you I could.' The look on his face makes it clear he's trying to chat me up, and doesn't seem remotely self-conscious about it.

Do some guys just ... do this sort of thing? Could I be one of those guys?

'Technically, Sam and Silvia think we were anyway,' he says, and shrugs. His face is calm, his expression a picture of 'why not?'

'They won't actually believe it.' I hope that's true – that they'll accept it when I say I slept through the whole charade. I expect if they've hooked up next to me before they'll know it's possible.

'If they won't believe it, then what's the harm?' he says, like the only reason I might not want to jump him right now is the curious disapproval of my two best friends.

'Stop it. I'm done with this conversation, it's getting weird.' Talking about it so blatantly feels too real, too open, too not-accidental.

'Liz'd hate it if you actually enjoyed yourself, wouldn't she?' he says and offers me the bottle.

He needs to stop being quite so on the nose with his comments. It's creepy how well he reads me. Or is it? Maybe it's just Minder things again. I feel myself closing up at the thought, the tendrils of friendship curling back inside me. 'I don't care what she thinks,' I say and wave the bottle away.

He turns and tosses it back towards his bag. 'She probably expects you to mope around and pine after her, wank into one of her old T-shirts and cry about how sad and lonely you are.'

'Are you trying to chat me up or depress me?'

'Perhaps neither. It's late, we should turn in,' he says, and peels himself off the mattress. 'It's been entertaining, Te Maro, but the booze is making me sleepy and you're being very boring.' And just like that, he sucks his straw clean, then sets his mug on the floor, reaching for mine as well. It's empty, its contents already burning a happy hole in my gut.

What just happened? Had he been serious? Did he actually want to … And now I'm supposed to just, what? Sleep next to him? Continue raising our egg-baby and making his breakfast and pretending that he didn't just blatantly proposition me in my own bed, while we were uncommonly alone together, all soft and careless with alcohol and fatigue?

He doesn't offer to swap sides, even though he's in my spot. He doesn't even switch our pillows over, just plumps mine, arranging them just so before leaning over to check on Meggan. He settles back, smoothing the sheet over the edge of the duvet and burrowing down. I still haven't moved.

'Are you coming, Te Maro?' he says, and reaches out for my jaggy little piece of quartz, which I'd put on the bed end. He taps it and it dulls to a barely discernible glow. The audacity of him touching it barely registers.

I don't know how to move like a person anymore; my body feels weird and his body feels too close and too … possible. And he's expecting me to sleep on his pillow. I wriggle into position between him and the wall, jerky and awkward like a half-drunk Great Dane trying to climb into a Christmas stocking. I slide further under the covers, hyper-aware of where my knees are and just how much space there is between us.

His elbow encroaches on my side of the bed for a second and I wonder if we'll just lie here all night, side by side, staring up at the ceiling, not touching. Then I feel the bed dip and he's moving and my heart bangs in out of nowhere, assuming he's going to kiss me in the dark and I won't be prepared. He doesn't, of course, just rolls towards the baby, and as my eyes adjust I realise I'm over here with nothing. And all these inches between my hands and him. Too many inches to excuse an 'accidental' touch. And why has this even happened? This morning he was merely conventionally good-looking and surprisingly inoffensive to spend time with. Then he goes and says one stupid thing and my whole outlook shifts. Why am I like this? Blind for an entire lifetime 'til something clicks into place and then it's all I can think about.

Elliott Bloody Parker – giant pain in the arse for our entire schooling until about two minutes ago when he says, 'Come over here and prove it,' and my entire body is suddenly like, YES, PLEASE. And then he laughs and says, 'We should turn in … you're being very boring,' and then …

this. *This*. Lying in the dark staring at the line of his neck and knowing, somehow, what he'd feel like pressed against me. I can guess what he'd *taste* like. And there's literally nothing stopping it from happening, except for the fact that the whole thing scares the shit out of me.

CHAPTER 10

IT'S ONLY NATURAL

Breakfast is the same as every other morning. Except that I'd woken up hard and forgotten Elliott was there for a second. My usual practice of self-comfort was interrupted by a mild heart attack when my knuckles brushed his hip and I ended up staring into his wide grey eyes with my fingers wrapped tight around my dick, both of us wondering what the hell was happening. So breakfast is actually a little uncomfortable. At least Silvia and Sam haven't arrived yet and we don't have to deal with their un-subtle eyebrow waggling and casual questioning of 'how we slept'.

'How do you feel about baked beans?' I ask, assessing the various dishes on our table.

'Negatively.'

'OK.' I wonder if beans have become a metaphor. Maybe he just wants to say no to me since I said no to his offer last night.

'Just a bacon roll will be fine.' He sounds as tired as I feel. It's been days of not sleeping now, and our midnight chat didn't help any.

'Right. Bacon roll with aioli. Cool.'

'Thanks.' He pauses. 'You seem weirder than usual this morning,' he says. 'Is it what we talked about last night?'

I just look at him, a pair of tongs in one hand and a soft, round bap, fresh from the oven, in the other. The roll is supple and warm in my hand and it feels exactly like I'd imagine grabbing his butt would feel.

'I guess,' I say, since that's probably less weird than telling him I almost accidentally had a wank beside him twenty minutes ago.

'Will you stop being weird soon or do we need to talk something out?'

'I might be weird forever.'

'That does seem more likely.'

He doesn't try to make me talk again, just eats his bap with one hand and coddles our egg-baby with the other. All morning, he pretends like nothing is wrong; I can tell he's pretending because he doesn't look me in the eye once.

He talks to Blake in first period, which is worrying. Manaia is with them, grinning like a cat. I'd say it was a bad omen, but I don't know how things could possibly get weirder than they currently are. Though it does make me wonder how I'd feel if Elliott and Blake became civil again while Liz and I still aren't talking. I can't even look at her without my gut turning over. It might be guilt. Shame, perhaps.

Silvia ends up answering the unasked question of what Elliott and Blake were talking about. There are new living arrangements, apparently. Not new in the sense that Elliott's going to be vacating my room anytime soon – quite the opposite. He's moving in with me. Sam's moving in with Silvia and Manaia is taking Elliott's place by moving in with Blake. I don't know how they organised that, or what they've all done to convince Blake it's a good idea. Or Manaia. Is she doing it just to terrorise Blake? Or as a favour to Silvia? Does she just want a bit of drama in her life? There's going to be more than drama if we get caught. No-one's dared do anything like this before, and I'm somehow not surprised it's the three of us testing the limits of our luck. I wonder if our parents will hesitate to expel the lot of us, though, if it comes down to it. I guess we'll finally find out if anyone actually monitors the cameras in the girls' corridor.

When I mention the risks, Silvia assures me it's all just for the duration of the assignment. Another three weeks. Not permanent. She adds, 'Don't mention it to anyone, Tim, especially your mum – I know you trust her, but she'd have a professional obligation to do something about it and we shouldn't put her in that position.' Silvia swears she wouldn't be breaking the rule herself, but really, 'Why is there one rule for the straight students and another for everyone else?'

She insists that she'll take it seriously when all the bisexuals (myself included) are locked up by themselves in case they accidentally sleep with someone, since that seems to be the driving force behind the typical gender segregation. I'm not remotely convinced that's the reason she's going along with it, but I'm hardly going to argue with her. Not now. Not when I'm still entertaining the idea of temptation and Elliott Parker and the thrill of illicit, no-strings hook-ups. Not when he still manages to look irritatingly good on just as little sleep as I've had. When his stupid oversized cardigans looks like they need to be snuggled against and his hair is begging to be tousled. When his hands are suddenly a thing that would be better off all over me and his mouth seems far too empty without my tongue. Not that I'm getting carried away.

I don't say much for the rest of the morning, stuck as I am in my head, and Elliott scolds me again for being boring and takes Meggan from me so he has 'someone to talk to'. I've been replaced by an egg-baby who only makes seven different sounds, all of them seemingly dependent on how shit I feel. I don't know what bizarre magic they've all been infused with, but she's creepily accurate at reading my mood.

Elliott and I walk to lunch together, and I imagine another version of us stealing back to our room to make out instead of sitting down to bolognaise and garlic bread and a bracing cup of PG Tips. No such luck. Maybe I could suggest it. Apparently *he's* allowed to suggest things.

We sit with my friends; Hana, Nikau and Matt are arguing about indoor netball (again) and Ana's focused intently on her phone. Silvia and Elliott somehow end up nattering about osmosis and I wonder how he can dare call me boring when he's literally talking about the properties of water right now. Silvia's an Alchemist so she's right into it, and I think of all the times I've zoned out while she's talked endlessly about crystals and night-blooming herbs. I suppose it's nice she has someone to talk to.

When I look up at Sam so we can bond over a blokey sort of eye-roll, he's glaring at something over my shoulder, which turns out to be Lizzie and the new love of her life. I take a moment to enjoy Sam's stubborn loyalty – he and Lizzie used to get on fine, but he's refused to talk to her since we broke up. Nikau's been slightly less obvious in his loyalty to me, probably so he doesn't hurt anyone's feelings, but I still feel like he has my back. I don't know if their support would ever extend to me indulging my new curiosity about Elliott, though.

For some reason, probably stupidity, Lizzie and Blake are coming to sit at the table right next to ours, when normally Elliott's presence has been enough to keep at least Blake at bay. There's one of Lizzie's Year 12 friends with them, someone I don't really know but I'm pretty sure is in her extracurricular dance group. She seems to be hanging on Blake's every word, more even than Lizzie is herself.

'And so now I'm stuck with a *lesbian* for a roommate,' he finishes as they approach, sounding monumentally annoyed about it and loud enough for us all to hear.

I expect our new rooming situation will be over soon.

All respect to Manaia, and it's obviously her choice, but she shouldn't have to put up with that for three whole weeks. Attitudes like his shouldn't even exist anymore. It's amazing she hasn't punched him. Though I'm betting she might actually do so in the future. Or at least she should. I'd like to. Even Lizzie looks like she might have a go. It's Silvia, though, who speaks for all of us.

'What's wrong with being a lesbian?' she says, nice and clear, and half of the surrounding tables fall silent, the hush permeating the adjacent Year 11s as well.

'Nothing *wrong* with it, I just – well, you know.' Blake curls his lip in obvious disgust and Liz is looking at him like he's the gelatinous inside of wētā and I feel a sudden thrill at the thought of what might be about to happen.

'If there's nothing the matter with it,' Lizzie says, her voice a carefully controlled chain of dynamite – it might go off, or you might get away, but the odds are definitely not in your favour – 'you'll need to explain your tone, because I'm quite confused.'

'My room smells like sandalwood and patchouli already and she's only been moved in for an hour. And everything is plaid,' Blake whines, foolishly thinking that the truth, and not a simpering apology, is the right course of action. 'She wears men's shirts and flannel pyjamas and has all these books about gender politics and feminism and there's a bloody great locked chest under her bed that I expect isn't for her diary, if you know what I mean. She's the worst kind of girl and I hate it.'

'You mean,' Sam starts, and I'm all ears, because Sam's not the most tactful guy but he did hug me for almost an hour when I came out to him last year, so surely – 'she's the kind of girl who doesn't want to go out with you?'

Oh wow. Call the paramedics.

'No, that's not what I – I don't –' Blake looks dreadfully uncomfortable and I'm drinking in every second of my ex-girlfriend scowling at him in disbelief. Yes, Elizabeth, this is the shithead you left me for.

'Blake?' Ana interrupts, as she's prone to doing. She's the only girl Defensive, now, and not someone I'd mess with, even if she is kind of skinny. I wouldn't be surprised if she had a personal stake in this. 'Does the best sort of girl smell of cupcakes or something? Wear frilly, see-through nighties and read magazines about make-up and clothes and how to please a man?' She slowly rips a piece of garlic bread in half.

Everyone at our table – along with half the people at the adjacent ones – is staring at him now. This is fantastic.

'That's not what I said, I don't actually –'

'Blake, are you upset that lesbians don't have any use for you?' Silvia asks, and this is why she's one of my best friends. Relentless and righteous.

'Do you think we don't *all* have flannelette pyjamas?' Ana asks, right on the tail of Silvia's question, starting everyone in on a barrage of subtle, scathing mockery.

'You do realise flannelette pyjamas are *warm*, right? And that we live under a *glacier*?'

'Does gay have a smell?'

'I'm amazed he even knows what gender politics is.'

'Come on, I –' Blake starts to look a bit worried, and it's well past time for that.

'No, mate.' Nikau shakes his head, a pitying smile on his face. 'Just let it go.'

'But I –'

'Best you shut up, really,' Liz says, and pats him on the arm. He looks at her like he doesn't understand why she's suddenly turned on him.

'Fine,' he says, and wanders off, bewildered, towards the Minders' table.

Everyone starts talking at once and there's a general consensus of not quite knowing how he's made it this far in life without being cellotaped up in a pride flag and rolled into a volcano.

After the noise dies down, Ana asks, 'So is Manaia single, then?'

Several interested pairs of eyes flick to Elliott and wait. 'I wouldn't ever, in a million years, speak for her,' he says. 'She is her own woman and all enquiries regarding her personal life should go through her.' He takes another bite of garlic bread and fixes his eyes on his plate 'til everyone goes back to their own food.

Only Ana is left distracted, staring across the room at Manaia and tearing her garlic bread into smaller and smaller pieces.

CHAPTER 11

INTO TEMPTATION

The rest of the day passes in a tired blur. Meggan grizzles almost constantly and it's probably my fault. I want nothing but to sink back into bed, but every time I think of it, I remember I'll be there next to Elliott and I'm assaulted with mental images of him flushed and messy and gasping and I feel immediately more aware of my own body. Skittish. The underlying knowledge that it's not so far-fetched makes it all the more dangerous to think about. It's not theoretical, it's an actual choice I can make, and I don't know if it's a path we should go down. I don't know if that's something I want. I've never really had anything casual, and finding out I don't like it while we're rooming together would be awkward.

That said … Finding out it's good while we're secretly rooming together and guaranteed some privacy would be awesome …

'What are you thinking about, Other Tim? You look confused.' Manaia says. We're sitting with her this evening, at Elliott's request. She's stopped eating her dinner to stare at me, fork held loosely in her hand. As much as I'm starting to like her, hanging around her is like swimming with stingrays. She's too sharp for my own good. And she's still calling me *Other Tim*. 'Are you not sleeping?' she asks.

'Not a lot,' I admit, hoping she's just fishing. She's an Elemental so I'm pretty sure she's not quietly fossicking through my thoughts.

Elementals have cool powers, but Dad and I always reckoned they were too specialised. Until their magic has fully matured, they're a bit useless if they're not near any actual elements. Air can only do so much. (Naturals are the same – cool powers, but pretty limited in a city, unless they're really into pigeons.) I've seen one of the Elemental tutors turn a jug of Raro back into powder, but that sort of thing takes years to master, and so far they're just really annoying to share a bathroom with. Maybe one day they'll manage something more useful than dicking around with the water in my shower cubicle, or making wobbly little orbs from whatever they're drinking, but not before they're apprenticed.

That said, if ever there was an Elemental to be afraid of, it'd be Manaia. She hasn't orbed my tea yet, so maybe she's found better things to do with her capabilities.

'What about you?' I ask.

'I dropped my egg-child for a reason,' she says. 'I sleep peacefully.'

'Will you, though, in the same room as Blake?' Elliott asks. 'Or will you have to drop him head-first onto concrete too?'

'I think I'll enjoy antagonising him far more than anything else,' she says, and lets us in on her plans to annoy the living hell out of him. The excessive patchouli, it turns out, is a torture device and not a personal preference. She's magicked it so she can't smell it herself. It's just another stereotype, she says, and weaponising all of those is giving her 'a very deep, very gay, sense of satisfaction'. She's so organised and I'm so impressed, I forget about my own problems for a moment. Even the confirmation she isn't straight comes second to the realisation of how much Blake is going to suffer at her hands. It's the mention of 'leaving lube lying around just to confuse him' that reminds me of my own rooming arrangements and, like a punch to the gut, that underlying skittishness comes back.

Towards the end of dessert, Manaia spots Blake and Lizzie heading for the door and leaps out of her seat, scampering away to ruin their chances of being alone in his room. I find myself liking her more and more. Maybe I should ask her what she thinks of Ana. They'd be a formidable team.

'Meggan's been in a bit of a mood today,' Elliott says, just as I'm wondering what lesbians get up to in their own time. 'Did you notice?' I get the feeling he was waiting until we were alone to mention it.

'Oh. Yeah, I –'

He puts his fork down but keeps his eyes on his plate. 'I think it's because you're being weird, and I think that's maybe my fault, and I should apologise.'

'Oh.'

'I realise I might be more comfortable with … things … than you're ready for. Considering. You know. Your level of experience.'

'Right.'

'So. I'm sorry. I've resolved to be a little more discreet about my … ideas.'

'OK.'

'But I want something from you, too.' He turns his head and looks at me. 'Could you just tell me next time if I've pissed you off? So we can deal with it and not have our daughter be a cranky little madam all day?' He turns his attention back to her, sitting in his lap wrapped in her little green blanket.

'I'm not pissed off.'

'You seem pissed off.'

'I'm not.'

'Care to explain, then, why you're so quiet and you won't look at me? And why every time I look at you, you seem to be trying to scowl your own eyebrows off?'

I'd obviously rather not. Not in the dining hall, anyway, where we could be overheard, or seen, or anything. 'Not here,' I say.

'But you admit there is something bothering you?'

I sigh. 'I've been thinking.'

'That explains the pained expression.'

'Can we just' – I wave my hand towards the large double doors – 'like, go?'

'Fine,' he says, and stands, tucking Meggan into his side. 'Where are we going?'

I haven't thought this far ahead. Hadn't thought I'd have to say anything. I honestly didn't think he knew me well enough to notice if I was a bit off. It makes choosing somewhere to go all the more difficult, because anywhere we can be alone is going to look like I'm taking him somewhere we can 'be alone'. We can't go to the lounge or library because they'll be full of people soon, and we can't go back to my room because seven o'clock is a bit early to be turning in and that'll draw far too much attention. We can't go outside, it's freezing, and I don't want to take him to my dad's. That leaves a bunch of old tunnels I'm not setting foot in at night, some empty classrooms, or the photocopy room, which doesn't exactly set a mood. 'I don't know. Where do you go when you want a private conversation?'

'Your mother has a whole apartment down here and you're asking me for ideas?'

'Yes, since my mother is *in* that apartment and she's capable of hearing through walls and also wondering what I'm doing behind them with you. So, no. Bad idea.'

'And there's nowhere else you've discovered in however many years you've lived in this place? Really?'

'Nowhere that I'd go without a torch and a blanket.'

'Well, *that* sounds romantic,' he mutters. 'Fine. I have an idea. But you're not allowed to tell anyone.'

Elliott leads us along dim corridors towards the admin area, then past it, through the little atrium that leads to the shuttle bus that goes into town. Just beyond that, he takes a narrow corridor on the right, and if he hadn't disappeared down it I might not have seen there was a corridor there at all; I've always thought it was a dead end. As, it seems, I was meant to, if there's something else back here. An impressive piece of magic.

'I came here a bit at the beginning of the year,' he says as we reach a heavy wooden door at the end of the dimly lit passage.

I'm intrigued as to what warrants being hidden from the entire student body, but he pushes the door open to reveal what looks like nothing more than a small mechanic's workshop, complete with a familiar-looking Toyota Camry up on blocks. It's somewhat anticlimactic and hopefully not a sign of how this conversation is going to go.

We must trigger a sensor because the overheads come on with the eerie, clicking flicker of fluorescents, and I flinch. I'm glad Elliott's in front of me and doesn't see. I probably look like enough of a dick being moody and weird all day.

There's another door on the left-hand wall, possibly leading to a storeroom or a bathroom or something. Beyond the Camry there's a fridge, an old, tired-looking lounge suite and a bench covered in grubby tools. The entire right-hand wall is a roller door, which explains how the cars get in and out of here. It also explains why this is all hidden. The temptation of a midnight joyride would be too much for some people. Exactly the sort of people Elliott was friends with last year, and I expect that's how he knows about this place. A whirl of doubt tickles in my gut.

'So what is it, Te Maro?' Elliott says.

He walks over to the corner and sets about making a nest out of limp, grey cushions on the armchair for Meggan. She's still grizzly, but far quieter than she has been today. Am I calmer already, just from him apologising for coming on to me and making things awkward? Even though I'm kind of OK with that now? Or is it just because I'm staring at his arse as he's bent over the chair?

A particularly impulsive part of me wants to pin him down on the car bonnet and do what I've been thinking about all day. The image of it springs readily into my head, the heat and the sound of his panting breath in my ear and the thrill of another male body under mine. Except ... well. How's it going to happen? How will I even suggest it? *Hey, former nemesis, about what you said last night – wanna hook up?* That'd go down well. I bet he'd go down well. No. Stop. I'm getting ahead of myself.

'I'm sorry I've been in a mood,' I say to his back, because that's probably easier.

'OK,' he says. 'I am genuinely sorry if I made you uncomfortable.' He turns from the chair, Meggan settled in a mound of sad, drab velvet. 'And – I also wanted to apologise for something else. I remember being where you are now, and it was shitty of me to question your sexuality for my own amusement.'

Oh. *Oh*. He thought I was pissed off about that as well? About accusing me of not being bi?

'I wasn't upset about that, I kind of got the impression you were just trying to goad me into … you know.'

'OK. Good. What was the bit you were actually annoyed about?'

'I told you, I wasn't annoyed.' I eye the couch, wondering if it's too much to have this conversation sitting side by side in a secret room. It might almost seem romantic, except for the mess and the smell and the horrible lighting. 'It was just a lot to deal with, having you … suggest things when I haven't really … entertained the idea of someone else, yet, after Lizzie.'

'But I'm guessing you did today? Entertain the idea?' He looks smug, the bastard.

'I … thought about it a bit.'

'And?' He cocks his head to the side.

'It's a bit risky, considering. I mean. We're roomed together, we're doing this assignment. It could get awkward and we'd still be stuck together all the time.'

'I think you're missing the point, Te Maro. If there's no feelings involved, it doesn't get awkward. And when you're stuck rooming together, it's kind of perfect.' Yeah, OK, I had actually suspected that, hadn't I? 'No-one questions you spending the night in the same place. How do you think me and Blake started off?'

'You and Blake ended disastrously. You hate him.' Another thought occurs to me. 'And didn't he give you some sort of sex-disease? Or did I completely misinterpret what you were doing in the sick bay that night?'

'Oh my god, Te Maro, I don't have an STI. That stuff is an antidepressant. Blake violated the out clause, not my physical health. We had an agreement and he ruined it.'

'Out clause?'

'For you and me, it'd be simple.' He takes a step closer and I have to look away. 'Once the assignment's over and we go back to our own rooms, we stop doing whatever it is you've been thinking about all day.' He takes another step. 'Are you going to tell me what that was?'

'Nope.'

'What if I agree to it anyway? Whatever you want and no more? I won't pressure you to do anything you don't want to, just –' He sighs, takes another step, so close I can see the exact colour of his eyes, the cool grey separating into a collision of blue and silver with deep black pupils so wide I could drown in them. 'Whatever you want.'

He thinks I'm timid. Innocent. Inexperienced. Like I don't know what I'm doing at all. Maybe I don't. Maybe there's a huge difference between girls and boys and I'm too new to know what it is. I've kissed both before, though; it shouldn't feel this difficult. But it does.

I nod anyway.

Maybe there's just something about Elliott – I can't even look at him right now without my gut twisting. Maybe it's being this close to someone and knowing he doesn't actually like me like that – knowing that everything I do, every move, is going to be judged without even the rose-tinted haze of a crush. Am I afraid that Lizzie was right and I'm just inherently unsatisfying?

The thought of her having an opinion on this is so infuriating I go back to wanting to shove Elliott against something solid and prove her wrong. He might even let me. Except, when I move to reach for him, he steps closer at the same time, and his hands find my waist, and my hands settle lightly on his chest instead. It feels far too intimate to be touching him so softly instead of shoving him, and I don't know what to do or where to look. His lips are right there, and there's a light sparkle of stubble on his jaw, and the sound of his breathing is close enough to drown out the pounding of my heart. He leans in until our lips are almost touching and I barely even need to move; it's just a tilt, another centimetre to close the space. His mouth is soft and slow, undemanding, and his hands are light on my back. Almost like he's expecting me to pull away, or get spooked, or change my mind. Against all expectation, our first kiss is kind of gentle and wholesome and totally at odds with who we are.

'Elliott,' I whisper against his mouth.

'Tim?' he purrs back at me, his breath tickling my chin.

'I'm not actually an innocent little flower petal.'

'Good,' he says, and surges in, unleashed.

CHAPTER 12

IT'S ON

Our second kiss is a lot more like I'd expected. Slightly too rough to be comfortable, an almost competitive edge to it. I push my fingers up into his hair, looking for some sort of control, and it's so soft I almost want to compliment him before I remember that's not part of the deal. It's not a relationship; we don't need to like each other. No strings, no feelings, no awkwardness. A thrill shoots straight through me at the lack of expectation, at the way kissing him doesn't come with a commitment or a promise or my mother gazing fondly at the two of us from the staff table. It's just a kiss. A good one.

His teeth press into my bottom lip and his hands fist in my jumper, pulling me closer. I must make some sort of sound when he does that, because he pulls away a second later, panting slightly. My mouth tries to follow him and I'm left reaching into the space between us, needy.

'You OK there?' He sounds overly pleased with himself, and my defences leap up from where they've puddled on the floor.

'No, I really need to sit down,' I deadpan. 'Knees a bit weak and all that. This is all a bit, you know. New.'

He rolls his eyes and lets go of my jumper. 'Couch, then?' He looks over at the dilapidated velvet. 'Or do you need a moment?'

'Shut up,' comes out of my mouth automatically, which is good, because most of my thoughts are currently focusing on whether we're about to lie down together and whether this is going to be an embarrassing repeat of what happened with Mareko.

I sit on the couch, hoping he'll sit next to me and I'll be able to keep the state of my pants to myself for the foreseeable future. He doesn't, though, of course. He moves in and props one knee on the cushion beside my left thigh, then the other on the right, so he's straddling my lap, and then he tips my chin up and kisses me again. I hear his hands hit the back of the couch on either side of my head, and his weight shifts and he's all over me. Lizzie used to sit in my lap like this as she covered me with strawberry lip gloss and a false sense of security. Elliott is a whole other thing, heavier, his thighs firmer, a slight prickle of stubble in his kiss and no chance of emotional security at all.

It's different – easier, somehow – than it ever has been before, and I don't want it to stop, maybe ever, so I put my arms around him and hope that's not too much like actual affection for whatever our new arrangement is. And apparently it's fine, because he *doesn't* stop, just keeps kissing me. I feel brave enough to let my hands wander, to feel the sharp planes of his shoulder blades and the flat warmth of his chest. And he does the same. It's like he's actually enjoying it, which is both wildly unexpected and also very lucky, because I *definitely* am, even with the truckload of doubt unloading itself in my head.

It gets harder to focus on anything like that, though, the longer it all goes on. The more his lips soften against mine, the more he relaxes against me, the more real it starts to feel. He must notice the shift as well, the niceness that's creeping in, because he pulls away, not quite looking at me.

'You're not bad at that,' he says, and sits back, discreetly smoothing out his shirt where I'd been playing with it.

'Yeah,' I say, trying to readjust my jumper to cover my lap. 'You too.'

Over on the chair, Meggan makes a happy cooing sound and we realise what we've been doing in front of her. Thank goodness she doesn't have eyeballs.

'See,' he says, and backs up off me, still not meeting my eyes. 'Even the baby thinks it's a good idea.'

'I'm a bit dubious about taking advice from an egg.'

'Well then, take it from me,' he says, and his gaze flicks

over my lap before his grey eyes rise to meet mine. 'This is a very good idea.'

That night, the tension of expectation permeates the usual bedtime routine until I'm almost twitching out of my skin. Standing alone in the communal bathroom down the hall, brushing my teeth, I try to breathe like a normal human, willing my heart to calm down. It's not a big deal, it's just two people who are sort of friends, doing whatever. It doesn't mean anything and, he said it himself, he's not going to make me do anything I don't want to do. Not a big deal.

Regardless, the walk back to my room is terrifying in a fun, new way, and I almost completely bypass my door to go and get a cup of tea instead. As it is, I stand outside for almost a minute. When I finally go in, he's sitting on the edge of the bed in his fancy soft pyjamas, patting Meggan in her cot and looking completely harmless.

'She's almost asleep,' he whispers, and I close the door as quietly as I can.

'Probably a good thing,' I say, because even though Meggan isn't an actual human child, it still feels weird doing anything in front of her. 'If we're ... you know.'

Elliott raises an eyebrow. 'If we're what, Tim?'

I can't tell if I've misjudged how this works or if he's just being an arsehole. 'Or not, whatever,' I say, and feel my cheeks heat. 'Sorry I said anything.' I don't know if I'm embarrassed or annoyed, or annoyed at being embarrassed.

I should just climb into bed and pretend it's not a big deal, except seeing him sitting there is sending my brain into overdrive. A bed is very different from a shitty old couch, and right now it seems very hard to ignore the fact that we're not wearing anything under our pyjamas. I'm defenceless except for a bit of fabric. Just because he said we won't do anything I don't want to do, doesn't mean I'm going to know what's going on. What if I misinterpret something and he thinks I'm giving him the go-ahead and I'm not?

Hideously, it seems like I'm *not* sorry I said anything and I actually desperately want to keep talking about it.

Maybe it can wait until the lights are out and I don't have to look at him while I talk, with his stupid hair falling in his eyes and his nice face and everything. Or maybe being in bed in the dark is going to make it harder. Either way, I've been standing here staring at him for too long. I tap my quartz *on* where it sits on the bed end and then turn off the overheads. *Mood lighting*, a part of my brain says, but another part that sounds like Silvia snaps back that *we can't exactly sleep with the lights on, can we?*

I climb onto the bed, staying as far away from him as I can without it looking like I'm doing it, and resign myself to the wall-side again since he's still sitting and fussing over Meggan. I get a whole minute to try to arrange myself in a way that might look attractive without looking too eager before he slips under the covers, lies back on my pillow and throws his ankle over mine.

'Hey,' he says, looking over at me in the dimness like he hasn't a care in the world.

'Hi.'

'You OK?'

I don't answer right away. Dr Peters said it was OK to think about questions before I answer them, but the evidence so far has suggested that normal people disagree. Elliott is, apparently, normal.

'Tim?' he says after a moment, and he sounds ... hesitant. It's encouraging.

'Should we talk?' I ask.

He sighs. 'Second thoughts already?' he says, looking up at the ceiling. 'Ouch.'

'No. I just –' Shit. 'I don't know what the rules are. How does this work?'

'You Defensives and your rules.'

'You Minders and your disregard for them.'

'Again, ouch. Can we make rule one that we're nice to each other?'

That's probably a good one, and covers a lot of my concerns. 'Agreed.'

'Rule two, stop worrying, this is supposed to be fun.' He pokes me in the ribs and my skin tingles where he's touched me.

'Easy for you to say – you've done this before.'

'You've had a girlfriend before, it's not that different.'

'It *is*. She *liked* me. I didn't have to wonder if she was judging me all the time.'

'Tim,' he says, as he rolls onto his side and looks down at me, eyebrow raised, our legs tangling. 'You're overthinking it.'

He's very close, and he's warm and smells of mint and reckless decisions, and he's just hovering there, staring at my mouth and waiting for me to grab him by his stupid silky collar and pull him down – so I do.

It's different here, in the dark, under the covers, the thin fabric of our pyjamas magnifying the undeniable presence of another body. He's more polite than I expected – his touch light, hesitant – and he rolls onto his back at some point, pulling me with him and leaving me in control as he busies his fingers in my hair. And that's where his hands stay until we're slow and sleepy and both gagging for a drink of water. I fall asleep with his hand heavy on my stomach and it's about the most intimately that he's touched me all night.

That lack of handsiness, so noticeable in the darkness, disappears in the light of day, and with it go the doubts it had quietly planted in my brain. Saturday morning I wake to him draped over my back, snoring softly into my neck, and the day only gets better. I get a smack on the arse on the way to the shower, a rather gratuitous cuddle when I come back shirtless and half-frozen, and his avid attention when he realises I actually have core muscles and demands I flex for him. It's bizarre and pleasantly invasive and nothing like how Lizzie used to be at all.

We have a small amount of homework, which Silvia insists we do immediately after breakfast, and I'm so distracted that

I just go along with it and it only takes an hour. Elliott sits across from me, his foot resting against my ankle, and it feels like a promise of more to come – but it also goes against everything I'd expected for this arrangement, which was for all affection to be restricted to the times we're properly alone.

A group visit into town is littered with similar confusion. He's the same, mostly, as he is when we're alone, even though Silvia and Sam are there, and I wonder how much he was flirting with me before and I didn't notice. He teases, nudges my shoulder every time I get lost in thought, always pulling me back to him and Meggan. She's tucked out of sight in his immaculate red JanSport (trust him to have a needlessly expensive backpack) and I don't know if he actually thinks she needs monitoring or just wants me close to him. His hands are always somewhere, adjusting my seatbelt in the shuttle, holding me in place while he whispers in my ear, a light pressure on my back as we walk through the hidden pedestrian tunnel that leads into the bush. Did he always touch me this much?

The path is soft from recent rain and the cool air smells of ozone and loamy soil. It's perfectly picturesque, as usual, but slightly squishy. I'm glad I wore boots; it'd be a hundred times more embarrassing to stack it in front of Elliott and have to walk round town all muddy.

Sam pulls me out of my head with, 'Who are we feeding today?' It's a normal thing for the three of us on our walks into town, but I didn't know if we were going to do it in front of Elliott.

Sam pulls a handful of sunflower seeds out of his pocket and Elliott turns to me, questioning.

'We take turns summoning different birds,' I explain. 'It's good practice.'

'Practice for what?'

'Being able to summon birds.' I shrug. 'Pacific magic thing. Your Western European skillset is probably more aimed towards, like, pillaging.'

He glares at me, but doesn't argue. At least he's self-aware.

'Tim wants to be a Disney Princess,' Silvia says, 'and who are we to deny him?'

'Disney is morally corrupt,' Sam reminds us. 'We *should* deny him. But you're welcome to be Shrek instead.' He grins over his shoulder.

'Bring me a kōkako.' I glare at him.

'See, this is why you don't have your own bird anymore, Tim. You have impossible standards,' Sam says. 'Pick something that's not extinct or I'm going to let Elliott choose.'

'You know, actually,' Elliott interrupts, 'it'd be better for the birds if you summoned all the rats and killed them.'

We all stop walking and stare at him. He's not wrong, it's just kind of … brutal.

'Not in front of the children, Elliott,' Silvia says, putting a protective hand over where Leda's ears might've been. 'Pick a *bird*.'

He frowns. 'I don't know … the big pigeon. Thicc boi of the forest. Begins with K.'

'Kererū?' Sam says, with only the tiniest amount of mockery in his voice. 'OK then.'

Sam closes his fingers around the handful of seeds and Silvia holds his free hand so he can use some of her magic as well. It still makes me a little jealous when they do that. He shuts his eyes for a moment, focusing, while walking slowly along the path. We stay quiet, stepping more softly over twigs and leaves, breathing low. Meggan coos from inside the backpack. After a minute we hear it – an unmistakable, thrashing wingbeat. I lay a hand on Elliott's arm and we all stop and wait. Sam opens his hand, holding it out, and the intimidating whoosh of half-a-metre's worth of bird comes thundering out of the trees and lands violently on his wrist. Sam's arm sways a little under its weight, but the bird stays put, her claws gripping the thick woollen sleeve of his Swanndri. She eyes us all for a moment and deems us collectively unthreatening before turning her back and eating out of Sam's hand.

'It's huge,' Elliott whispers.

'That's what she said,' I whisper back.

He smirks. 'Lucky you have lube.'

Silvia raises an eyebrow, but doesn't look at me. She just smiles.

We stop at Four Square and Elliott buys Meggan ridiculous things: a unicorn-shaped teething ring she can neither hold nor bite, stewed apples I'm pretty sure he intends to eat himself, and a couple of picture books – one with dragons and one about a witch called Meg and her cat, Mog. I never even knew they sold that kind of stuff. The whole time we're in there, he pulls me around by my wrist.

He hasn't got any less tactile by the time we get to the cafe for lunch, and Silvia pounces the second Elliott goes to the loo, getting in while Sam's at the counter ordering food.

'You two seem pretty cosy,' she says, and the look on her face makes it an accusation.

'We're friends, I guess,' I say, since that in itself is probably a big enough surprise after years of us all thinking the whole group of them were awful. It's possibly even bigger than the truth – our arrangement – since it doesn't have a built-in expiry date.

'Since when are you friends?'

'Since we managed to spend time together and no-one got throat-punched.'

'That's your minimum requirement for friendship these days? You'd think you'd be drowning in social invitations.'

'I'm too tired for social invitations,' I say, and she looks dubiously at the quietly burbling backpack on my lap. '*Meggan*'s fine. It's just. I'm constantly with Elliott, every minute except for when we're in our separate classes, and it's exhausting having to be "on" all the time.'

'So you're friends with him but you don't like being around him?'

'I – I mean, he's fine. But he's not you,' I say, hoping to distract her with flattery.

'I'd hope not, after what you were up to the other night.'

Shit.

I'd forgotten about the fake hook-up underneath the secret real ones. Silvia had let it drag out for long enough that I'd dropped my guard. She's prone to doing that. Wily cow. I wish I had the sense to be friends with stupid people.

Sam arrives back at the table just in time to hear me fumble a rebuttal. 'That wasn't – I was asleep. Elliott was just trying to get you guys to stop what *you* were doing.'

'Sounded more like he was trying to join in,' Sam says, and Silvia cracks up laughing. They're terrible friends, but at least it doesn't look like they thought Elliott and I were actually doing anything.

Silvia steers the conversation away from their indiscretions. 'I do think you and Elliott make a good couple, Tim. You know, as parents. Don't you think, Sam?' She gives me a look and I try to keep my face from giving anything away.

'I guess,' he says, throwing his arm around Silvia and Leda. 'But we're still going to win this, aren't we?'

'I don't know,' she says, 'they're definitely keeping the bar high.'

'It's just an assignment, guys,' I say, trying to derail her scrutiny. 'It's not a big deal.'

Meggan coos despite the churn of different emotions making a mess of my chest; maybe my relief at being a good egg-daddy is slightly more intense than my desire to crawl under the table and die.

'Yeah, but there's pride on the line,' Sam starts as Elliott sits down beside me, his knees casually spreading until we're touching under the table. Sam rattles off a list of strategic predictions of why all the other teams are going to lose. When he comes to us, he says that, yes, we are doing well, but, 'Think about it – it'll be a real couple that keeps their baby alive the longest, won't it? Because they're going to stay focused and they have a real reason to want to see it through. All you random pairings are just going to get bored and careless and you're going to slip up.'

Elliott smirks but doesn't argue, just slings his arm around the back of my chair and leans over to peer into his backpack and pat his egg-daughter on the head. 'Don't you listen to the nasty man, Meggan, he doesn't know what he's talking about.'

And I realise he's right. For the first time in my life, Elliott Parker knows more about what's going on with me than Sam does. And it doesn't feel very good.

CHAPTER 13

CAN'T GET ENOUGH

Later that night, as we're tucking Meggan in and Elliott is singing her some ridiculously dorky-sounding lullaby, I decide to bring it up again – the fact that we haven't told our friends. Or, at least, that I haven't told Sam and Silvia, and I usually would've. I don't tell Elliott I'm still undecided on whether I want them to know. He counters with a declaration that maybe Sam wouldn't want to know what we're getting up to. He goes on about all the many reasons this might be better kept a secret: our exes, our illicit sleeping arrangements, the threat of expulsion, the proximity of my mother. Neither me nor him being properly out yet, the fact that it's not anyone's business – certainly not yet. The freedom from expectations, from societal

124

opinions, the thrill found in the secretive nature of the relationship ... and that word, *relationship*. Is that what this is? Are we in a relationship? Is that how he sees it? The word falls so easily out of his mouth that I start to wonder if he cares about the list of reasons he made before he said it.

Then he tugs at the hem of my shirt and I remember what he *does* care about.

'Is this the signal, then?' I ask, and lift up my arms so he can pull the shirt off over my head. I mean it to sound humorous, but he just looks at me like I'm a bit strange.

'Signal?'

'Yeah.' I feel a blush coming as I lower my arms. 'You know. Whether we're gonna ... I dunno.'

'Do you want there to be a signal?' He frowns. 'I figured we'd just ... go with it.'

'OK. I just –' I have the words in my head, but my mouth refuses to say them, like some sort of latent self-preservation instinct. Maybe, historically, humans really could die of embarrassment and this is my body trying to save itself from certain death. I take a breath and fall back on something I know is true. 'I don't know what your boundaries are. It's making me nervous.'

'Well, what're yours?' he asks, like it's a trick question. 'You brought it up. You talk.' He reaches for the waistband of my jeans and holds onto it, not moving, eyebrow arched. 'Is this OK?' There's a smile at the corner of his mouth and I'm pretty sure he's making fun of me, but maybe that's the best way to have this conversation – by pretending it's not nearly as important as it is.

'Yeah,' I say. 'Kinda expected more from an expert like you, though. Did Blake like it like this?'

Elliott's expression puckers and his eyes narrow, and he slips his fingers a little deeper and yanks me closer. 'I thought we agreed to be nice to each other?'

'And I want to know how *nice* we're planning on being.' It's still a bit baffling that he wants to do any of this with me at all, but I guess without Blake, and if he doesn't like girls, his options are limited. Except I don't actually know whether he likes girls. I never asked him, and now doesn't seem like the time.

'How *nice* would you like to be?' He cocks his head to the side. 'You're the novice. It should be up to you.'

'Fine.' I reach out and undo the button on his trousers. He doesn't flinch, so I double down and do the zipper too. The sound of it sliding open sets something off in my gut and I can't tell if it's fear or excitement or both, since I've just undone a boy's trousers for the first time.

'That was *helpful*, I suppose,' he says, and he glances towards the bed before looking pointedly down at my hand. 'I don't know if I'd call it *nice*.'

He's egging me on again, and I wish I wasn't falling for it, but I probably need *something* to make me brave right now. Besides, this is the point of the whole thing. To experiment; to explore who I am and what I like. And if he gets something out of that too, then fine. He probably deserves it. I don't know if I'll be any good at doing it this way round, but it can't be harder than girl parts, can it?

That said, I don't know if I can touch him while he's *watching* me.

'I'm being nicer than you've been so far,' I say. And when he looks up, all indignant, I lean in and kiss him, and it's significantly less scary than it was yesterday. At least in comparison to what I'm about to do.

On Monday Elliott and I have four classes together in a row, and there are still vivid images of our weekend together dancing around in my head. Worse, he spends our entire Maths lesson nibbling on the end of his pen with his knee against my thigh and his free hand intermittently reaching towards my lap to pat Meggan on the head. It's nice she's there for multiple reasons, but mostly to hide my interest in having him reaching for anything of mine again.

In our Magical History and International Relations class it's his turn to have her and it's not really any better. His long fingers absentmindedly stroke her dome as we listen to the teacher summarise about four weeks' worth of 'How Magical Culture Impacts Interpersonal Relations', and all I can think about is our own interpersonal relations and whether there's a spell to determine if someone is ultimately bad for your mental wellbeing in the long term, even if you find them attractive. Just like Taylor Swift, I knew he was trouble when he walked in, and yet here we are. As least she's profiting from her debatable choices. I don't think my future regrets will be worth anything at all.

Lunch is a welcome respite from having to sit touching him, except that instead, I have to sit opposite and watch him assemble a hot dog. By hand.

'Can you make me one too?' I ask, since it's my turn with Meggan and it might justify the fact I'm staring.

'Take this one,' he sighs, and goes to hand me his.

I hesitate before reminding him I like tomato sauce, and admitting I'm not *that* fond of mustard.

'You're not fussy at all, are you?' He gives me a look before picking up a fresh bun and sliding a hot dog into it. 'How many millilitres of tomato sauce would you like?'

I want to laugh but I'm hungry and flustered, and it comes out like a grim chuckle. 'You're not being very self-aware right now.'

He scowls at me as he squirts sauce on my hot dog, then asks how many sprinkles of grated cheese I want before deciding for me. He hands it over.

'That wasn't so hard, was it?' I say.

'It was pretty hard, actually,' he says, and smirks the very tiniest amount, so no-one else notices. 'I got sauce on me.' He holds my eye and licks a drop of tomato sauce off his thumb, far slower than is strictly necessary.

I make it through Food Tech by force of will alone, but at least I can see him starting to suffer as well. He's flushed the whole time I'm washing our carrots and courgettes.

He cringes a bit when I start grating them. The tall pepper grinder seems to push him over the edge when it comes time to serve up, and he sits with his stool so close we're touching from shoulder to ankle.

We don't make it back to our room after class. I pull him in the opposite direction once no-one is looking and drag him into a maintenance cupboard. I place Meggan gently in an empty mop bucket. He doesn't bother asking what I'm doing, just locks the door behind us, rests his lit quartz on top of a giant pack of toilet paper and waits for me to shove him up against the door and kiss him.

It takes the edge off. We make it through 'til bedtime without acting weird in front of our friends, at least. And Meggan is happy. Happier than Ana and Matt's egg is. They decided to shut it alone in Matt's single room where it can't bother anyone and leave it there, damning themselves academically if there's any sort of parental proximity sensor.

Elliott and I make sure to act as platonic as possible – sniping at each other every so often, sitting at opposite ends of the couch. At ten o'clock we brush our teeth at a perfectly normal speed, and don't walk to our room too quickly. Or hand in hand. Or even together. I go first with the baby, and he wanders off to hang out with Manaia for a bit before our dorm supervisor, Lorraine, drops in for her curfew check and packs everyone off towards their gender-appropriate corridors (still not knowing, hopefully, that some of us will be redistributing ourselves once she's gone). I consider starting by myself after twenty minutes, but Elliott shows up not long after, looking harassed, and pounces on me immediately.

My previous nervousness is nowhere to be found. The dam's been broken, hesitation banished, and Elliott's shameless enthusiasm has me flying off the edge of reason, eyes closed and arms outstretched like I might actually grow wings. There's a lot to be said, it turns out, for hooking up with someone who has the same parts as you. It's a thousand per cent more exciting because it's another person, but you already have a comfortable understanding of how things work, what's good, and at what point you should probably stop before it gets messy. Or not.

The next day I manage to concentrate in my morning classes, since Elliott isn't in them, but Magical History is almost a write-off again before I remember I actually need to know this stuff if I want to do any sort of law enforcement apprenticeship. I ignore Elliott's glare and stick my headphones on, letting Fat Freddy's Drop get me in the zone for a rehash of *Chapter 7: Intercultural Bonding Practices in the Southern Hemisphere*. I read the whole chapter and it's a bit creepy in parts and dead boring in others, and I learn far too much about the romantic habits of people my nan's age. Elliott spends a lot of time trying to distract me instead of doing his work, and I wonder what he's planning to do with his life. Maybe he could be a nanny, or someone who irritates people for a living. Maybe politics would satisfy both.

There's a movie night organised for the evening, and Lorraine, along with my mum, are in the senior lounge handing out popcorn and growling at kids who aren't being quiet. It's horrifying to be in the same room, on the same couch, as Elliott and his wandering limbs when my mother is there, and he notices I'm tense and milks it for everything it's worth. Lorraine, of course, is around most nights before curfew, helping with homework and keeping an eye out, and she's used to Elliott and I being friends now. Mum isn't. I get a lot of strange looks from her – usually when Elliott is being inappropriately touchy, which is saying a lot since there's five of us on a four-person couch and it should look perfectly normal for us all to be overlapping somewhat. He makes it look dodgy, though, and I message him from my seat to get his bloody arm off the back of the couch behind me. He sends me an eggplant emoji followed by a lollipop emoji and I die a little. He ruffles my hair and I adjust Meggan's blanket on my lap and fume in silence.

He makes it up to me later. He's better at that than Lizzie was.

On Thursday night, we beg off early with homework and the hideous port comes out again and Elliott ends up giggly and handsy and we get almost no studying done. I decide not to complain and let him do as he pleases, which ends up pleasing me more than it does him, and he declares that I owe him one. I tell him he's only getting his precious reciprocity if he can keep his hands to himself in class the next day so I can concentrate. It makes Friday a lot easier academically and a lot scarier emotionally as I realise what I've agreed to. I end up sneaking off to the loo and googling some stuff. I'm not sure if it helps, but I'm not risking any 'instructional videos' on the school wi-fi.

We have nachos for dinner that night and I pick at them, eating so little that Ana and Silvia start shooting me worried looks and I have to shovel a bunch in just to avoid questions. It's not like I could answer them. Certainly not at the dinner table. Or in the crowded lounge after. It'll be hours until we can go to our room inconspicuously, and for once I don't mind. This'll be the first time we end up doing something I've never done before, and it feels like a bigger deal than anything else has so far.

Elliott doesn't seem remotely worried. 'What's up with you?' he whispers.

I stare at him. 'I have something I have to do later.'

'It's kinda late to be doing anything.'

I raise an eyebrow. Idiot. 'Reciprocity?'

'Oh.' He rolls his eyes. 'You don't have to do that. Especially not if it's going to make you all weird and quiet.'

'It's fine, I want to.'

'You really don't have to, though.' His brow wrinkles. 'You get that, right? We came to a pretty clear agreement. Whatever you want.'

He looks so carefully worried I feel the urge to hide my face in my hands, but I settle for just pushing all the loose hair out of my face. 'I want to try?'

'Fine.' He smiles. 'If you ask nicely, I guess I might let you.'

'Right. I'll beg for the privilege, shall I?'

He blushes then, and my heart skitters and I look around. Enough people have gone to bed that we can probably leave without drawing attention. Having Meggan helps – we should probably get her down soon if we want her to have a decent sleep and not give us hell tomorrow. I stand up.

'Night,' I say to the rest of the group. They're sitting on their phones, mostly, though there's a fairly high-stakes game of Spite and Malice happening on the floor. Manaia looks like she's winning and Ana looks like she might resort to violence if she does. I turn to Elliott. 'You want me to take Meggan or are you coming to bed?'

'I can carry her,' he says, playing along. 'I'm not incompetent.'

'Whatever.' I walk out and along the hall, then brush my teeth and try to calm myself down. When I get to my room, Elliott has put Meggan in her cot and changed into his pyjamas.

'My turn,' he says, and it seems a bit blunt considering he just said I didn't actually have to, but then he just slips out the door towards the bathroom and I cringe at myself. His turn in the bathroom. My turn to feel like an idiot.

I get changed and get into bed and put on some music. I turn it off again. I pull my pillow over my head and quietly scream into it. I wait, unable to decide if I'm more scared or more excited. I hear the door squeak, and close, and the lock clicks, and there's a spark in my belly that gives me the answer.

CHAPTER 14

GREEN LIGHT

He falls asleep before me, hours later, his hand pushed into mine. I find myself watching him, like if I stare long enough he'll start to make sense. His behaviour is no less confusing after a week of dishevelled clothing and hidden hickeys and finding excuses to be alone together. Since the beginning, he's been affectionate when it's just us, and after his fun time teasing me in front of my mother during Tuesday night's movie, there seems to be no boundaries in public either. I find myself thinking more about that than the physical stuff.

We've chipped away at my curiosity so thoroughly, there's really only one thing we haven't even talked about doing – something I'd never expected to try for the first time with a guy I wasn't even going out with. But each night that we've fallen asleep all tangled and soft and he's murmured goodnight into my hair, I've wondered if it matters that we aren't really going out – that we're the opposite of committed, or that I'm thinking about using up my last first time on someone who might not really deserve it. Because apart from that, he's been kind of perfect. Or at least, he's been very good-looking and very patient. I feel like I'm waiting for something to go wrong, and the fact that it hasn't yet is making me nervous.

The next morning is Saturday so we stay in bed, just cuddling, Meggan wedged between us like we're a family of gay penguins. It's kind of lovely, but I don't really enjoy it properly because I don't know what lovely means. I wonder if my mood of uncertainty is obvious enough that he's just trying to keep the peace by not trying anything, or if he's getting sick of me, or if it's just general sleepiness (or chafing). It feels a bit like a transition into something else, and I wish I knew what, but asking seems like admitting it matters, and that's not the point of all this.

I'm conflicted enough that I go to see Mum after a late breakfast, as I do in times of uncertainty, and she comes too close to spotting a telltale mark on my neck and I don't know what I'll tell her if she asks about it. That I got back with Liz? That I have a secret lover? That I have a temporary boyfriend? A lab partner for the world's least school-appropriate human biology experiment? I change the subject to needing socks, and her maternal instincts kick in as she plans a shopping trip. I let her presence soothe me into thinking everything will be OK. I don't, obviously, ask her about sex, or Elliott, or sex with Elliott, even though it's on my mind. I don't know if she'd be quietly condemning or embarrassingly supportive. I don't even know which of those is worse.

She offers me a sausage sandwich for morning tea, and I'm in my head the whole time we're eating, remembering things. I walk with her to lunch and it's meatloaf loaded with a cheese centre. I get no respite. My brain is in horny, obsessive overdrive, wondering ... When? If? Is there a limit to how far this can go? Should I try to satisfy all my curiosities while I can? Should I put a limit on it and save myself for someone who actually wants to go out with me? Will I even like it? Who'd do which thing? Does *he* want to do it? Can I *ask?* Then I wonder how Lizzie and I lasted as long as we did when my focus was clearly elsewhere.

Whatever you want, Elliott said. So on the way back from lunch, I nod towards the corridor that leads to the workshop, and he smirks and pushes me ahead of him, checking no-one's there to see us slip away.

He obviously isn't expecting to *talk* when we get there, because he pushes me up against the closed door and kisses me before I can say anything. My confidence ratchets up a notch as his fingers slip under the edge of my waistband and I really, *really* want to see what comes next if all of *this* has got so comfortable so easily. There's far less of the awkward fumbling I had with Lizzie; he's so sure of himself, even if I'm not, and he doesn't seem hampered by anything so trivial as emotions. Only thing is, I hadn't expected peppered kisses down my neck to be part of our arrangement, and yet ... that's happening. It tickles.

'I want to have sex,' I say, and his lips freeze where they are. 'If you do.'

'What?' He pulls back. He looks nervous. *'Now?'*

'No, like. I dunno. Whenever.'

He rolls his eyes at me, and I ask him if he's done it before and we end up having a tiny argument about what I mean before he admits to what he has and hasn't done. I'm surprised, a little, but my assumptions were based on his implications, and bravado is a part of him I'm familiar with. He and Blake hadn't gone the whole way, apparently. He knows what to do, technically, but hasn't done it either. It feels like a big thing, deciding we both want to. A mutual first that's probably a bit too monumental for someone you're not really going out with, who plans to leave you sometime soon. It changes the way I feel about touching him, and we sit in silence for a while on the shitty old couch, my eyes tracing scratches in the glossy paint of the Camry.

'We don't have to do it,' he says after a time.

'I want to know what it's like.'

'Yes, but if it's going to make it weird between us, is it worth it? I'd rather carry on as we are than have some hideously awkward attempt be the last thing we do.'

'Are you scared?' I ask, surprised to find myself thinking he might be.

'No, I'm appropriately wary.'

'We can talk about it some more. I usually feel more scared about things when I can't be really honest about them.'

'I see your recent visits to the school counsellor have worked wonders.'

'You don't have to be a dick about it,' I say, not willing to talk about Dr Peters and how many wonders he actually did manage to work.

'Fine then, Te Maro, go ahead, lay your every thought on the table.'

'I'm worried it'll hurt. For whoever's … you know.' I feel my face heat.

'According to the brochures, to avoid discomfort, one should ensure they have adequate time, water-based lubricant and trimmed fingernails.' He holds his hand out to me, palm down. His ring is more intricate-looking close up, almost delicate. 'I can promise the first and the third. Apparently lube is your department.'

His nails are, indeed, extremely short, and I wonder if they're always like that, or if he's been thinking about all this stuff as well. I hold my hand under his so our fingertips are aligned. His fingers are longer than mine, but slimmer, and I don't hate the thought of them. He pushes into the delicate webbing until he's holding my hand, and it shifts the mood of the whole conversation.

'Lube was the Year 10 Health curriculum's department – remember our very informative sessions with the school nurse?' I say, and let our joined hands sit against my thigh.

'All we have to do is relax.' I look around the room, realising our missed opportunity. 'Do you think there's any alcohol stashed in here?'

'There was ...' Elliott's other hand is busy with the fraying edge of the cushion. 'But at the beginning of the year I was ... not in the best place. I don't want to do it drunk, anyway.'

'I'm not suggesting drunk, just ... more relaxed. And not with your vile port.'

'We can buy something else more *relaxing*, then, if you'd prefer?' he says. 'Next time we go into town. Manaia's eighteen. Though I don't fancy trying to buy condoms in front of her.'

'I have some,' I say, and the agreement feels more solid now that we're talking logistics. My gut flares with anticipation. It feels like a weird sort of sexual Christmas, and now that it's real I suddenly don't know how I feel about it. I say it out loud to see what it's like. 'Cool. So, we're gonna do it.' The fizz of anticipation rolls over in my stomach. 'When should we ...?'

'Manaia said she had an essay due that she hadn't started, so I doubt she'll be free today before the shops shut, and the liquor store isn't open on Sundays.'

'OK. Next weekend, then, I guess?'

Elliott nods. 'And what'll we do right now?' he asks, looking at me like he knows exactly what. 'You made me sit through the most awkward conversation in the world, so you owe me.' He gets up off the couch and turns to stand in front of me.

I think he's going to stay there, looming, but instead he comes forward to straddle my lap like the first time we were here. This time I grab his hips and pull him flush against me. He kisses me, and it's too easy to slide back into the rhythm of him and forget where we are. I daydream about what we're going to do later, and he bites at my neck, and the flood of endorphins makes us bold, or forgetful, and it goes way too far considering we might get caught in here. Eventually, we bundle a happily gurgling Meggan out of her cushion nest and sneak back into the corridor.

We find Manaia in the lounge surrounded by half-done English homework and manage to arrange a trade: I'll sit down 'immediately, for the love of God', and help her with her essay, and she'll come into town with us *this afternoon*. The week I thought I had between me and massive life-changing events evaporates into proverbial dust and robust discussion. My nerves ratchet up a notch, but Elliott looks completely unbothered so I guess I'm suffering alone.

Manaia and I spend an hour sitting in front of the heater, drawing thematic parallels between *Whale Rider* and *Hunt For The Wilderpeople* while Elliott lies on the floor beside us, one hand keeping hold of Meggan, the other glued to his phone. He's browsing Reddit, and keeps interrupting to lean over and show me things, or read out idiotic comments, and it's worse than when we were with my friends. Clearly, he's more than comfortable being affectionate with me around Manaia. I wonder what she'll make of it: the familiarity of his socked foot digging into my side or the back of his hand resting on my knee while he wiggles his phone at me.

He's not acting like a friend with benefits, he's acting like a boyfriend. Maybe that's the way he wants it – one hundred per cent like it could be, but on a fixed schedule. But what about his insistence that no-one should know? Why bother with that if he's going to be like this? A week ago I was thinking we could avoid anything remotely romantic, hoping our feelings wouldn't catch on to what we were doing. Instead, he seems to have some sort of ability to turn them off and on at will, and no regard for whether I can do the same.

CHAPTER 15

YOU GOTTA KNOW

Our second excursion into town together is much the same as the first, his hands everywhere, except that he also refuses to let me pay for the hipflask of rum I ask for, insisting it's a gift. He simply hands over his debit card and Manaia comes back with my rum and a fancy-looking 40oz bottle of whiskey. He even buys me a Coke at the petrol station when he decides that I 'look thirsty'. He gets one for Manaia too, but it's not enough to divert her furtive looks. I can only hope her loyalty to him extends to not publicly speculating on what we're up to, because she's not stupid and I don't know what her shining a light on our arrangement will do.

She seems especially smirky when Elliott decides I should summon a fantail, and marvels a little too much at my ability to do so, even though I can't coax it down to my hand since I have nothing to feed it. It just flits about our heads for a bit, then buggers off back into the forest. I can't tell if her gaze is assessing my magic, or assessing the way Elliott is treating me. Eventually I decide that's his problem. Even if I'm confused by it, I'm enjoying someone being really nice to me, after Lizzie. And if I say something about how obvious he's being and he decides to dial it back, I might actually miss it.

Thinking about being alone again makes me needy, and all the walking makes me tired, so once we're back home and out of Manaia's earshot I suggest an early night. His expression says a lot. I spend the hours between then and dinner trying not to think about what might be coming and what a big step it is for the both of us. I fail. Both Silvia and Manaia keep throwing sly glances our way and I can't even remember what normal behaviour looks like for me, so I probably act extra weird. I don't eat much. My stomach is in knots. Elliott looks completely relaxed, but he's stopped touching me now and it's the only indicator that he's on edge as well.

After dinner, back in the lounge, we wait until Silvia's at the loo, then turn in with a declaration of being exhausted by our trip into town and the whole parenting malarky. Sam says, 'Are you still not sleeping through the night?' and I can safely say that, no, we aren't, because whenever we're awake at the same time, we tend to get distracted. If there was any chance Elliott's Minder skills could cause inhuman horniness, I'd assume it was him making me avoid my friends and lie about where I'm going. Just like now.

This time, though, at least we've planned it for a reasonable hour. The door is locked. Meggan has had a bath, a bedtime story and a lullaby, and is making tiny little snoring sounds. If you think about it a certain way, we're nailing this assignment. We have the happiest fake baby in the class.

On the other hand, we're also subjecting her to an awful lot of adult activity playing out right by her bed.

'So,' Elliott says, taking off his jumper and shoes, then loosening all the extraneous buttons on his shirt. 'Are we doing this now?'

He's nervous. It's comforting, because all the easiness of the week has just shattered into tiny pieces and I'm not feeling a hundred per cent confident myself. Maybe fifty-five per cent, at a stretch.

'Only if we want to,' I say, and I still don't know if *I* do. 'We planned for next week, so it can wait. Meggan and Leda and a bunch of the other eggs are still alive and well. Assignment's not over.'

'True,' he says, and shrugs. 'Though, anything could happen between now and next weekend.'

'How about,' I say, 'we try the first bit, and then after that, make a decision on the whole –' I make a vague gesture with my hand. 'The main event bit.'

'That seems sensible.'

'And talking about it, telling the truth, will make it less scary, remember. Even if it's weird to say it out loud.'

'Yes, Dr Te Maro. Let's just have a drink, shall we?'

'I think you should call me Tim,' I say, because if it's going to be awkward anyway, we should start with something small. 'I feel like we're past surnames.'

He looks a bit spooked, even by that, and I wonder if the name thing was one of the parts helping him switch his feelings off. I also wonder if it'll be a bedroom thing only. It might be a bit telling for those on the outside – he's only ever called me Te Maro. Manaia would probably read into it if he called me Tim in front of her, even though *she* calls me Tim already. Girls seem to have different rules.

'I guess I can try,' is all he says, muttering an incantation over our mugs, still stained with port from last time. 'You're having rum, I assume?'

'I'd like to try your fancy-pants whiskey, if you don't mind? See what a dollar a shot tastes like.'

'I doubt your palate is sophisticated enough to discern any difference from common bourbon. But by all means, let's try it. Who knows what your mouth is capable of?' He smiles to himself as he looks around for the backpack that we smuggled in this afternoon, heavy with our two bottles of illegal alcohol.

I roll my eyes. 'Thanks,' I say, and wonder if he's purposely honed in on the one thing I'm even less confident about or if he's just trying to lighten the mood.

'Fortunately, you know what you're doing with your hands, at least,' he says. A compliment, almost. My shoulders relax slightly. 'I assume that decides who's doing what. Unless that's something else you think we should awkwardly discuss?'

'It doesn't necessarily dictate who does what. But if you want me to do the prep and, um … be the insertive party … I can. I've done it before. Once. Almost.'

'Makes sense that one of us should almost know what we're doing.'

'Cool. There's, um, an incantation, for …' Honestly, just kill me now. 'Internal cleanliness. Mareko explained a few things after we, um, hooked up.'

'So it's a family trait, the lecturing?'

'It wasn't a lecture, it was just advice – like an oral guidebook.'

'An oral guidebook? You'd think you'd be better at that then.'

'Shut up, I tried.'

'Shall we start with the incantation then?' He leans over and slides the large whiskey bottle out of the backpack. 'Or shall we start with the underage drinking?'

'I need an empty shell, hang on.'

Testament to our increasingly weird magical education, he doesn't question that, just pours a measure of whiskey into each mug and takes a sip while I fossick around in a box of extra mea looking for something appropriate to help focus my energy.

I come up with a small kākara, which seems oddly well-named for what I'm doing with it. 'Can I?' I gesture at his belly.

'Sure,' he says, and lifts up his shirt, which is both distracting and unnecessary, but it's not like I'm going to pass up a chance to touch him.

His skin is warm and smooth, and the tiny hitch in his breath soothes my ego in just the right way. I close my left fist around the white seashell and let my right hand slide down and spread out until my fingertips are just under the waistband of his jeans. 'Ready?'

'Do you need a hand?' He offers me his open palm – an offer of his own magic. I hesitate.

Does he fully understand what he's doing? Letting someone draw on your power is pretty intense. I've shared with Sam and Silv before, and Mum and Dad when they were teaching me how to do stuff. Once or twice with Lizzie. Silvia and I experimented with blowing things up, mostly. Sam daisy-chained on to us once and we turned a dead stump into a pile of splinters. But we were *friends*. Even considering the physical closeness of mine and Elliott's relationship, it's not a given that we would ever share magic. It's not insignificant that he's offering, but who knows what it means, coming from him. It's easy to lose knowledge when the magic skips a whole generation – especially for complex social customs like this.

I decide I don't care either way; I've felt the very edges of his magic and I want to know what it's like to get inside it. No-one needs to know we did it.

'OK.' I lay my fist in his hand and his fingers close around me like an anemone.

I feel the familiar tingle, and then, immediately, he lets himself go. The thrum of his magic surges, twining around my own, dancing over my bones, strong and soft and strange. His magic is more than I expected – fuller, denser, more ... shiny. *That*, I guess, I *could've* expected.

I take a breath and focus on the shell in one hand and the depths of his belly with the other. I hold the idea of both in my mind and recite the incantation Mareko taught me. I feel the pulse in my hands and Elliott twitches under me, startled.

'Wow,' he says, and lets go of my hand. 'Seems that worked.'

'Yeah.' I feel his absence in more than my skin. 'Do you want to do an, um, exterior one, or should I?'

'Something else Mareko taught you?'

'Just seems sensible. Clean.'

'Then go ahead.' He offers his hand again, and I put the shell in my pocket and lay my palm down against his.

Superficial cleaning is easier; it's a natural inclination and rarely needs a mea. It really doesn't need any extra power either, but it looks like we're ignoring that. I'm more than happy to touch his magic again, and that's ... new. Sharing power before has always been an exploration of magic, of our capabilities. It never felt like an exploration of each other. Not like this.

I slip my hand off Elliott's stomach, back over his hip, into the dip of his lumbar. His hand tightens around mine. He lets go of his magic again and it swirls through me, waiting for me to do something with it, and I – I *really* like it. I let my hand slip lower and he shifts towards me, supplicant. We're not even doing anything and already my heart is pounding. I whisper the incantation and he sighs against my shoulder. He doesn't let go of my hand.

It's good we did this now, the cleaning stuff. It seems naive to have thought I'd have the mental capacity to perform any magic effectively after we'd started. Even simple incantations require having blood in useful places, like my brain, and right now it's enthusiastically starting to flow somewhere else.

'All done.' I step back, releasing him. I feel heavy.

'Well, that was an experience.' He pours himself more whiskey.

'It's important to be prepared,' I say, and unzip my hoodie and chuck it on the bed; it feels warmer in here, all of a sudden. I beckon him forward. He comes to me slowly, without meeting my eye. 'You OK?' I ask.

'Fine.' He hands me my drink and sips at his own. 'Stop treating me like I'm fragile, Te Maro.'

'Call me Tim, would you?' I take a sip, remembering to hold it in my mouth to taste it better.

'Fine, *Tim*,' he says, watching me drink. 'What do you think of the whiskey?'

'It's nice,' I say, and he snorts.

'You'll have to come up with a better adjective than that, or you'll owe me a dollar for every mouthful.'

'It's very nice.'

'That's still a dollar.'

I take another sip and hand my cup back to him. The vapour is filling my nose, making it tingle. 'Fragrant.'

'Acceptable.' He tips his own cup back, draining it, and sets them both on the wide wooden frame of the bed end.

I reach for his belt and he lets me unhook it, pulling the leather free and leaving it to hang so the buckle tinks against itself in the quiet. It sounds different tonight. More significant.

'OK?' he asks, and I nod, not trusting my voice.

It's easier to kiss him than to think about everything I'm feeling. Easier to read into his touch than the way he's looking at me. Easier to get us where we're going if I just let my body take over and tread the familiar path into comfortable, instinctive oblivion.

I pull back and flick off the overhead lights, draping the room in darkness. My gut thrums a little, my heart thumps, and he drags me back in so there's nothing but darkness and quiet and his mouth on mine.

Then there's a soft tapping sound, the lock clicks, and the door opens with a squeak. Light floods in and suddenly we're not alone anymore.

CHAPTER 16

BE MINE TONIGHT

We both turn and find Sam silhouetted in the bright light of the doorway.

'Gimme a second,' he hisses down the hall, gaze averted just long enough that Elliott has a chance to put some platonic distance between us before Sam turns his attention to the room. He startles when he sees me. 'What the hell are you standing around in the dark for?' he says. 'I thought you were going to bed?'

A valid question when we're both still fully clothed, but the lights are off. Shit.

'Shush, we're trying to settle Meggan,' Elliott whispers before I can come up with anything. I admire his quick thinking – he's turned to lean over the little purple cot, lending legitimacy to his claim and also hiding the fact his belt is undone. 'Could you keep it down?'

'Sorry.' Sam raises his hands in surrender, grabs the blanket off the end of his bed and leaves, though not before shooting me a very curious look. I really, really wish he was a bit stupider – I'd be getting away with this a lot better. I also probably wouldn't be doing quite so well in some of my classes, though, so it's a double-edged sword. The door clicks shut behind him.

'Did you not think to maybe *lock the door?*' Elliott asks, and I hear the telltale sound of his belt being refastened. 'That was very nearly very bad.'

'I did lock the door. He still has a key.'

Elliott lets out a long-suffering sigh. 'You staff kids are a law unto your own. I gave my key to Manaia, and I assumed you'd given me Sam's. Nice of you to mention there was a third one.'

I wonder if I should tell him we all have master keys, Sam, Silvia and I. Not legitimately – we really, honestly, shouldn't – but when you teach a bunch of teenagers to replicate small, inanimate objects and someone (Silvia's mum) happens to leave a master key lying around (OK, it was in her handbag) then what do you expect? Maybe I'm better off distracting him.

'Sorry. I have somewhere else we can go if you want. Somewhere a bit more private.' At least, I think it is. I'm pretty sure Mum gave me the only key to those rooms.

There's still the masters, but at least no-one has any reason to go looking for me in there.

Elliott raises an eyebrow. 'I'm not having sex with you in a tunnel.'

'That's not where I'm taking you. Come on.' I get up and put my hoodie back on, wondering if we can get away with taking a blanket, since I don't know what's left in Dad's rooms. I pull a light woollen one out of the wardrobe and hold it out. 'If we wrap Meggan in this, no-one will question us taking it with us.'

'Where are we going that we need a blanket?' He scowls at me.

'We can stay here and just go to sleep if you want.' I shrug to prove I don't mind, just in case he's getting cold feet. I don't know why I'm not. Maybe it's too much to process now and I'm beyond normal feelings. Maybe Sam interrupting us made me realise how much I wish he hadn't.

Elliott sighs again instead of answering, then gently scoops Meggan out of her cot and hands her to me. I see him lift his pillow, grab the sachet that's still stashed under there, and slide it into his pocket. He eyes the backpack. I hope he's not going to try bringing the 40oz of whiskey with us; we'll get flayed if we're caught, and it's much harder to hide a bottle that size than a hipflask.

'The rum, not the whiskey,' I say, and he grunts in reluctant agreement, fishing around for it before nudging the backpack under the bed. He turns around with it in his hand and looks down, hopelessly, at his pockets. He's too

153

skinny to hide anything even that small under his clothes, and going out in an uncharacteristically baggy jacket is just going to look suspicious. I hold a blanket-swaddled Meggan out to him. 'We can hide it in my pants, my jumper will cover it.'

I'm expecting him to take the baby, but instead he reaches for my waistband, manages to grab both my jeans and my underwear, and unceremoniously shoves the slim glass bottle down the front.

'What the hell?' I gasp as my ardour withers. The glass is bloody cold and I could kill him. 'You could've warmed it up first, you bastard.'

'That'll teach you for lying about the key.' He pulls my jumper down over the bump and turns for the door.

'I didn't lie,' I say, following him into the corridor. 'It was an omission.'

'Your *benefits* will be an omission if you do it again.'

I let it go – we're almost in earshot of the student lounge. I give Silvia and Sam a nod in passing as we walk through.

'Where are you going?' Silvia calls after us.

'Taking Meggan for a walk; see if that helps her settle,' I say, and hope they don't notice that she's completely silent right now. Or notice when we're gone for an hour. Or two. Or however long it takes, what would I know?

She looks appeased, even if Sam doesn't, quite. I try to act normal and just keep following Elliott. He speaks again once we're alone in the corridor.

'So where are we going?'

'Staff wing. I have a key for my dad's rooms.'

'Won't your *mother* be there?'

'What? No, he had his own separate rooms as well.'

Elliott's quiet for a moment. 'Why?'

'I guess he got offered them and said yes? Dad wrote textbooks and articles and stuff, so he used it as a quiet space to work. Plus, the apartments are pretty small – they probably appreciated some time away from each other.'

'Sounds healthy. I can see why their relationship was so successful.'

'Shut up, Elliott.'

'This is the worst date ever.'

'It's not a date,' I say, but I'm not sure of that now that I'm saying it.

'Well, then, it's the worst one of whatever you think it is.'

'Let's just have a look before you get your knickers in a twist. It might be fine.'

'"Fine" sounds so romantic. I can't wait.'

I stop walking. This isn't how I'd pictured it going. He takes a few more steps before he realises I'm not keeping pace with him anymore.

'What now?' he says.

'Are you OK?' I ask, pushing my own frustration down. If he's being snarky, it might be a sign, and I don't want to be that guy. My mum didn't raise no peer-pressuring sleazebag. 'Seriously. We can just go for a walk and get a tea if you want. Try again tomorrow. Or later. Whatever.'

He takes a breath, not meeting my eyes. 'It's fine, let's just get this over with.'

'I don't want to *get it over with*.'

An announcement about extracurriculars comes over the tannoy just as Elliott opens his mouth to respond, and he glares at the tinny old speaker until it stops. 'Can we stop having this conversation in the corridor, at least?' he says.

I shrug, and we walk, and neither of us says another thing until we're behind closed doors, in my father's living room.

'Te Maro ... are you sure he's gone?' Elliott asks, and when I don't answer immediately, he corrects himself: 'Sorry. *Tim*, are you sure he's gone?'

I have bigger things on my mind than what he's calling me. Like why my dad's lounge still seems to be furnished, and full of his stuff, including his wall of books and his couch and his computer perched on his writing desk. My heart stutters and I hold Meggan a little tighter. Comfortingly, there at least seems to be a noticeable layer of dust on everything, so I'm not imagining that he left. There's just ... something else going on, maybe.

'Doesn't look like he lives here anymore,' I say.

'Yes, but it does appear that he left everything behind.'

'Yeah.'

It's very, very weird, but I try to focus on the fact that something of him is still left here for me. A Dad bubble. I might actually be able to use the space without crying – this is far less depressing than a completely empty room would've been. And his books might be useful for studying. Maybe it's even evidence that he and Mum might get back together, eventually – proof that he knew there was no sense in moving all his things. I can't help smiling at the thought and, honestly, it would explain a lot of things about how it went down with them.

On a more immediate note, the big leather couch in front of us is going to be miles better than the shitty couch in the workshop, or being interrupted again.

Elliott is apparently thinking the same thing. 'Why didn't we come here the first time? Instead of the workshop?'

'Wasn't really ready to see it without him in it,' I say, and he nods, accepting that without saying anything else.

Instead, he walks over and opens the nearest door, revealing a small bathroom that's almost identical to the one at my mother's, and in the same position as hers too. I'd imagine all the staff rooms are pretty similar. Hanging on the wall between the vanity and the shower I can just see an orange hand towel, and its presence seems superfluous if my dad isn't planning on coming back. Another good sign.

Elliott moves towards the next door along and I find myself following, curious to see what the bedroom holds since I know Dad never slept here. Curious if there's a bed and if it has sheets and everything or if it's just a rusted frame and a moth-eaten mattress, leftover from whoever lived here years ago.

I've often wondered what this place was before it was a school, but Mum just looks at me funny when I ask, even

157

though there's a whole wing that no-one goes into because it just feels wrong. I'm getting a similar feeling now, deep in my gut, and I'm almost scared when Elliott wraps his hand around the doorknob and twists.

I needn't have been. It looks like a completely normal bedroom, if a little sparse. There are boxes stacked to one side, a dresser with nothing on it, a heater and a neatly made bed. The bedside tables are completely barren except for a layer of dust. No lamp, no books, no generic box of tissues, nothing. I look up. There's not even a lightbulb in the socket. I take the rum out of my pants and turn the heater on one-handed, Meggan still held close. The boxes are full of more books, of course. Typical Dad.

'Looks like an abandoned motel room,' Elliott says. He pulls out his pale, flat piece of rose quartz and places it on the corner of the dresser. He taps it and the room glows pink. 'Give me your hand.' He reaches out and wiggles his fingers at me.

'What for?'

'I'm going to do a spot of dusting,' he says.

He scoops at the air in front of him with his other hand, trapping some in his fist. It's a familiar move, but not one I expected to see him using as a Minder – it's Elemental magic. Curious.

I take his hand, but I hold on to my own magic as he says the unfamiliar incantation and blows across his closed fist. The gesture makes sense for what I know of Elemental magic, and magic in general. We use gestures a bit in Defence, like recently with shielding, but that's advanced stuff; we've only been learning it this year, so it seems odd that he'd know it. Learning magic from other Specialties isn't against the rules, it's just really, really uncommon, since the teachers don't have time for free lessons outside of class. It relies very heavily on another student being capable of teaching you: you both need the time, and to be good enough. I wonder if Elliott could teach *me* things ...

I let my magic go. His gentle eddy of wind immediately picks up, the bedspread rippling and flapping, the pillows flopping over, a visible whirl of dust forming over it, spinning and twisting. A part of me feels itself curling through him, exploring all his corners and being drawn into his hands, directed by his intentions. It's nice. He's calm and confident and my magic feels safe in him.

He reaches behind us, pulls a drawer out of the dresser and holds it against the edge of the bed, pulling on my magic to coax the little tornado across the mattress until it's dropped inside. When the swirling dust slows and flops down into a small pile in the bottom of the drawer, he turns again and slides the whole thing back into the dresser. He drops my hand.

'Where did you learn that?' I ask. His control seems well beyond what a non-Elemental should be able to achieve, and he did it while messing about with the drawer as well.

'Manaia.' He shrugs.

'It seems pretty advanced considering it's not your Specialty.'

'We're both quite clever.' He smiles. 'Besides, most of our other friends were expelled, so we found ourselves with a lot of free time this year,' he says, bending down to take off his shoes. 'Had to fill it with something.'

'Fair enough.'

He looks up at me from under his lashes. 'I could probably teach you,' he says, and that's what I'd hoped for so I can't help smiling.

The moment hangs there between us, my impressed affection adding itself to the mix of emotions, seeping into the confusion and longing of being in my father's space. The weirdness of finding his rooms like this can wait; he left and he's certainly not here now, but Elliott is, and so am I, and half an hour ago we had a solid plan.

'Teach me later,' I say, and reach for his hand again.

The pink light makes his skin look warmer, richer, and his hand feels comfortable in mine, and I kind of want to just push him down into the mattress and kiss the living daylights out of him. I still don't know how he's feeling, though, and we need to find somewhere to put Meggan, and it occurs to me I've completely forgotten to bring condoms with me anyway, so that puts a cap on *that*. I can still kiss him, though. So I do.

Meggan is a hard lump between us when everything else about his kiss is warm and sweet; more like the first time we kissed than the last. It's not long before he steps back, turns and opens a different dresser drawer, gathering up our daughter and placing her inside. He touches the piece of rose quartz for a moment and the light dims. He comes back to me, pressing close, one hand sliding into my hair and his mouth soft on mine. His fingers find their way under my jumper and they're cold, but I don't care.

'Do you want to talk about anything?' I ask between kisses, and he answers by grabbing me by the shoulders and shoving me down on the bed.

'Nope,' he says, and climbs up after me, following me as I shuffle back towards the pillows. 'You?'

'No.' My heart is pounding, partly adrenalin. 'I'm all good.'

'Good.'

'I forgot to bring condoms,' I blurt.

He smirks, reaches into his pocket and brings out the lube and a Durex three-pack – the sort I've only ever seen in petrol stations. Things click together in my head. The Coke and the random declaration of my *thirst* suddenly make more sense. I almost laugh, but he kisses me again and I lose my hold on time.

We might be there for hours, slowly shedding layers, retreating under the covers when we get too cold, systematically covering each other in hickeys like we're stalling for time. His skin is warm and the fabric of his boxers is smooth under my fingers. I still find myself marvelling at the sharp angles of his body, the light stubble on his jaw. The coarse hair of his legs is still a thrill even after all the time we've spent tangled together in my bed. And all the while, our little stash of supplies burns bright in the periphery of my senses. This is different from the other times and we haven't even really done anything yet.

He sighs above me, pushing his hips down, and my heart pounds deep in my chest at the blatant display of want. His forehead is damp against my own, and he's still for a long time, just breathing. Now that my eyes have adjusted to the dimness, I can't stop looking at him. I wonder if this might be it for the night, but I'm wrong.

'Are we doing this?' he whispers, kissing gently along my hairline, licking my temples, nipping softly at my brow.

Probably. I don't want to *not* do it, I just don't want it to be scary. And this is different from Lizzie, because Elliott doesn't love me – so he's not going to instantly forgive me if I'm crap at it, or if I do something wrong.

'This might be a good time to talk about the next bit,' I say, my voice sounding too loud as my hands find the small of his back.

'I have no complaints so far,' he says, flexing his hips again with a sigh, eyelashes fluttering against my cheek.

'"No complaints" is not consent.'

'Well, then.' He threads his fingers into my hair and pushes it back so he can look me in the eye. 'I consent. How's that?'

'Very clear, thank you.' I say. It's awkward, but his smile is warm and fond and comforting in just the right way. A rush of warmth sweeps across my skin. One look from him and I've gone from worrying I won't be any good, to worrying it'll be *too* good. Despite the number of problems

Lizzie and I had, that wasn't one of them. Kind of telling in hindsight.

The whole time, I keep noticing all the other ways he's not like her. All through the awkward bits and the awesome bits and the times I can't even string thoughts together. He's not passive, he's not leaving everything up to me, he's not holding back on what he wants. He doesn't treat any of it like he's indulging me, or doing me a favour, or like we're not completely equal in every moment. I kind of love it. I mean, yeah, of course I do, but I swear it's never been like this before – honest and careless and easy. The freedom is like a drug, the comfort a welcome surprise, and the bone-deep satisfaction on a level entirely new to me. All I can think is, this was *definitely* a good idea.

CHAPTER 17

KNOW YOUR OWN HEART

I wake up in my dad's bed sometime during the night. It's disorienting for a second, but Elliott's rose quartz is still glowing softly on the dresser and he's still draped across my chest. It doesn't take me long to come back to myself.

The similar layout to Mum's rooms helps my feet find the bathroom in the near-dark – my own quartz is somewhere in my trousers, which are somewhere on the floor. The bathroom light blazes in comparison, and I pee mostly blind.

I don't notice until I go to wash my hands, when my eyes have adjusted, that there's something sitting beside the sink.

A wide gold band, painfully familiar.

All the hope I had for my parents reuniting vaporises into a thick cloud of despair. It fills the tiny bathroom like steam until my throat feels like it's closing up. I pick up the ring, turning it over to make sure. It's very definitely my father's wedding band. I can't just leave it here, lying around like it means nothing, so I slip it on, and somehow that feels worse – more final. Like he's never coming back for it.

I don't expect to be able to sleep anymore, so I wake Elliott and we gather our things, and our egg-baby, and sneak back home. The corridors are dark and cold and Meggan wakes and whimpers, so I cuddle her closer, wishing someone would do the same for me.

The second time I wake up is better. Elliott groans a little and stretches and pulls me towards him and slides his ankle over mine and I nuzzle at his neck, dropping little kisses and nipping at his skin until he's properly awake.

We end up losing another hour to each other, not a thing between us but the memory of what last night was like. It's weirdly intense for first thing in the morning, and yet afterwards he wonders aloud about whether the petrol station sells lube or if we'll have to use WD40 next time, and I laugh and it's just … fine. It's nice, and not awkward, and I don't regret anything we did last night like I was afraid I would.

On Monday, we walk to the dining hall with Meggan bundled in Elliott's arms and me carrying both our schoolbags, then cruise through our usual breakfast routine.

It reminds me a little of my mother's stories about her and Dad and me as a tiny baby, and I try not to think about Dad's ring, still on my finger. We have Specialties first, and Elliott's is way safer than mine, so I part ways with the two of them until morning tea, not quite able to get either of them out of my mind the whole time we're practising shield formation. I get hit in the head a few times, but not with a snow globe or anything, so I'm still up on last month.

I think about Elliott: unbuttoning his shirt cuffs, resting his knee against mine, absentmindedly patting Meggan 'til she falls asleep. Then I imagine him sitting in class, learning how to lie, how to affect other people's thoughts, and I wonder, again, if that's what he's doing with me. The churn of potential regret flares in my gut. What if he was so needy after Blake left him that he latched on to the next available body? Maybe he's manipulated me into going on this mad journey of self-discovery with him. Well, except the discovery has mostly been mine, I suppose, up until recently. Or not – maybe he knew I'd find it easier if he said it was his first time too.

'You with us, Tim?' our weapons instructor asks, and I turn to find him standing over me where I'm sitting cross-legged on the floor, my classmates spread out around me. Stu's an ex-cop so he misses nothing, which I suppose is good, but I could do without his practised attention right now.

'Yeah, sorry. Was just thinking about something.'

'Anything you want to ask me about?'

I don't know if he's actually assuming it's about class stuff or if he's offering to listen to my personal problems, but the issue is technically both, so I try him. 'Minders,' I say. 'Would this sort of shield work against them?'

'Good question,' Stu says, and scans the rest of the class. He lifts his hand, and each of the little foam balls we've been practising with freezes in the air. All the other Defensives turn to face him, and he continues. 'Who reckons this shield will work against a Minder?'

Corey makes a crack about whether the Minder is throwing a foam ball at him, but in general the discussion is sensible, and Nikau's the one who summarises (correctly, apparently) that no, this particular shield is essentially useless against non-solid objects. It won't even block magically manipulated air, which makes it a bit of a write-off if you tried to use it against some Elementals as well, since that might be their whole thing. Stu assures us it does work against water and earth, though, and goes on to teach us the variation for blocking fire. After last year, the teachers have all been a bit twitchy when it comes to open flames.

None of it really helps with my question, though, so I hang back after class. 'Stu, can you tell if someone is manipulating your thoughts with magic?'

He sighs, a look of understanding passing across his grizzled features. 'Depends. How good are they?'

'I don't know. Pretty good.'

'Student?' he asks.

'Yeah. Theoretically.'

He doesn't give any indication of buying that, but he indulges me anyway as he cinches the storage bag closed on the class set of foam balls. 'It's highly likely that a student in Year 12 or 13 would be good enough to get into your head, but it's less likely that they could do it without you noticing. That takes skill and practice, and I don't think any of that lot are breaking any records this year.'

'What does it feel like?' I ask, and isn't that the topic of my life right now. 'When they get in your head?'

'Depends on what they're trying to do. Any of them ever get you before?'

'Yeah, they made me see spiders one time. I knew it wasn't real but I freaked out anyway.'

'Mmh.' He nods, and it's kinda nice to feel validated, like that sort of thing might happen to everyone. 'They rely on your instincts to trick you; they can't change the way you feel about things, but they can make you see something you already have a strong emotional response to. Which is why that shield doesn't work. The spiders aren't real. If they were real, it would work.' He pauses, and misinterprets my silence for a lack of understanding. 'Think of it this way: use the shield, and if it pushes the spiders away, the spiders were real but they're gone now and you're safe. If it doesn't push them away, they were never real, and you were always safe.'

It's a valid tactic, sure, but my mind is snagged on the first thing he said, and the rush of calm that came with it. 'They can't change the way you feel?'

He raises an eyebrow. 'Who's messing you around?'

'No-one. Just curious.'

'Right.' I see him waver, then decide he doesn't want to know. 'Good. Stay curious. It keeps you from being stupid.' He nods and gives me a gruff goodbye, like we've just had an awkwardly pastoral conversation that he wasn't ready for.

I follow him out and head for the dining hall, comforted by the fact that Elliott hasn't been violating my mind. I hadn't realised how much the doubt had been weighing on me. My heart skitters with unbridled contentment when I see him already sitting at our usual table, chatting to Sam.

I drop down opposite them and Elliott hands Meggan over, and she sits in my lap and burbles while her other daddy butters us scones. He even warms them without being asked. The butter is melty and delicious, and I enjoy the small act of service all the more now that I know there's nothing nefarious behind it.

Life Skills is after morning tea, and we arrive to find Van Mill and an array of weird, technical-looking mea laid out on the table. She explains none of them, which seems like a wasted opportunity to actually teach us something. Instead, she just waves her hand over everyone's egg-babies, doing her checks, and is overtly 'just thrilled' at our results.

I bet my entire collection of mea that she's surprised to see Elliott and I near the top of the class. Half the egg-babies are out of the game already, but our group is all doing pretty well. There's Meggan; Sam and Silvia's Leda; Nikau and Hana's Buttercup; and Matt and Ana's egg, Humpty. Matt did apparently almost drop Humpty in the shower, which didn't really surprise anyone but did make us wonder what he was doing in there with it.

Outside of my immediate circle, the only remaining eggs are Blake and Lizzie's Agatha, and Fabergé, who belongs to a Minder couple I don't know very well but who are probably dickheads. Then there are three other eggs, hilariously named Pēkana, Gonad, and Cedric Diggory, all belonging to people I know and like but on a pretty superficial level. We've been stuck underground together for ages, and you learn who you can get along with for extended periods of time and who you can only deal with in small doses. We're as friendly as any year group is, but I can feel the drift already as some of us prepare to not see each other ever again after December.

Our table discusses the current results (and various egg-deaths) over lunch, throwing around ideas about who'll win and who'll be eliminated next – and whether it'll be by innocent fumbling or Manaia-level self-sabotage. We bring up whether or not there's any sort of prize (and if there isn't, there should be). The decision is made that whoever lasts the longest out of the group gets a bowl of chips shouted to them at the cafe.

Elliott declares to all who will listen that he and I are going to win, and Sam shakes his head and repeats his earlier assertion that we aren't a real threat because we aren't a real couple. It seems tactical this time. I see the look Silvia gives me as he says it, tempting me to disagree, pointing out that she knows something's going on between us even if I won't talk about it. I get the feeling they might've been comparing notes on us.

Elliott is oblivious to it, and goes on to list all the reasons we're less likely to drop our baby than Sam is (which basically boils down to: we're both determined to prove him wrong and the baby's not a book). His ankle is resting against mine again and he refills my tea without being asked and, overall, I reckon I can probably cope with my friends knowing so long as it doesn't change anything. I realise I haven't thought about Lizzie dumping me in ages and I've barely even remembered the fact I'm sad and alone – and it occurs to me then that I'm *not* sad and alone.

Not anymore.

CHAPTER 18

SETTLE DOWN

When I get to our room that night, Elliott's there already, reading *Meg and Mog*. He's doing all the voices and I can't help grinning. It wouldn't be a bad life, actually being with Elliott. He's obviously not so prickly once he gets comfortable – quite the opposite. And he's ridiculously hot under all those expensive clothes. And smart, and respectful, and shamelessly cute with Meggan. All good things. Things that are going to make breaking up with him utterly horrible, but it's what I signed up for, so what else can I do?

Thinking about it is too hard and I don't want to ruin an otherwise good day, so I pluck the book out of Elliott's hand, throw it to the end of the bed and pull him on top of me. He's warm and enthusiastic and perfectly distracting.

His hands snake under my pyjama shirt, pushing it up and over my head, and he whips off his own, too, throwing both to the floor. Meggan starts to snore softly, contented in her bed as our own happiness lulls her to sleep.

'When do we get to do it again?' he whispers, his breath cooling my damp skin where he's been nibbling at my neck.

I stare at the ceiling and wonder how dangerous it is to get used to this, then decide I don't care. 'Now's good,' I say.

'That's the answer I wanted.'

I shudder at the confidence in his voice, the knowledge of what's coming and what it does to me. 'We should put something in front of the door,' I say, because I really, really don't want to be interrupted this time.

He hums his assent and backs up off me, bare-chested and ruffled and gorgeous. He looks around the room and frowns. 'I think we're going to have to drag Sam's bed over.' He steps onto the floor and examines the heavy wooden bed frame. 'Help?'

'Sure.' I wrap my right hand around my pounamu and utter the incantation for increased strength. A shiver cascades through my muscles; it tickles, and I have to shake it out. He frowns at me, confused, but I just smile because I finally have the chance to impress him.

I shift Leda's cot out of the way, squat down at the middle of Sam's bed and grab the underside of the frame. It's like moving a cardboard replica – same sense of unwieldiness, but the weight is insignificant and it slides easily across the threshold, blocking the door from opening. I adjust it slightly to make sure, then stand up.

'OK …' Elliott says, looking at me. 'Two things: What was that? And since when do you wear a ring?'

"The ring's Dad's. I found it in his rooms. And *that* was increased strength.' I shrug, and step towards him.

He nods, not pressing for more. Instead, he points at my chest. 'You used that as a mea?'

'Pounamu is one of the strongest types of stone. Used for cutting things, traditionally. Plus Dad gave it to me and he was …' I trail off, the sadness creeping in.

'He was built like a brick shithouse, yes, I remember.' Elliott lays a hand on my chest, close but not quite touching the small, carved mere. 'You know, I'm glad he doesn't know what we're up to, come to think of it. Though your mother probably wouldn't be too thrilled about it either.'

'Not up to them,' I say, refusing to think about what he's really saying – that we don't belong together. I reach out for him, running my hands over his hips, right down until I reach the top of his thighs, then I scoop him up off the floor and into my arms. He squeaks. 'Time to shut up,' I say.

He leans down and kisses me and it's bizarre and kind of wonderful. I want to throw him on the bed, but I have to be careful with him until the magic wears off, so I stay where I am and just let it all happen. He pulls my hair loose and twists his fingers into it and it feels like he's everywhere at once.

'OK?' he asks between kisses, and I nod, not together enough to make real words. 'Do you want to put me down?'

'No,' I say, and it's scary how deep that thought goes. That I might not want to put him down *ever*, even though I know I have to. I feel my arms squeeze reflexively, pulling him closer. It's scary, the suddenness of all these feelings. I don't know if I'm rebounding, or if I've been secretly into him for a while, or if this is just what happens when someone accompanies you on your trip of self-discovery. Maybe it's just the confirmation that I can trust him that's finally sinking in. I take a deep breath.

'Are you sure you're OK?' he says, and I can hear the grin behind it.

'Just – go slow, yeah?' I say, and find the edge of my mattress with the backs of my legs. I take his weight in one arm and ease us down with the other.

He doesn't answer, just kisses the tender underside of my jaw, the soft silk of his hair tickling my skin. I pull him in close and hold him to me and none of it makes any sense. It feels personal but it isn't, it feels safe but it shouldn't, and I feel irrepressibly happy about all of it.

CHAPTER 19

FALL AT YOUR FEET

The following week is a blur of classes and sweaty tangled limbs, and I have to really try to keep the contented grin off my face or risk giving us away. Elliott is still being attentive and nice and blatantly affectionate in public and I'm still not sure what to do with it, but I fear it's beginning to wear down whatever walls I had in place. I know if I accept all his small gestures and just go with it, everything will get messy and our inevitable separation will be emotional and tense and I'll end up heartsick and really missing him. It's already clear I'll miss him physically. We barely make it through the door these days before he's pulling at my clothes. I'm frequently distracted over dinner, waiting for when we can be alone.

Friday, we get our first night out by ourselves – Sam and Silvia are babysitting Meggan in exchange for us babysitting Leda tomorrow night. They have her until ten in the morning – ostensibly because we've said we don't know when we'll get back from town, but actually because we'd like to spend one night without her listening in.

We get the shuttle around four and walk the rest of the way into town, headed for dinner at the restaurant attached to the pub and an evening playing darts or something else inappropriate for small egg-children. Our waitress recognises us from school – she's only a couple of years older – and she points us out to a guy called Noah, another ex-student from her year. He comes over looking for gossip about the teachers and ends up telling us all about his apprenticeship in Queenstown. He tells regular people he's a meteorologist, but he's actually an Elemental, and now he's one of three graduates making ski season happen at the right time and keeping things safe for the unwitting public. When he's done talking about himself, he introduces us to his cousin, Dave, who he's staying with down the road in their grandpa's old house, and we end up sneaking into the pub with them and playing doubles in pool. Noah covertly buys us drinks and sends unsubtle looks at Elliott and I'm not sure how I feel about it.

After a couple of hours, we follow Noah and his cousin back to theirs, a group of other pub-goers in tow and far too much alcohol in me to be thinking sensible things like how we're going to get home if we miss the last shuttle. All I can think of is whether Elliott's going to ditch me for this older guy and whether or not I'd leave him here if he did.

The rest of the night starts with old records blasting under dim, dusty lights and our pick of beers out of someone else's fridge. At some point Noah makes his move on Elliott while I'm sitting alone on a shitty old couch, watching what might be the worst thing to happen to me all year. Then, in a way I hadn't hoped to imagine, Elliott starts laughing and points at me across the room and Noah looks devastated that he's messed up. He kneels drunkenly at my feet and apologises profusely, then runs off to fetch me an 'apology beer'. Elliott sits next to me and I remember that the worst thing to happen this year should probably have been my girlfriend leaving me. Whatever emotion that realisation provokes, it gets lost amid the overwhelming feeling of having had too much to drink and I throw caution to the wind, no longer caring if we get home, or if I even keep my food down, so long as Elliott keeps telling random older guys he's with *me*.

There's only snatches of memory after that: a platter of chicken nuggets, Elliott wearing a blanket on his head, someone telling us to be good to one another. There's a guy wearing sunglasses inside and I'm so drunk I'm pretty sure I can see through people, and then, so late it's almost early again, Elliott and his blanket settle over me on the couch and we fall asleep to the light of a lava lamp and the sound of someone snoring in the next room.

I wake up on the same couch only a few hours later with a sore back and a full bladder. Only one of those things is easy to fix. I think I'm still drunk. I don't feel hungover yet so I must be. I should drink some water.

'Elliott.' I sit back down on the couch after I've been to the loo and got a drink. 'Wake up. I brought you water.'

'No,' he says, voice low and husky. 'Come back to bed.'

I'm tempted to point out that this isn't really a bed – that we have one of those back at school, a brisk, two-hour walk away since, unsurprisingly, the shuttle doesn't run at stupid o'clock in the morning. But then Elliott slips a hand around my waist and his touch is like warm water and the thought of having to trek through the dark and the cold is too much, so I crawl back under the blanket. I can't help but curl into him and lose myself again in his kisses. I'll take the five million detentions if we get caught – I don't care.

It's different this time, kissing him, letting it escalate. It's slow, gentle, and my chest is aching like I'm not remembering to breathe enough. The whole room seems to glow with a warm light as we move together, still in our clothes, his tongue sliding hot and wet on my neck and the soft scrape of teeth sending me over the edge in more ways than one. When I wake up again, hours later, I see the outline of him and smile without thinking, before I realise what I've done with a force so brutal it pushes tears from my eyes, and my heart flutters with panic.

I've fallen for him. Right off the cliff's edge we've been walking this whole time.

And I'm alone.

CHAPTER 20

BETTER BE HOME SOON

By the time we get moving, it's almost six-thirty and we decide to wait the few minutes for the cafe to open so we can get a coffee and a pie and try to make ourselves human again. It's weird, because everything between us looks fine on the surface but I'm slowly dying on the inside. At least the physical pain in my head aligns nicely with the internal crumbling of my heart.

I message Sam and tell him we're hungover and still technically in town but we're not dead, in case anyone noticed we were gone, and he sends back a vomit emoji and a thumbs up. It's a long walk back to the hidden door in the bush, but Sam has worked some sort of magic and his grandad is waiting for us in his van with a book in his hand, sipping from a thermos of tea. He lifts a disapproving eyebrow but doesn't mention that we look like death warmed up or that we were obviously out all night. I don't volunteer any information, either: not the underage drinking, the going home with strangers or the missing of our curfew. I definitely don't mention getting off on said strangers' couch the next morning, or the fact I've fallen for my roommate. Who I'm not meant to be rooming with.

We manage to get back to our room without anyone asking any incriminating questions, then strip to our underwear and fall into bed, not even bothering with pyjamas. It's all too soon that we're woken up again. There are two very familiar voices whispering and the contented burbles of two egg-babies. Elliott is spooned up behind me, his face buried in the nape of my neck, his bare arm draped over my waist.

'Oh, look. Tim's awake.' Silvia sounds smug, which is never good.

'So can we leave Meggan and go now?' Sam says.

'Please do that,' I murmur, hoping Elliott doesn't wake up and I can get away with never telling him that we got caught cuddling.

'Mate, you look wrecked,' Sam says, and he sounds almost sympathetic.

'I expect he *is* wrecked. Lord knows where the two of them ended up last night. I told you we'd need to bring them hangover remedies,' Silvia says, and I hear a comforting rustle and a clink.

Oh, she's a goddess. I hold my hand out for the little bottle, and the cool, smooth press of glass is enough to make me whimper with relief. I crack an eye open, uncap the bottle, and carefully tip it into my mouth without sitting up too far.

'The pub,' I say when the bottle is empty. 'Then some guy's house.' I lower my head back onto the pillow, wincing.

'Shh,' comes a sound from behind me, and a slim, pale hand reaches up to pat my mouth.

'Right,' Sam says. 'So, Meggan's here, in her cot. We'll see you at five when we drop off Leda.'

'No, Sam, we'll see them at morning tea in fifteen minutes. They have a responsibility as parents to be awake to look after their child.'

'Whatever. I'm not enjoying seeing them now, so I'm leaving, and I'm taking our daughter with me.'

Silvia tsks and says her goodbyes, and there's shuffling and the sound of the door. I hear them start to bicker as they walk off down the hall, along with the soft grizzly gurgles of our egg-daughter sharing our feelings. I open one eye to check we're definitely alone before saying anything to Elliott.

'We should get out of bed.'

'We should not. You are, as usual, wrong.'

I am, but not about this. I'm wrong to have feelings for him when we said we wouldn't, or to be pathetically happy that he's still clinging to me despite the interruption, or to be secretly glad that my friends didn't seem to mind too much that they've just got confirmation something's going on.

And yeah, it's wrong, and I'm an idiot, but it's also not my fault. Not when he made me feel this way with his relentless affection and attention, and every single kiss he poured himself into like there was nothing else in the world but me. Not with the enthusiasm he has for our egg-baby, and his faith in us that we'll win, and the fact he hasn't, not once, reminded me we have an expiration date. Maybe he thinks I shouldn't need reminding.

I need to be away from him for a bit, so if he wants to stay in bed, then fine. That works for me too. Maybe I'll feel normal when I'm alone.

'I'm going to go have a shower. Silvia's right, we should eat something.' My stomach rumbles slightly in agreement. That pie barely touched the sides, and it was hours ago. 'Any chance you could unclamp yourself from me so I can get up?' I try to push his arm away.

'You flatter yourself,' he says, retracting his limbs. 'I was merely holding on to the nearest solid object to keep the room from spinning.'

He's trying to be funny but it stings, and I can't think of anything else to say that won't come out shitty or give away too much of what I'm feeling, so I just throw back the covers and look around for something to wear. I settle for my dressing gown and his slippers, since that means he'll be without and I want to be petty right now. I throw him the second bottle of hangover remedy that Silvia left, though.

He'll be impossible without it, and I still have a tiny bit of self-preservation instinct.

'Are you going right now?' he asks, before he knocks it back.

'Yes.' I grab my towel off the back of the door.

'Wait,' he whines, and I ignore him and leave anyway.

CHAPTER 21

SILVER & GOLD

He's dressed when I get back from the shower, looking tired and rumpled and sort of helpless. I feel guilty for being mad at him. I suppose it's not his fault that I think he's good-looking or nicer than I expected. I retreat under my towel, drying my hair more thoroughly than usual. When I pull the towel off my head he's standing there, stock still, looking at the pounamu around my neck like he's surprised to see it. My hand drifts automatically to the gap in my robe, seeking out the carved stone. He looks up then, and our eyes meet, and I see my own confusion mirrored there.

'What?'

'Nothing. I thought I remembered something, but it's

gone.' He goes back to fussing with Meggan, but I'm left with a weird feeling of unease.

It's as I'm getting dressed that I notice Dad's ring isn't on my finger anymore. My right hand is completely bare; there's not even a dent to say it was there. I panic, hard, because normally I might've been able to find it, to retrace my steps through the corridors and classrooms. But the last eighteen hours have been well out of the ordinary – a trip to town, to the pub, to some random dude's house, to the cafe, and all the way back through the woods again. It could be anywhere. It could've come off in the shower and be gone forever down the drain. I check my other hand, just in case.

It's a different ring I find there. A silver one. Still familiar, but not the one I was wearing when we left yesterday. Elliott's ring. The one he once casually mentioned was worth almost a grand. The one with the black stone set in it – the very distinctive, very much his, silver ring. On my left hand. Fourth finger. Ring finger.

I look over at him and see a flash of gold as he bends to push his feet into his shoes. My panic subsides. Something else blossoms in its place.

I want to ask Elliott what he knows, but I don't want to hear his answer. Don't want to be teased for thinking we might have made some sort of commitment to each other last night – or, worse, to have him share my suspicions and see him openly regret whatever led to us wearing each other's rings. I don't want to be mocked for wishful thinking. *You wish you were sleeping with me,* he'd said. *You wish.*

And what if I wish for more than that now? I don't want him to see my feelings written across my face like it was a billboard for badly kept secrets. So I shut my mouth and look away from my dad's ring on his finger, and pretend I don't know anything at all about the silver one on mine. I have time.

It's easy for a while. I don't need my hands for walking. I keep them buried in my pockets, out of sight. I insist on sitting at an empty table, far from Sam and Silvia's laser-guided eyesight, and I eat food that doesn't need buttering. I use only my right hand; the left is jammed between my knees. Elliott is distracted with Meggan, grizzling in his lap. We make it through almost all of morning tea. Then we don't.

'What do you want?' Elliott snaps at someone over my left shoulder. I turn and find Blake. Here. Near me and my hand and the world's most visible scandal.

'Just wanted to say hello,' he purrs.

'I'm no longer interested in saying hello to you.'

'What?' Blake puts on an air of mock offense. 'You only say hello to Te Maro now? Is he your new special friend?'

'Don't see why you care,' Elliott says. 'You broke up with me.'

'Now, now, we had an arrangement, Elliott, and it had stopped being mutually beneficial.'

'If you'd kindly go away and let us eat in peace, I think that would definitely be mutually beneficial.' Elliott takes a casual sip of tea. 'Mostly to you, because I won't be forced to curse you.'

'You're very cranky, sweetheart. Did we finally come across something Te Maro isn't good at? Other than weather charms and keeping a hold of his girlfriend?'

'Bugger off, Blake,' I say, giving him the finger, and it should be because he's giving me shit, but I fear it might be because he's calling Elliott 'sweetheart' and I hate that and might have to kill him ... But also myself, because Blake grabs my left wrist, the one I just brandished at him, and –

'*Oh*. What's this, Elliott? He's wearing your ring? Don't you think it's a bit soon?' Blake smirks, and I don't really see what happens but his laugh cuts off in an instant, and Elliott has his left hand clutched around something and a glare on his face that reminds me too much of our past. It's the first time he's come to my defence, though, and I don't know what to make of it.

Blake drops my wrist and stomps off back to my ex-girlfriend, and Elliott puts whatever it is back in his pocket. 'Sorry about him,' he says, staring at my ring finger like he hasn't seen it before.

'All good,' I say. 'Not sure it won't backfire on you, but thanks.'

Elliott doesn't say anything; his gaze is fixed on his own ring finger now.

'Tim,' he says, his right arm wrapped around our egg-daughter and his left splayed out on the table.

'Yeah,' I say, because I want just another second where I don't have to face this.

'It's ...' He looks between the rings. 'You don't think ...'

188

'You'd certainly hope not.' I try to laugh, but it comes out rough, like a lie.

'And yet.' He rubs at the gold ring with his thumb, turning it. His voice goes quiet, worried. 'Swap back?'

I feel a tiny, ominous twist in my gut at the thought of removing his ring, oddly worried I might lose it, but I hold the silver band tight and slide it free. The second it leaves my finger, it's like handling a tiny razorblade, and I drop it on the table.

It gets a thousand times worse.

'*Ow.*' I barely even hear my own voice.

My insides feel like they're melting, my vision is dark and cloudy, and behind it is a feeling of dread – visceral horror at an unknown thing that sends my heart into double time and makes me want to curl into a ball and hide under the table. My subconscious automatically undoes its last action, grabbing the ring again; the horror eases back to the tiny razorblades. I look at my hand and I'm not bleeding, and I can't decide if that's good or if it's even more ominous than what just happened in my head.

'What?' Elliott says, reaching across the table.

'It's bad,' I say. An understatement. 'When I drop it.'

Unease is flooding my gut and I have to test it again – have to know for sure. I place the ring on the table and lift my fingers, and the unearthly nausea and wrongness come back. I'm ready for it this time, but it's still unfathomably horrible. I lay a single finger back on the ring and the feeling goes away. It's pretty clear. It's not a good outcome, but it's clear.

'It's bad how?'

'Everything feels horrible. Like someone's put bad magic on it.'

'Is there any sign of that? A mark? A carving?'

I pick it up and turn it, tiny razorblades be damned.

'It –' Shit. It's a hundred times worse than I thought. 'It has today's date engraved in it, and our initials and the words – shit.'

'It says *shit?*'

'No. It says, *"mō āke tonu atu"*.' I grin, but it's a weak attempt at convincing myself I'm not having a mental breakdown. I slide the ring back on and feel mostly normal again. Or, at least, only as crap as I already felt this morning.

'I'd hope it goes without saying, but that wasn't on it before. I don't even know what those words mean.'

'I do.' I reach into my shirt and pull out my pounamu, easing the plaited cord over my head. 'Here,' I say, turning the carved mere over and holding it out so he can see the same words etched into it. 'It means "forever". The pounamu was my grandfather's originally – his best friend gave it to him when they went to war together. My grandfather gave it to my dad when he came back alone.'

'Oh,' Elliott says, and his brow furrows, his expression understandably strained. 'Check mine,' he says. He wiggles his left fingers at me, right arm still wrapped around Meggan. Apparently academic curiosity wins over whatever else he might be thinking.

'It's going to feel bad if I take it off.'

'We're not going to know anything more if you don't.'

I take his hand. With nervous fingers, I ease the gold ring loose and watch his reaction, waiting to see if he feels it too. He's not exactly calm, but he looks unbothered. Maybe touching someone who's touching the ring is enough of a connection for it not to hurt, like an electrical current. I keep a hold of him just in case. It won't look good in a crowded dining hall, but what choice do I have? I look at the inside of Dad's ring. I sigh. 'Same thing. Date, initials, "forever". Written in English this time.' I slide the ring back on his finger and there's something undeniably not unfamiliar about that action. Something I'm hoping he has an alternative explanation for, because my own is a little bit crazy. 'What are you thinking?' I say.

'That potentially getting done for underage drinking and staying out all night might be the least of our worries, considering.'

'Considering what?' I ask, drawing out my wilful ignorance for one more moment. Enjoying the feel of it as I prepare for its loss. Wondering if there's any sense in hiding my feelings anymore.

He sighs and his fingers flex under mine. 'Considering that it appears we're married.'

CHAPTER 22

ONWARD

Elliott and I try taking the rings off a few more times throughout the day to see if anything's changed, and it hasn't. It aches to lose contact with them – it even hurts a bit when it's on a different finger. Feels *wrong*. The attempt to put Elliott's on a chain around my neck is vastly uncomfortable, like tiny razorblades swinging past my heart. On the upside, when we retreat to opposite corners of the school there are no weird twinges or pains or urges to get back to each other. It's a relief to be away from him, actually, and all the looming questions.

We don't talk about the implications of having got into this situation at all, just the physical issue of the rings and the pain and how much trouble we'll be in if we have to explain what happened to a teacher so they can fix it. We *do* talk about the similarity it bears to some of the stuff we've been studying in class lately, and the seemingly brutal way that ancient magical cultures around the world used to forge alliances.

Despite Elliott's suggestion that we might be married, we focus on different sorts of *platonic* bonds. We also consider the fact we might be cursed. Maybe Noah didn't handle rejection quite as well as we thought. Both of us ignore the fact that it looks like we accidentally signed up for a magically enhanced commitment in a relationship that, by its very definition, was meant to be the avoidance of commitment.

Once we finally think to actually get in touch with Noah, he and Dave are already on their way to the airport to fly home. They don't have contact details for anyone else who was there last night, and neither of them remember anything about us swapping rings. They're useless, but at least it probably wasn't either of them who did this to us.

I have a horrible suspicion it was *me* who suggested whatever it is we've done. Because despite the shit situation – despite the stress and awkwardness and physical pain – a tiny part of me kind of loves it. The idea of having someone by my side forever. Of having someone who likes me enough to be tied to me by magic, not just by habit and history. Or maybe I'm just chickenshit and I'd rather this than ever having to build up the courage to tell Elliott I like him. He can't reject me if it's not my fault that we can never break up.

We spend the afternoon 'studying' Magical History in the lounge, seeing if there's anything in our textbooks that might give us some insight into how to fix this without needing to tell anyone about it. We sit there for almost two hours and, while there are a few mentions of things that have taken on new meaning now that we've learnt about them in class, nothing goes into enough depth to be of any use. That said, I'll probably do really well in the exam.

We wander down to dinner together and sit at my usual table, with the usual people. Manaia's already there when we arrive, sitting between Silvia and Ana, so I guess she's becoming usual as well. I wonder if Elliott's told her anything about the nature of our friendship – or the new nature of our rings. She doesn't show anything on her face, so who knows.

Across the room, Blake and Liz are at the Minders' table, Agatha the egg sitting on Liz's knee while Blake laughs and jokes and stokes the fires of my own private hell. I hate him knowing something I haven't even talked to my friends about; it feels like a violation. At least he doesn't seem to have told anyone.

Judging by Silvia's expression, though, other people are perfectly capable of figuring it out on their own.

'You going to tell me about your new jewellery?' she whispers from beside me. 'And your new boyfriend, by the looks of it.'

'Later,' I tell her, and tug my sleeve down to cover my fingers before adding 'we're not going out,' just in case my heart starts to get ideas.

Ana looks up from the other side of the table, but she doesn't say anything so I have no idea if she heard that or not. Or if Elliott did. He has his head down while he eats, his left arm tucked around Meggan, fingers hidden by the blanket. I doubt Silvia's noticed he's wearing Dad's ring yet – I don't even think she noticed when I was wearing it – but I don't know how long that'll last.

I nudge Elliott with my knee and he looks up at me. He's so gorgeous it hurts and it's a wonder I never noticed before this year. Maybe it's the fact he has a greater range of expressions nowadays: more than just rolling his eyes at me, or sneering, or that little judgemental curl of his lip that used to make me want to punch him.

His lips don't do that anymore. They have a whole variety of other occupations when it comes to me. One of which seems to have been saying 'I do' and making this whole thing infinitely more complicated.

'Where are you guys going tonight?' I ask Sam, hoping an unrelated conversation might ease my nerves.

'Out to the clearing for a picnic,' he says.

'For dessert,' Silvia adds, wiggling her eyebrows.

Sam sighs and adds, 'Actual dessert. I got permission from Carol in the kitchen and I made tiramisu. We're going to eat the entire thing and sit in the woods looking up at the stars in absolute egg-free silence.'

'Tiramisu and silence go quite well with a nice whiskey,' Elliott says.

'Oh?' Sam asks.

'Yes, if you're up for it, I have some I can donate to the cause. Since we were late getting home, it seems only fair to compensate you.' Elliott smiles and I'm surprised by his generosity. 'It's under Tim's bed – you still have a key, apparently. Feel free to grab it on your way out.' Oh, there's salt attached to it.

'Thanks. What are you two planning tonight?' Sam asks, ignoring the dig.

'Sleeping sounds good,' I say, only half-meaning something else.

'Research into dealing with our new predicament might be slightly more pressing,' Elliott says quietly, and his gaze flicks over to where his ring sits on my finger. A tiny part of me twinges at the implication he might not wholeheartedly want to remain stuck with me forever.

'What new predicament?' Silvia interrupts. Ana looks up again.

Shit.

I catch Elliott's eye and he looks like I feel – sprung.

'You didn't ...?'

'No,' I say. 'Of course I didn't tell them. When would I have?'

'Well,' Elliott says, still keeping his voice low. 'Blake saw Tim wearing my ring and thinks we're together, which is a bit of an issue, since he might randomly decide to tell everyone and make a scandal out of nothing.'

'When in fact Tim's wearing your ring for some other reason?' Silvia asks.

Elliott hesitates for only a second. 'Yes.'

'And that reason requires research?'

'Yes.'

'Has it got anything to do with the fact you're wearing Tim's ring as well?' Sam says, and I curse inwardly. 'Seems odd you wouldn't just take them off.'

'We tried. We can't,' I say.

'Is this to do with where you were last night?' Silvia asks.

'Technically, yes.'

'Why won't you tell us?' She looks more confused than hurt, thank goodness.

'I will tomorrow.' I say. 'Talk about something else. We're one person's magically enhanced hearing away from being in a heap of shit.'

Ana looks thoughtful but keeps those thoughts to herself, bless her. Sam and Silvia just look at us with matching expressions of suspicion and I'd put twenty bucks on them spending the rest of the evening trying to figure out what's going on. They drop it, though, and we discuss the merits of tiramisu while we finish dinner. Elliott lets me take Meggan out of his arms after a while, so he can eat in peace. Soon after, Silvia and Sam get up to leave. Leda is handed to Elliott. He looks slightly taken aback at the honour, but

Silvia simply rattles off their egg-daughter's usual bedtime routine as Sam tries to tug her away, their jackets thrown over his arm and a carefully packaged tiramisu hanging from his elbow. The servery switches to dessert, people eat and leave, and eventually we're alone – two egg-babies instead of one, two bowls of trifle on the table, and an elephant between us.

'Don't tell Sam what was on for dessert,' I say. 'He'll never go out on a date again.'

'Is that what they're doing – a date?'

'Well, yeah. They're together, so isn't it automatically a date?'

He shrugs, his expression dry. 'Was last night a date?'

'If you'd wanted it to be, I'd imagine you wouldn't have suggested the arrangement we actually have.'

'Would you have acquiesced if I'd asked you out instead?'

'Of course not, we'd barely spoken to each other before. Plus, we kinda used to hate each other with our entire souls.' Now, though, of course I would.

'Who else would you have ended up with?' he scoffs. 'None of the other guys in our year are remotely queer except Blake.'

'I'm bi, I could've gone out with anyone.'

'Oh, you could?' He sounds unflatteringly dubious.

'You know what I mean.'

'That you're arrogant?'

'No.' I let my anger slide away; I have no room for it at the moment. 'I probably wouldn't have dated anyone.'

'The whole rest of the year? Wouldn't you have been insane with frustration?'

'Probably,' I say. 'But I also wouldn't have ended up accidentally possibly married to someone who asks a lot of questions, so the pay-off might just have been worth it.'

'You'd be lonely without me,' he says to his dessert, and his voice has lost its edge.

'I certainly would tonight,' I say and bump my ankle against his. It's almost a lie, because I'll probably miss him for the rest of my life when this is over, but I'm hardly going to vomit all my new feelings on him now. Or, like, ever.

'So what are we going to do?' he asks, mashing sponge into his custard.

'Eat too much trifle, get fat, waddle back to our room, put the babies to bed and fall asleep?' I suggest. 'Research, perhaps, if we're feeling spritely.'

'So much romance in this relationship, I'm overwhelmed.'

'Shut up. Neither of us signed up for romance,' I say, hoping he doesn't see how genuinely sad I am about that. I scoop some trifle into my mouth, trying to drown the sadness in carbohydrates, but the gloomy thoughts are unstoppable.

'We definitely did not.'

He sounds disappointed and I want desperately to read into the fact that he's dishing himself more dessert before he's properly finished his first bit. Maybe we're both sitting here thinking the same thing. In a perfect world, maybe he'd have the balls to tell me he's changed his mind, and we'd be upstairs already, acting sappy and making plans for our future while staring into each other's eyes. Maybe we'd cry and cuddle together instead of it just being me, crying alone in the dark.

'Shall we pick up some books on our way home?' I ask. 'Library's open.'

'Sure. I suppose we should try to find out something actually useful,' he says, then picks up his phone and proceeds to ignore me.

I eat the rest of my trifle in silence.

CHAPTER 23

BUSINESS TIME

We head from the dining hall to the library, Meggan and Leda burbling at each other but the two of us quiet. I kept thinking back to our conversation and wondering if I'd imagined the disappointment in Elliott's tone. I want to try something reckless, see how he reacts. So I reach for his hand. He flinches slightly in surprise, but lets me thread our fingers together with nothing more than a weird look and a soft blush. There's no-one around but, regardless, I loosen my grip and let our fingers slip free once we're in sight of the carved wooden library doors, just in case.

The librarian isn't behind her desk. Instead, there's a Year 12 student sitting there whose expression turns to interest as we walk in side by side, doubly laden with blanketed bundles. I get paranoid about Blake having blabbed, and I throw out the idea of asking her where we might find information on magical marriage and bonding rituals. No need to pour fuel on the fire.

Elliott seems to know where he's going anyway, steering me with a warm hand on my waist, and I wonder if that's helping the situation. It takes all my self-control to not look back and see if she's staring. I feel distinctly more comfortable once we're behind the stacks.

It's rare for me to be in the library without the looming pressure of assignments, so it's probably the first time I've appreciated just how nice it is. The lighting is warm and soothing, the air is dry but cool, and the silence is almost palpable. I feel like I couldn't speak if I wanted to. When Elliott does, it's in a whisper.

'Can you hold on to both girls, or shall we put them on the floor?'

'I think we've established I can't even hold on to one girl.'

He gives me a tired smile and pushes Leda into my arms before walking back out of the aisle and off to the right. He reappears pushing a book trolley. I wonder just how much research he thinks we're going to do.

'I think it'll be safe,' he says. 'I don't want us to kill their baby – everyone will assume the lure of a free bowl of chips was overwhelming and we did it on purpose.'

It takes a second, but I realise he intends the trolley for the eggs. He settles the girls in the top basket; they fit snuggly next to each other and the sides are high enough that they won't fall out. We can fit books in the bottom basket if we want to. And apparently he does want to, because we end up at a table with seven hand-bound manuscripts and various other publications ranging from *Bonding Ceremonies and Rituals Around the Globe* to *Enchanted Objects and Cursed Treasures of the Pacific*. Apparently, we won't be going anywhere near *Love and Other Cultural Conflicts*, which is actually a comfort. I feel like any more conflict might finish me off.

'So we're bypassing anything about marriage?' I ask, trying to get my thoughts back on track.

'I did that research already.'

'How?'

'I Googled it. In New Zealand, after 1951, you need a marriage licence before you can be legitimately married, and that licence has to be lodged with the Births, Deaths and Marriages Office,' he says, and I feel guilty for thinking he was ignoring me when he was on his phone before. 'Do you remember doing any of that?'

'No.'

'Me neither. So we aren't technically, legally, married, according to New Zealand law.'

'OK. So what are we looking at?'

'It seems fair to assume there's magic involved, so I reckon we focus on any sort of bonding ceremonies with rings that make the wearer want to die when they try to take them off.'

'We should get Sam's take on this; he's the Philosopher.

He knows way more history than I do.' Dad would be even more helpful, but apparently he had somewhere else to be.

Elliott nods, much to my surprise. 'We can, but those two deserve some time off and we can manage by ourselves for one night.'

We manage a whole twenty minutes before the girls require cuddling, and even then, they're fussing again by eight o'clock. Calling it, we check out the pile of reading material we've yet to touch and return the others. The Year 12 on duty looks at us with something akin to suspicion, but says nothing beyond 'hello' and 'you have two weeks to return them'. She doesn't mention the use of her trolley as an egg-pram.

Settling both babies at once takes some effort, and we climb onto the bed with relief, even if it is with boring library books. Elliott has made us drinks and, much to my surprise, pulled reading glasses out of his leather bag. They're kind of hot and I end up ogling him sitting with his mug of tea and his fancy silk pyjamas and a faint bruise on his neck from where I bit him last night. And my dad's ring, of course, with those ominous words engraved in it, destined to live on his finger for eternity. Or as long as it takes us to find a way to fix it.

We make our way through all the articles, bound theses, journals and books, taking notes where necessary, working until we're both yawning. I shut the last book with a satisfying *whump* and collapse sideways on the bed. He huffs and glares at me from over the top of his glasses.

I ignore him and decide Sam's bed is the best place for all the stuff, because it's appropriately respectful to the years of scholarship and dutiful research that went into publishing it. Also because my desk is covered in crap and I can't be bothered tidying it. I pluck the last article out of Elliott's hands and put it on the pile. He doesn't bother to fight me on it.

I strip and get into pyjamas, crawling under the covers and cuddling up to him, reading over his shoulder as he flicks through the notebook we've been using to record our findings. We last all of two minutes before the notebook is thrown aside and his glasses are placed carefully next to Meggan in her cot, and we descend into the hazy bubble of distraction our proximity offers. I can't help but notice the weight of it now, the bare reality of what we're doing. The fact we're connected somehow by some sort of magic, and –

'Elliott,' I say, placing my hands on his shoulders. 'Stop.'

'What's wrong?'

'One of the essays I read mentioned consummation. How in certain instances it can solidify a bond. Make it harder to break.'

There's a long pause, his face in shadow, and I wonder if he's busy marvelling at how I didn't think to mention it sooner.

'Tim,' he says, and leans back in to nip at my throat. 'Allow me to apply logic to that.' He licks the line of my jaw. 'We presumably got bonded at the height of the festivities last night, which we don't remember. And what we did on the couch happened *after* that, which I know because I *do remember*. Everyone else had gone to bed. So.' He kisses me again. 'Theoretically, even if we are married – and I don't think we are – we can do everything up to and including what we did on the couch without endangering ourselves any further than we already have.'

'But – neither of us know what bond this is, or what counts as consummation. What if it relies on time spent doing the thing, or what if you have to do it twice, or on a full moon? And I don't remember which ring I was wearing when I got up for the loo, what if –'

'OK, OK.' He retreats. 'We don't have to do anything.'

'I read –' My mouth is suddenly host to his. His kiss is long and sweet and soft and his hand is curled around my jaw.

'It's fine,' he whispers. 'Don't worry about it now. We can do some more research in the morning.'

'What if – what if it *is* too late, and what we did on the couch last night … meant something?'

'Then you're stuck with me forever. You'll cope. Relax.'

I feel him shift, rolling away, but he reaches for my arm and tugs at me until I'm spooning him, and he brings my hand up to kiss my fingertips and I melt a little. *Relax*, he says, like it's easy. Like I've ever been able to make sense of his rules and his contradictory level of affection. But I try it; I just … stop holding it all in for a second, and hug him tightly in the darkness instead, my blood thrumming through me.

I let myself imagine that he secretly *wants* to be stuck with me forever – that all of this is for keeps. That we actually, maybe, might have already made this whole thing somewhat more than temporary. I pretend he feels the same way about it as I do – that his grip on my arm, wrapped around his chest, is somehow possessive, needful, and that I'm not alone in this mad, teetering whirl of emotion. The possibility is simultaneously horrifying and exhilarating. My emotions slip out of me, every breath a thought of what could be. I feel it like a physical thing, an unfurling of all of my defences; every shuttered thought and feeling, every tightly stifled wonderance, finally let free.

It's a long, long time before I can fall asleep, trying to cram everything back inside.

CHAPTER 24

EVERYBODY KNOWS

We're awake early for a weekend and in the dining hall before the majority of students have bothered getting up, so we're safe to talk about things without being overheard. The notebook is open in front of us, and Elliott has fashioned my jacket into a nest so Meggan and Leda can sit on the table between us. I pour the tea and he butters some scones – uniformly shaped for him and dark-edged and crispy for me.

'Why don't we read the whole list of things all together and see if anything links up?' he says. 'It'll be a start. Once we know what questions to ask we can do some more specific research, ask a teacher or something.'

'D'you think it's safe to ask one of them? Won't it be obvious why we want to know? I can't imagine that standing in front of my mum with our fake baby and your ring on my finger is going to be remotely subtle.'

He *hmms* in assent. 'Have you talked to her about any of this?'

'No, of course not. I haven't even seen her this weekend. And I don't want her to find out I've done something embarrassingly stupid unless I have no other choice.' I push my hands through my hair and try to reset my brain. 'Let's just start.'

He looks up at me from under his fringe and the sheer beauty of him hits me again, right in the gut. '"You cannot create a bond with someone who's already dead",' he says, looking me in the eye.

'You also –' I turn the notebook towards me, trying to get back on task. '"Cannot create a bond with someone without their consent".'

'Folie à deux, as expected,' he says, and I don't bother asking him what the hell that means.

'"You cannot create a soulbond with someone who is already soulbound to someone else",' I continue, '"already promised to be soulbound, or not yet born".'

'All sensible rules. And I doubt this is a soulbond.'

'I was being thorough.' I give him a pointed look and he shrugs, so I continue. '"One can only rely on the fortitude of a marital bond –"'

'I thought we decided we weren't married?'

'*You* decided. I don't trust everything I read on the internet.' I find my place on the page again. '"... If the parties are of sound mind, of true heart, betrothed to one another or confined by parental shackle ...'" I pause. 'What do you get from that?'

'If that's our bond, the "of sound mind" bit is something of a surprise.' He smirks at me.

'That wasn't the bit I meant. Could a ceremony – the magic – recognise Meggan as a parental shackle?'

'I don't know. When did you research marriage stuff?'

'I didn't, specifically – this was in *Bonding Ceremonies and Rituals Around the Globe*. New Zealand law obviously doesn't legally recognise most of what was in there,' I point out. 'Some of it sounded familiar and some of it definitely didn't and then there was a bunch of stuff where I couldn't even tell if it was magic at all. Anyway. Do you think "true heart" means "honest"?' I mull it over. *True heart* ... it reminds me of something dragony. 'It sounds like a movie about a knight who gets given a sword.'

Ana and Manaia arrive then, and the conversation shifts to movies as Elliott tucks the notebook out of sight and we pretend that's what we were talking about all along. The others drift in: Nikau and Hana with Buttercup, looking enviably domestic, then Matt, with a hot water bottle and a blister pack of ibuprofen. Sam and Silvia turn up as we segue from talking about dragon depictions in media to discussing specific TV shows and whether characters can be considered queer canonically if the showrunners said no, but the writers and the actors hinted very blatantly at *yes*.

'Morning,' Silvia says. Her and Sam have probably had

a very romantic start to the day again, if the extra fluff in her bun is anything to go by. Or Sam's smile. Ugh. At least I didn't have to be there for it this time. 'Were they OK last night?' she asks, and lifts Leda out of the jacket nest for a cuddle.

'Minor grizzling at about four,' I say, 'but otherwise fine. We took them on an exciting trip to the library.'

'Tim,' Silvia pats me on the arm. 'You do know they can't read, right?'

I give her my best withering look.

'I expect they can hear if you talk, though, otherwise talking to them wouldn't settle them down,' Sam says. 'Who knows, they might be listening to everything we say and reporting back to Ms Van Mill.'

I panic and look over at Elliott, hoping nothing Meggan has heard us doing has made it back to any of my mother's colleagues. He gives me half a second's glance before focusing on Sam.

'Well. I can assure you, we did not make them listen to several thousand words of dry, tedious information about bonding and cursed jewellery,' he says quietly, and passes over the teapot.

Sam's eyes light up and the egg-spy theory is forgotten. He leans in, ready for new information. 'Is this about the rings?'

'Unfortunately, no,' Elliott says. 'None of it really seems to be. We've done a lot of research, but none of it seems to fit what these rings are doing.'

'But they're *doing something?*' Silvia leans in, right beside Sam. 'Tell us what's happening. From the beginning.'

She's forgotten to be quiet and now everyone at the table has gone still, waiting. I look around and see mostly worry, not the thirst for scandal I'd expected. Even Manaia looks concerned under the frown she's directing entirely at Elliott. Presumably he hasn't kept her up to date. Meggan grizzles from her nest and Elliott pulls her into his lap to comfort her. I wish he'd do the same for me.

'We don't really know,' I say, loud enough so it carries the length of the table but hopefully not beyond. The nearby tables are only sparsely occupied, so we should be fine. 'We went out, got drunk, woke up with each other's rings on.' I hold my hand up just enough so they can see, and Elliott does the same.

Silvia frowns at the gold band, then back at me. 'You don't normally wear a ring.'

'It's Dad's. I found it a few days ago with his things.'

Sam freezes halfway through buttering some toast. 'His things are still here?'

'Focus, Sam.' Silvia flaps her hand at him. 'Are they giving you visions? Can you communicate telepathically? Are you having the same dreams?'

'No, we, um …'

'We can't take them off,' Elliott says.

'What? At all?'

'They can technically be removed,' Elliott explains. 'But we experience a vast and horrific sense of unease if we lose

212

contact with them. Almost like emotional vertigo. Nausea, despair, et cetera. Imagine depression, but condensed and turned up to eleven.'

Ana grimaces sympathetically, her tiny hand reaching out for Manaia, but Sam looks thoughtful, which is why I wanted us to get his help in the first place.

'Even if you keep hold of it, the edges of the ring feel sharp, like a blade,' I say. 'Though no actual damage seems to be done in either case.'

'It punishes you if you take it off?' Sam asks, frozen knife-deep in a jar of Pic's peanut butter.

'I guess.'

'That's not normal,' he says.

'That's pretty far past *not normal*.' Silvia's lip curls. 'Why would you need that if both people wanted to be bonded to each other?'

Sam hesitates. 'Maybe it's not meant for two people who *want* to be bonded.'

'Are you thinking master-slave stuff?'

'Not specifically. I'd need to think more about what the benefits of the bond might be before I made any sort of hypothesis.'

'Are there benefits?' Silvia turns to me again, and I don't have an answer for her. I see her lip twitch when she realises what she's just said, and I don't have an answer for that either.

'None that I can think of.' I say, straight-faced. 'Like I said, no telepathy, no visions, no dreams. No magical GPS, no night vision. Nothing.'

'Maybe it's not a punishment then,' Sam says. 'Maybe taking the ring off does something else and you just happen to feel bad. Correlation, not causation.'

'Maybe it's just the drunk teenager special?' Elliott suggests. 'Saved for idiots who drink too much without thinking about the consequences. Doomed forever to be reminded of the need to be sensible.'

Silvia smiles. 'It would serve you right if it was, wouldn't it?'

Elliott directs his sarcasm at me. 'Your friends are so supportive, Tim, I can see how you did so well at life.'

'Hey,' Silvia says. 'We never said we weren't going to help you figure this out.'

'Yes. Food first, though,' Sam says.

'Us too,' Ana pipes up from the other end of the table.

'Whatever we can do to help.' Manaia nods and goes back to her coffee, seemingly unbothered that she's been volunteered for something without her permission.

'We have netball, but we can help after?' Nikau offers, and Hana and Matt nod encouragingly.

The weight of secrecy lifts with the promise of not having to tackle any of this alone, and Meggan goes quiet and calm in Elliott's arms. He shifts one of his feet so it's tucked between mine, and for the first time since we woke up yesterday, things don't seem quite so bad.

CHAPTER 25

MY DELIRIUM

The rest of the morning is dedicated to researching what kind of bond it is. With Sam at the helm, and Elliott more than happy to follow his lead, things quickly get far more intellectual than I can manage right now. A spreadsheet emerges from between where Ana and Manaia are huddled on the library's old blue couch, covered in textbooks and an atlas. After an hour, Silvia and I leave a note at the table and take the egg-babies for a walk.

She eventually lands on the topic I've been dreading and I shrug, not sure how to explain my feelings even to myself. 'You must really like him if you're not completely freaking out about this,' she says, with a hint of mischief.

'He's fine,' I say, and I feel the heat of the lie burn my ears. 'He's good with Meggan and he's been helping me with atmospheric charms in Practical Magic. He can cook as well, unlike Matt, so Food Tech is less hit-or-miss now.'

'Come on, Tim.' I hear the smile in her voice. 'We found you *shirtless*. *Cuddling*. It's obvious something else is going on.'

I decide to *not* mention we were also pantsless. 'It's not a big deal, Silvia.'

She makes a disbelieving sound and we walk in silence for a moment. Then she asks, 'Is this why you and Lizzie broke up? She always seemed really into you.'

I let out a sigh. 'Yeah. Well, things changed. I was dealing with some stuff, and it wasn't really … working.'

'But it's working with Elliott?'

'We're not going out,' I groan.

'Sure you're not. You've gone straight past that to married.'

'We're just *bonded*,' I say. I wish I cared as little as I'm implying, or that I could actually tell Silvia how I feel, but she might not get it.

'You guys are living together, sleeping in the same bed, and you've swapped rings. A hundred years ago, this would be a common law marriage.'

'Common law marriage doesn't exist anymore. Since 1951, you need a licence to be married in New Zealand.'

'And before 1951, you *didn't* need that.'

'We didn't go *back in time* the other night, we just went

to the pub. And it could be entirely coincidental that we used rings. It's not like either of us have other jewellery or anything else that would work for some other sort of bond.'

'What about your pounamu?' she says, all smug, and I glare at her 'til she gives up. 'Fine,' she says, like she's disappointed that my life isn't entertaining enough for her. 'Maybe you're bonded in an entirely non-marriagey way and we'll find some quick little unbonding spell and you can go back to living as lovers and being ten feet deep in denial.'

She makes it sound ridiculous – that it could be so simple. That I've been naive in hoping it will be. I can still hope, though. It's that or cry.

Silvia looks sideways at me, quiet for a moment, like she's trying to gauge how touchy I am right now. 'Do you want to be married to him?' she asks, and I wish I knew how to answer.

There's definitely a part of me that wants the epic, sweeping romance of being married young and throwing caution and modern conventions to the wind. I like the idea of being loved so much that none of that matters. But I'm not loved, and there is no romance, and it does matter. And lord knows what the rings will do if either of us want to get married to someone for real in the future. So I say, 'I don't want to be wearing a mental breakdown on my finger for the rest of my life.'

'Is that the only reason you want to fix it?' Silvia stops walking and I turn to check if she's OK, but she's just standing there staring at me like I'm incredibly thick. 'Tim. Seriously. Do you like him that much?'

I can't look her in the eye. 'It's not like it would matter if I did. We have an … arrangement, and it's only 'til the end of the assignment. We agreed.'

Thankfully, she doesn't nag me for more information, just says, 'Unless you're magically bonded forever …' and then goes quiet. It doesn't last. 'Tim.' She looks hesitant. 'For argument's sake, if it *is* a marital bond … Have you guys … you know … since you were bonded? I mean, it looked like you had yesterday morning, but I don't want to assume. Because according to what I was just reading, it would make a difference –'

'We didn't …' Oh my god, this is horrifying. 'It wasn't, you know, we just –' My face is on fire and I stare at the floor, wishing it would swallow me. 'We don't even like each other. We only hooked up because we'd both been dumped and we were sharing a room anyway, and I was curious.'

'Yeah, so you say. But are you still curious?'

Good lord, she's relentless. I look down at Meggan, clutched in my arms. Am I? 'No.'

Silvia doesn't say anything more, just bumps her shoulder against mine and stays close as we make our way back to the others.

When we get there, the librarian is gone and the same Year 12 student from last night is sitting behind the desk again, staring at us as we walk in. Sam is sitting at our table with Elliott, and Silvia leans over his shoulder to give him a hug. She stays there, whispering. He glances up at me for a second, his expression serious. Elliott keeps his eyes on his notebook and says nothing.

'Yeah, we were beginning to wonder that too,' Sam says, and my gut turns.

'Wondering what?' comes a voice from behind me, and I turn to see Ana, followed by Manaia carrying a stack of books. There's a particularly large hardback one at the bottom titled *19th Century Encyclopedia of the Occult,* which seems a bit intimidating.

I look at Sam, with Silvia still draped over his broad back, and he looks at Elliott, his eyebrows indicating very clearly that this is his news to share.

'Since we can't find any information about any non-marital bonds that fit the characteristics of this one, and a bunch of clearly marital ones that do ...' Elliott finally looks up at me. 'It's seems as though we might've actually got married. For real. Well, maritally bonded. Not legally married. I was right about that, at least.'

'Also, since you've engaged in some sort of sex since, you might have a hard time breaking the bond,' Sam adds.

My gut falls out of me and crashes through the floor, into ancient bedrock and closer and closer to hell. The feeling of doom is edged with frilly lace, though, and a soft, sappy feeling that I'm pretty sure is my latent romantic side. Somewhere else in there is also the horrifying realisation that Elliott has been talking to Sam about our private life, and Sam's now just announced it to Ana and Manaia as well. Both girls are silent and wide-eyed and I wish for a second that *all of me* could've fallen through the floor.

'Hang on. We don't actually know for certain what counts as consummation,' Elliott says. 'There's a reasonable chance this'll still be easy to undo and we just need to find the right information about how to do it.'

I'm torn between being pleased that the two of them are getting along and the ouchy feeling of my maybe-husband clearly hoping he won't be my maybe-husband much longer.

'OK then,' Sam says. 'I propose we concentrate on finding out what constitutes consummation in marital bonds, and whether marital bonds work for same-sex couples. If we happen to come across a divorce ritual, we'll keep it to one side in case we need it.'

'Sorry,' I blurt. 'And thank you all for helping.'

Elliott pushes the chair beside him out with his foot and motions for me to sit. 'It's not your fault.'

'Knowing what we do, it's probably both of your faults,' Sam says.

'My mum is going to kill me.' Elliott drops his head into his hands, and my insides hurt.

'Oh shit,' Silvia hisses, straightening up. 'Speaking of mums ...'

CHAPTER 26

DON'T FORGET YOUR ROOTS

'Hello Silvia, Sam.' I look over my left shoulder and the principal – Silvia's mum – is right there. We have zero chance of hiding any of the wildly incriminating literature spread across the table.

Behind Mrs Sisilia, I see the librarian claim her desk back from the Year 12 and realise we've been betrayed. Technically, we're allowed to look at all the restricted books now we're seniors, but quite a few of the ones we've grabbed are from the special collection they keep for visiting uni students. This is the only library in New Zealand with books about magic, so it gets used a bit by people doing their Masters by correspondence and stuff. I didn't know the librarian monitored them so closely.

'Hello, Timoti,' Mrs Sisilia says. 'Elliott.'

I look around and Ana and Manaia have disappeared, melting back into the stacks. Good for them, but they could've warned us. Though, to be fair, maybe not without drawing attention to themselves.

'Hello, Mrs Sisilia.' We utter our greetings with the enthusiasm of the condemned.

Despite all this being about Elliott and I, I think Sam's probably feeling the worst of it right now, with books about bonding all over the table and his girlfriend having just swiftly disengaged from a hug. Silvia's mum has never quite let him relax about dating her daughter, even though Silvia's dad is about ready to adopt him. It's bloody lucky we aren't obviously researching marriage, or Silvia might've been locked in her room for the rest of the year.

'It's been brought to my attention that you've been doing some research into ritual magic,' Mrs Sisilia says, and summons herself a chair from the next table – just extends her arm and it slides swiftly into her waiting hand. She sits down and scoots herself closer. Maybe it's not meant to be menacing, but the casual use of magic and her disregard for the audible scrape of a heavy wooden chair – in the *library* – seems like it could be a power move. A reminder of who's in charge, and of how much effort the same manoeuvre would require from any of us – not to mention we'd need to use both a mea and an incantation. Elliott must be reeling; at least the rest of us are sort of used to having parents do stuff like this. I keep Meggan clutched in one arm and drop the other down, letting my fingers skim over his thigh.

'It's important that we don't hide information from you kids,' Mrs Sisilia starts. 'We're here to teach you about how the world works, as well as your own cultural history, and part of that is where your magic comes from. But it's also important that you treat that information with respect. You're at the beginning of your journey into magic, and you don't have enough control of your abilities yet to be playing with any sort of serious rituals.' She looks at each of us in turn, then her eyes alight on the stack of occult books Manaia left on the table. She sighs and picks up the top one. 'Do you understand how magic is not always a power of good?' she asks.

'Yes, Miss,' we respond in chorus, except of course Silvia says 'yes, Mum' and sounds even more resigned than we do.

'Getting too close to some things is dangerous, even for someone of my experience.' Mrs Sisilia places the book back on the table, open to a drawing of a young woman surrounded by wispy shadows, a burning leaf hovering above her open hands. 'Magic is not good or bad in and of itself: it depends on you – your focus, your intent.'

I can no longer tell if she's here as a teacher or a mother – I've heard those words so many times at school while learning new incantations and how to do new things. It's like a teacher's mantra. *You have to focus, you have to mean it. Keep trying. Again. Focus.* But ... Mrs Sisilia's not exactly telling us off. And she looks worried. Meggan makes a grizzly sound in my lap.

'There are other powers that you do not control – that are out of your hands – and they don't always care about what you want.' She turns the page and the next picture is of the same young woman, cowering, the shadows closer and darker, flames licking at her arms, her hair.

OK. The metaphor's a little heavy-handed – don't play with fire – but point taken. We obviously aren't looking at anything like that, but there's no way to explain without telling her what we *are* looking at. It might be better if she just thinks we're collectively going through some sort of rebellious teenage edgelord phase.

'Sorry, Mum,' Silvia says, and we murmur our humbled agreement.

'I'm banning you from the library.'

'What?' Sam says, then slaps his hand over his mouth. 'Sorry, Mrs Sisilia.'

All hope drains out of me, and I look over to see Elliott staring, stiff and expressionless, at the tabletop.

'It's for your own good,' she says, and stands up. 'And also so I can sleep at night. Put your books back, I'll wait for you.'

She'll wait for us – as in, she'll keep a bloody close eye on us and make sure we don't sneak out with anything. Shit. Elliott picks up the pile of occult books and I follow him into the stacks. I can't help feeling we would've got away with this if Silvia wasn't here or her mother wasn't quite so protective of her.

'Hey.'

He looks utterly defeated. 'What are we going to do now, Tim?' he whispers.

'We'll think of something.' I take a couple of books off his pile and put them away. 'It could be worse.'

We're lucky, honestly, that her visit wasn't to do with either of our other transgressions: the fact we're involved in the chain of room-swapping that's violated the school's gender-separation policy, or, worse, the fact we were very recently out all night, well past curfew, drinking illegally (and ill-advisedly) and ignoring everything we've ever learnt about stranger danger. It almost serves us right that one of those strangers decided to punish us with matrimony.

'Let's go get a tea,' he says, sliding the last book home.

'Yeah, sure.' I stay where I am, just looking at him, wondering what's going through his head.

Is he horrified? Disgusted? Is he secretly holding it against me? Is he worried we're not going to find anyone to help us without getting in more trouble? Is he really worried about what his mum will say? Does he regret coming anywhere near me? He looks upset. Really upset, actually, and I'm ... not being very supportive, probably.

Up until now, I've been focusing on how it affects *me* if he doesn't want me in his life like this. I haven't thought about him or his needs. How he might still want me in his life in some other way. I haven't been a good friend to him, basically, and that's not OK, even if he might end up breaking my heart. That won't be his fault. My heart's not meant to have anything to do with this.

I tuck a still-grouchy Meggan against my side and hold out the other arm to him. He looks at me, unsure – maybe he thinks I'm going to try to kiss him in public or something – so I keep my head down and step in and hug him until he hugs me back. He feels tense.

'We can still be friends,' I say, and I don't know if it helps exactly, but he lets out a breath and pulls me closer and it's all OK for a moment.

'Are you boys done?'

We break apart and Mrs Sisilia is standing at the end of the aisle, her face not quite neutral. My heart starts to pound, even though hugging someone isn't particularly incriminating.

'Yeah,' I say, and she steps out of sight.

Just like that, I've made it worse. Elliott doesn't say anything the whole time it takes to gather our things off the table and be escorted out of the library. Mrs Sisilia leaves us at an intersection as she heads for the admin wing, and we slope away from her in silence with Silvia and Sam leading the way. Halfway to the dining hall, Elliott slips his hand into mine and gives it a brief squeeze before letting our fingers slide apart. My heart beats hard again, a mixture of surprise and sadness and who knows what else.

CHAPTER 27

NEXT TO YOU

Manaia and Ana catch up with us at the double doors of the dining hall and Silvia updates them on what just happened. They offer to keep researching for us, since they didn't get caught, and promise to be discreet so we don't lose the library completely.

Except … The school library isn't every resource we have. I might not be able to talk to Mum, and Dad obviously isn't here, but I still have access to his rooms and his books – we just need to read them all. There are hundreds. Might only take a year. There *are* nine of us though, if Nikau, Hana and Matt can help after indoor netball. I try to do the maths in my head.

I'm distracted enough that I forget not to push up the cuffs of my hoodie when I'm next to the servery, making tea. It's too late when I realise Elliott has rolled his sleeves up as well, and I've transferred Meggan to my right side. Our left hands are visible, right next to each other, and Carol is right there, topping up a plate of biscuits. She's known me since I was ten and probably thinks nothing of commenting that we're both wearing what look like wedding rings, and don't we make a cute little family, and why wasn't she invited to the wedding?

I manage to laugh it off and promise that when I find a wife, Carol will be the one making our cake so of course she'll be invited. I'm shitting myself on the inside, though. The last thing we need is people hearing her and looking too hard at us while we're still trying to figure out how to fix everything. Pretending to be straight might be a step too far, but she seems to buy it.

'Nice save,' Elliott says under his breath as we walk away, but he rolls his cuffs back down the second we're seated so it hurts anyway.

As we drink our tea, I bring up Dad's collection of books and Sam and Elliott nod, clearly having been thinking the same thing. We go to leave just as Matt, Nikau and Hana arrive, and Ana and Manaia offer to stay behind to fill them in before they go back to the library. It's weird letting Manaia help with something so personal, but I was right – her and Ana are a formidable team. Without them, we wouldn't have a spreadsheet cataloguing all the world's cultures and their different bonding traditions, key features and 'symptoms'. Though, honestly, finding out that some of those symptoms are certain death has been less than helpful.

The corridors of the staff wing aren't exactly deserted, and we pass a couple of teachers on the way to my dad's rooms, so it's lucky we're mostly staff kids and they're used to seeing us around here. It takes some creative manoeuvring to slip into Dad's rooms without being seen, but we manage it, and I lock the door behind us just in case. We really can't afford to be asked questions about what we're doing in his abandoned apartment.

'Your dad really did leave everything behind,' Sam says once we're safely inside, and drifts over to the bookshelf with Leda in his arms. 'Lucky for us.'

Silvia and I make more tea while Sam and Elliott sort four piles of books onto the coffee table, one for each of us.

'Silvia, we're giving you everything to do with the romantic stuff,' Sam says. 'Tim, you have myths and symbolism, I have magical theory in relation to the body, and Elliott's offered to deal with the poetry section.'

'Poetry?'

'Yes, an ancient, far-reaching and deeply metaphorical look at societal customs,' Sam says, and we all cringe except for Elliott, who picks up a book and wriggles back onto the couch with Meggan.

'Cultures say more about themselves in their art than anyone can hope to learn from just science,' Elliott says.

I can't decide if it's pretentious or sexy, and that's too much to unpack, so I put down the tea and pick up *Magical Symbology: from Inca to India* and sit next to Elliott on the couch. We only have an hour and a bit before lunch and we need to use it. I get through the whole volume without finding anything and start on *Myths and Magic,* looking for mentions of consummation, annulment, divorce, and any tips or tricks on finding out if you're actually married in the first place. Silvia has stretched out on the floor and Sam is sitting cross-legged at the coffee table making notes. Elliott has curled up in the corner of the couch, completely engrossed in whatever he's reading.

'You're not wearing your glasses,' I say, and he looks up.

'The light here is OK, and I'm not tired yet.' He smiles. 'Do you miss them?'

'Yes, absolutely. You look hideous without them.'

'Tim, if you think that's true, maybe *you* need glasses,' Silvia pipes up from the floor.

Elliott cracks up laughing, his tight posture breaking apart so his limbs loosen and drift towards me. His hand settles on the couch, just touching my thigh, and his legs stretch out to nudge against my shins. I flick a glance at Sam and he's smiling at my expense but not looking, and even Silvia has gone back to her book. I want to reach out and hold Elliott's hand and I think I probably could, but it's one more thing I shouldn't get used to.

I do it anyway. It feels like as big a deal as anything else because there are other people right here and we aren't hiding anymore. We spend the next half-hour with our fingers threaded together, awkwardly reading with one hand and not quite managing to look at one another.

We leave late for lunch to avoid being seen too often in the staff wing, and come back early for the same reason, filled rolls tucked in our pockets. Our piles of books are left waiting on the coffee table as we sit down in our places to eat. Elliott, apparently having reached a level of comfort I have not, stretches out his legs and settles them in my lap before taking a large bite of his roll. Too far. Neither Silvia nor Sam seem to notice, but I give him a look anyway.

'What?' he says, like I'm being needlessly fussy. 'I'm tired and this is comfortable.' He shifts slightly so his calf is touching me somewhere it shouldn't be in polite company. 'Besides, we're married now, darling; you have to indulge me.'

'I don't,' I say, and wish he'd stop calling me that, or that I could stop loving it. I push him off my lap and go boil the kettle.

After three hours we've got through eleven more books, another round of tea, and his legs are back in my lap. My phone beeps and I pick it up, happy for something else to think about.

'Who is it?' Elliott asks, and purposely flexes his calves against my crotch.

'Ana,' I say, and open the message. 'Apparently Nikau has something. They want us to meet them by the library, since we won't be able to talk at dinner.'

'You should go alone, it's less suspicious. We'll meet you in the dining hall,' Silvia says. 'We can talk about it after we've eaten.'

'I think we should stop now anyway; my ability to focus is gone,' Sam says.

I nod. I'm tired of sitting here; my brain hurts and my self-control is slowly diminishing. It's definitely too soon for Elliott and I to make out in front of my friends, but that hasn't stopped me from thinking about kissing him for the last hour. We leave our mugs by the sink and our books stacked on the table. I check the coast is clear and we slip into the hall. We stop in the main corridor with the dining hall down to the left and the library to the right.

'I hope Nikau's found something good,' Silvia says. 'We obviously haven't found anything, and I've almost finished my pile.'

'We only did the bookshelf, though,' Elliott points out. 'We haven't even started on the bedroom.'

Sam frowns. 'The bedroom?'

'Yeah, there's, like, eight boxes of books in there.'

Silvia looks smug and I cringe inwardly. 'In the bedroom?' she says. 'Interesting. I don't remember you going in there.'

Elliott realises what he's done and looks at me for a second, apologetic, before enthusiastically blushing at the floor.

We agree to return to Dad's rooms tomorrow, after all the staff have retreated behind closed doors to watch Netflix or knit or whatever they do after dinner. We can't risk anyone getting pissy about us spending too much time in their wing.

I head for the library – and hopefully some new information – looking back once to see Elliott looking over his shoulder, his cheeks still pink, his arms wrapped around our egg-daughter.

I'm still thinking about kissing him.

CHAPTER 28

VICIOUS TRADITIONS

I've calmed down a bit by the time I see Elliott again, and dinner is almost normal, despite the new information revolving in my head. Nikau keeps looking at me like he's sorry he didn't have better news, and I can tell Ana is frustrated by the need to eat dinner rather than test out her theory immediately.

My mother waylays me after dessert. It seems Mrs Sisilia had a sneaky mum-to-mum conversation with her, and it takes me twenty minutes to convince her I'm not joining a cult or practising bad magic, and that Elliott hasn't 'led me astray'. I mean, he has, but not in the way Mum's thinking. By the time she releases me, everyone is gone and I walk back to the dorms by myself.

Elliott's in bed when I get back to our room, despite the early hour, with Meggan burbling peacefully beside him. He's wearing his glasses again, reading the novel we're meant to be analysing for Pacific Arts and Literature, which I'll also have to read sometime soon if I want any NCEA English credits this year. It's not necessary for police college, but it'd be nice to prove I have some communication skills. My personal life only offers evidence to the contrary.

'Before you distract me,' he says, 'Leda had a sadly fatal little accident, and Silvia is devastated and we aren't to mention it in front of her, ever. Sam's ruling. They went to bed early.'

Oh no. 'What happened?'

'We aren't allowed to talk about that either. Best not to even *think* about it. What did the others have to share?' he asks, sliding an old receipt in to mark his page. 'Leda's demise put an end to any and all conversation.'

'Nothing good,' I say, and all I can do is look at him because I don't want to talk and be responsible for disappointing him.

I miss the times when I could kiss him and forget everything as he pulled me under. Now I have no choice but to acknowledge every single one of my feelings, including the fact that I want him, desperately, and I might never get to have him again. It's been two days but it feels like forever since I could even touch him without the dreaded weight of our own doom hanging over us.

'Nikau's nana also had a ring she never took off,' I say. 'She had to be buried in it. His mum tried to remove it after her tangi and she experienced The Despair. So on the upside, they have a built-in anti-theft feature,' I pull my jumper off, just to be able to hide for a second. 'But on the downside, we might be stuck together until after we're dead. Sorry.'

'Obviously not your fault.'

I smile, but it hurts – even though he's not blaming me, there's still an implication that something is wrong with us being together, and I'm tired and I miss him and my feelings are all over the place. I can't even trust my voice to work so I change into my pyjamas instead, and he goes back to his book. I catch him peeking and I wish I didn't like it, but I'm still human, even if I'm an idiot. I climb over onto the wall side and pull my hoodie back on – it's cold in here, and I have something else to tell him. The jumper feels a little like emotional armour.

'They also read about one way to undo a different kind of bond that *might* work. Manaia doesn't think so, but I guess it's worth a try.'

Elliott scrubs a hand over his face and drops his book to the floor. 'Interesting that that's not what you chose to lead with.' He wriggles 'til he's sitting up in bed. 'What do we do, then?'

'Apparently, we just swap back.'

He huffs out a resigned sort of laugh. 'It's embarrassing that we didn't actually try that already.'

'Yeah, well, it involved taking them off, which is painful, and I didn't want to.' I turn to face him properly. 'But we should obviously see if it works.'

He looks like he wants to object, and I want to have the courage to do it myself, but for different reasons. He nods, though, and slides Dad's ring off his finger. I pull off the silver one, and it's like tiny knives, same as before.

We align ourselves, fingers to rings, and simultaneously slide them home. Back to where they were before all of this went to shit. It feels like goodbye.

Elliott flinches as he takes his fingers off Dad's ring. My stomach turns. This doesn't feel better. There's no sense of satisfaction of having solved it – no rush of freedom, nothing. If anything, I feel worse.

I look up at Elliott and he doesn't look good at all. He's biting his lip and his eyes are wet, and when I let go of his ring he crumbles, tears streaming down his cheeks. I'm so busy hoping it's because he's sad he'll miss me that I don't notice it creeping up on me, too: bone-deep despair, cold and dark, a sharp, inhuman sadness. In a matter of seconds I understand his haunted expression and reach out for him, my hand on his knee, and it only helps a little. Even when I grab his hand, skin on skin, the darkness just ebbs for a second.

'I don't like it,' he says, his voice small and broken.

I take off Dad's ring and my hands are shaking, but I grab him again and shove the ring back on his finger. He gasps with what I hope is relief and I reclaim the silver ring with the black stone and bring it back to where it belongs. On me, apparently.

For a while, we just breathe, the shadows slowly backing away.

'That was horrible,' he says.

'Yeah.'

We sit, hands clasped between us, waiting for our hearts to slow, waiting for the dark to pass.

'Do you think the rings are sentient?' he asks.

'Let's say they aren't so I can sleep tonight.'

He fumbles around with his words for a bit, then says, 'We could – Can we … maybe just hug for a bit?' He blushes. 'I feel kind of hollow right now and touching you always makes me feel better.'

'We have to be careful …'

'We will be,' he says, and lies back in the bed, pulling me down on top of the covers.

He rolls to face me, nose to nose and toe to toe. He's so close he's just a blur and then he kisses me and I don't know what to do. We still don't know what constitutes consummation, but I don't want to be at fault if it's this, or whatever he's hoping for tonight. I break away, and his fingers tighten in my shirt like he's afraid to let go of me.

'I'm not going anywhere, I just –'

'Tim, *please*.'

He's terrible. He's beautiful and terrible and I'm hopeless and we're ruined. I send up a tiny prayer to whatever magical entity might be watching over us: that the winter-weight duvet trapped between us is enough to insulate ourselves from the awful truth of my intentions, and the fact I want him, now and always. Sooner or later my desire to not be at fault is going to be crushed by my desire for other things. We might not have consummated this bond, but I *want* to, and it's dangerous to even be near him.

And yet ... I let him kiss me.

Life Skills is first on Monday morning, and a bit of a mess. While Van Mill never announced that the egg assignment is a competition, it obviously is one among us, and the couples still in the game are even managing to write baby journal entries competitively. There's pride on the line. I wish I could commit to it fully, but my mind is elsewhere. Elliott seems to be sitting even closer than usual, our legs pressed together from knee to ankle, and I lose count of all his casual touches. Anytime he could elbow me for my attention, he uses an open hand instead, and usually it's right on my thigh, which is ... distracting.

Practical Magic is less noticeably different than usual because we're up and moving around. Elliott's still helping me with atmospheric charms and it's difficult magic, so most of our attention is on the work instead of on our other, bigger, problem.

Food Tech is all theory, though, and he's a permanent fixture against my leg again. When he leans in to comment on Graham's atrocious spelling, his fingers slide across the top of my quad and curl over my inner thigh, stroking a faint line there, so sensitive I barely hear what he's saying. By the end of the day I'm ready to throw him up against something solid and kiss him until he bleeds.

Except I can't, so I take the baby and visit my mother instead.

She asks questions about Meggan's sleeping patterns, and how my clouds are coming along, and how Elliott and I are going. I tell her we're doing well in the assignment, and I think I made rain, and that Elliott and I actually get on quite well now. I repeat what I told her last night – that he's a smart, sensible, caring person, and definitely isn't trying to get me into nefarious magic. She gives me a look, like I might've gone a bit far with it and everything I think I'm keeping secret is written on my face.

I want to exist in a world where I can ask her directly to help us, but she's too invested in my success to take it lightly. I don't need her reaction making me reflect on the severity of what we've done any more than I already am. I wouldn't have to evade the truth so much with Dad. He'd at least see the humour in it – that I'd got drunk and done something stupid. Also, having taught Magical History for so long, he might even know how to fix it.

So I ask Mum for help in the only way I can. 'Do you have any books about intercultural bonding for History?

The textbook is super vague and I'd like to get a good mark in this one.'

She stacks up a few books to take and keeps me occupied until dinner, teaching me to use air as a mea – to grasp it with purpose, then hold it in my palm and *feel* it. I manage to focus after a few tries, but it's far from easy. We sit on opposite ends of the couch, with Meggan wedged between us, and play catch, floating a scrunched-up ball of paper back and forth. I can't say I'm good at it, but I get a bit better and she promises, hilariously, to throw more rubbish at me later.

We walk to dinner a little early and the servery is just opening. Carol appears from the depths of the kitchen to say hello, and I panic. I'm still assuming Mum hasn't heard any marriage rumours, because she definitely would've mentioned it, but if anyone is going to accidentally start one, it'll be Carol.

We almost make it.

'I expect you're pleased with your new son-in-law,' she says to Mum, and winks at me. 'A nice handsome boy like that?'

I die, twice. Once because Mum is looking far too interested in what she means, and the second time because old ladies mentioning how handsome Elliott is only makes me feel dirty for agreeing with them. I cut my losses and forfeit grabbing garlic bread for the obvious benefit of walking away as fast as possible. Mum doesn't follow, but I catch her looking over at my table throughout dinner, a smug grin blossoming on her face when Elliott sits down beside me. Then he leans in, patting Meggan on the head while simultaneously draping himself over my shoulder. I wish he'd stop forgetting I'm not furniture. I also wish Mum would stop laughing at me from the staff tables.

None of my wishes come true.

CHAPTER 29

SEE WHAT LOVE CAN DO

We all linger at the table long after dessert, waiting 'til most people have left so we can plan our evening. Matt, Ana and Manaia have extracurriculars, but Nikau and Hana offer to go to the library and read through some of the older texts, since both of them can read te reo. Despite Dad being fluent, we spoke English at home most of the time since Mum knew approximately five Māori words when they met and most of them were food-related.

That leaves Sam, Silvia, Elliott and I back at Dad's until sometime before curfew. Elliott takes Meggan, I carry Mum's pile of books, and we make our way to the cardboard box library of Henry Te Maro. Hopefully, somewhere in there is a *scrap* of information about what counts as consummation and whether or not two stupidly drunk, queer teenagers are capable of achieving it.

Silvia makes us each a new pile, and it's immediately obvious there's something different about these books compared to the ones on the shelf. Several of them are falling apart, one is in literal pieces, and there are a few that look like back-alley, hand-bound, blacklisted texts from last century. Sam is in his element. Elliott is in my lap. Again. But it's Silvia who finds the first piece of information.

'Ooh!' she exclaims from her spot on the floor. 'Gay stuff! This mentions "unnatural urges". They're talking about how gay sex doesn't count because –' She cuts herself off mid-sentence but her eyes zip back and forth, reading further down the page. 'Oh my giddy aunt. These people are … Apparently consummation can only occur when there is "bona fide love, as witnessed by a man of the church", and "since the homosexual has no soul, he cannot experience love at all".' She looks up at us. 'What the actual fuck?'

'When was that book printed?' Elliott asks.

'Might also be worth asking *where* it was printed,' Sam says.

'Let's assume Hell, and throw it back in the fire,' she says, and tosses it aside. 'Next up, *Love in Other Languages*. Tim, where did your dad *get* these?'

'I have literally no idea.'

It's quiet again until Elliott gets up to make tea and Sam announces he's found something to counter Silvia's anti-love propaganda:

'"As in ancient times, the love between men has been well documented in the modern day, and within the magical community is no different. While societal attitudes have degraded in some regards over the centuries, the local community at Mount Hringur maintains its roots. The resort offers exclusive LGBT wedding packages, complete with marital suites and an optional consummation audience and refreshments, as was once popular amongst royalty in the north of Europe."'

'What on Earth are you reading?' Silvia asks.

'*Open Planet: Europe 1980*. I think it's a magic version of a Lonely Planet guide. That section was from a holiday resort in Iceland claiming to celebrate "the best of Europe's gayest bits in history". The fact it mentions consummation suggests it's possible for same-sex couples to be maritally bonded, and consummate.'

'I don't know how much I'd read into that.' Silvia looks exceptionally dubious and I can't help agreeing with her.

Beside me, Elliott's phone rings and he picks it up with a low-key, 'What's up?' and goes quiet for a moment while whoever's on the other end talks. 'OK, I'll meet you in five minutes. Try not to break anything.'

He stands up. 'That was Manaia. I need to go. See you at home?' he looks down at me and I want to know more but I don't want to pry.

'Sure. We'll be another hour or so, though, if you want to come back?'

He smirks, running his hand over my cheek. 'Oh, poor darling. Don't miss me too much.'

Smug bastard. I purposely don't offer to escort him out of the staff wing, and I pretend it's because he mocked me, but I worry it's actually because my mind is making up stories about him running off to Manaia for reasons other than being a good friend.

I don't quite settle after he goes. Sam gets up to make more tea after a while and Silvia comes to sit next to me with a very old fortune-telling book that looks a bit like a grimoire and apparently has a section for predicting things about your married life. I'm not sure I trust it.

'Can I see your ring?' she asks.

'It's not technically mine,' I say, but I shuffle closer and hold out my hand.

She takes it in her own, examining the silver band and the black stone, turning my hand over. 'I'm going to try something,' she says, moving the book so she can lay her hand flat on the page.

'Fine,' I say, before remembering the ring's prickly tendencies. 'It won't hurt, will it?'

'Only if you're secretly in love with him,' she says, and lays a finger over the ring.

I react on pure instinct, and I hate how naked it makes me feel as she looks up at me, her hand suddenly hovering between us and mine clutched to my stomach like it needs protecting.

'*Tim*,' she says, and a hot flush of pure dread burns my ears. 'I was kidding.'

'Please don't make a big deal out of this,' I beg, making it a thousand times worse.

'It's *already* a big deal.' She looks at me like I'm a bit simple. 'Sam, get over here.' She flaps her hand at him to come. When he doesn't appear, she turns and tries to get his attention. 'Earth to Sam. Are you reading or making tea? Come *here*.'

'Reading,' he says, but he doesn't look up. 'Guys ... I think I found something.' And then he just stands there, staring at the little book.

'Well, are you going to tell us?' Silvia asks. 'Sam? What's wrong? You're miles away.'

'Hmm? I'm one hundred and twenty years ago, actually,' he says, and leaves our cups and the steaming kettle and comes over to the couch. 'Tim, one of the books from your mum is a woman's journal. An old one. Listen to this: "The things I had seen in the ceremony at dawn – the private one, before the church service – almost made me believe it was magic. But lying with my husband for the first time was even more incredible than that. At the final moment, it was like the light broke through the clouds and our bedroom glowed gold like God was blessing us personally. My husband says it was the magic of our love, binding us together. He called it the midnight sun."'

Shit.

I try to act normal, when my life is anything but and my heart is racing.

'Do you remember anything like that, Tim? A golden glow? Seems like it'd be evidence as to whether whatever you did counted as consummation.'

'Tim?' Silvia says when I don't answer straight away. 'Are you OK?'

'Yeah,' is about all I can manage before I feel the need to curl into a ball and hide my face in my hands. I do it. It helps a bit.

'I'm guessing that's a yes, then, on the golden glow.'

'I'll finish making the tea,' Sam says, and I hear him walk away.

He comes back after a minute and Silvia tugs at my wrist 'til I uncurl. She puts a cup in my hand. It's comforting.

'So. You love him, and you've consummated the marriage,' she says.

'Yeah.'

'Tim, I hate to say it,' Sam says. 'But there's not a lot of point in us continuing to research if we know you've solidified the bond. You're going to need proper help. We could've managed something like an annulment, but even if we find a *divorce* spell, we won't be strong enough to make it work. If one even exists. I've seen no evidence so far and it's been two days.'

'Yeah.'

'Are you sure you're OK?' Silvia asks, and I feel my composure crack.

'Not really. How –' I don't know if I can say it. 'How can what we did count as consummation? It was barely anything at all, we still had all our clothes on.'

'But you love him.' Silvia points out.

'So?'

'Well. I guess it means more,' she says. 'Your feelings are more important than the specifics of what you physically did. If you think of it in vaguer terms, less science and more poetry, would you call him your lover?'

'Well, I'm not a poet, so no. Almost definitely not.'

'Keep in mind,' Sam says, 'the only reason we consider consummation to be "of the marital bed" is because of Christianity's influence. In some other cultures, simply living together is enough to consummate the marriage. And you *are* living together. And you *are* sleeping together, so even if you didn't *do it* that night, the general idea is the same.'

'We aren't in *some other culture*, though. We're in ours.'

'But you don't know who did this to you – bound you together. Or did this *for* you, I guess, if you wanted it to happen at the time. That person could've been from anywhere. Any sub-branch of magical evolution on the whole planet. The chance of their exact magical heritage responding to just one particular type of consummation was pretty slim.'

'You could've mentioned that earlier.'

'I did.' Sam says, and gives me a tight smile. 'In the library, I said you'd probably consummated. It was Elliott who said there was a chance you hadn't.'

'Right, let's drink our tea and we can tidy up and go home.' Silvia smiles into the silence, but it's edged with sympathy and I can't look at her for too long.

It weighs on me, the whole thing: the fact that we're stuck, and we need help, and that I'm going to have to tell my mum and she's going to be disappointed. Even the fact that Elliott's mum might be upset bothers me. I've never even met her. I walk back too slowly, Meggan awake and fussing in my arms, Silvia pulling on my jumper to hurry up, and it's like being dragged to my death. Because now I have to tell Elliott what we've done, what *I've* done, and even though it leaves us free to go back to our previous activities he's probably going to be too mad at me to want to.

'Are you OK?' Sam asks as we get close to the senior lounge.

'No. He's going to hate me.'

'He's got over that before. And it's not like it isn't partly his fault.'

'It's only partly his fault if living together is what did it. If it's idiotically loving him, then that's on me.'

'Takes two people to be lovers,' Silvia says with a wiggle of her eyebrows, and I smile in spite of myself.

But only for a second.

CHAPTER 30

GOOD INTENT

I get back to our room and Elliott's not there, so I brush my teeth, put Meggan to bed and tell her a depressing bedtime story about how her egg-dad is an idiot. I apologise to her for being about to ruin her short, fake life.

I realise I'm talking to an egg.

I get up and pull out my oldest, comfiest pyjamas. It's not going to matter if I look like shit anymore.

Elliott walks in as I'm changing, and his eyes rake down my bare chest.

'Hello, lover,' I say.

He looks at me quizzically and I don't bother explaining. 'What did Manaia have to say?' I ask.

He bends down and undoes his shoes. 'Nothing about us, unfortunately. I have no new info.'

'I do,' I say, and he straightens up, his face serious.

'About what?' He reads my mood, stepping over and sitting on the bed, waiting.

I finish buttoning up my pyjama shirt and flick my eyes up to his face. 'We found a book after you left. An old journal. With an entry about a wedding.'

The silvery light of my quartz is making his hair shine, and he clearly stole a pair of my socks this morning because they have a tiny hole in them and they look very, very familiar. It almost gives me hope. Maybe sock-stealing is a sign of love in his world.

'Do you remember a kind of golden, orangey light? When we were – when we were on the couch, at the house? Friday night? The room looked like it was glowing. I thought maybe I was still drunk, I mean, technically it was Saturday morning I supp–'

'Tim.'

'Yeah?'

'Spit it out.'

'The glowing light means something. They called it a midnight sun, it's –'

'Tim.' He sits down heavily on Sam's bed. 'Are you very ineptly saying what I think you're saying?'

'We've consummated it. We're going to have to ask for help.'

'Right,' he says. He won't look at me.

I babble, my heart going a thousand miles a minute. 'We talked about it on Saturday, remember? But we didn't know how it worked for non-het couples and – and then we got banned from the library anyway. And nothing we found on Dad's bookshelf was right, but then Sam found this in the pile from Mum and –' I take a breath. 'She, the woman who wrote it, talked about the glow, so, it seems it works the same way for any couple.'

'The same way?'

'Yeah. Remember, Sam found that reference to consummation being possible for same-sex couples? And then what Silvia's mum was talking about in the library when she kicked us out? You know, "magic isn't good or bad, it depends on your intent".'

'Intent?' he says, and his voice is flat, cold.

'Yeah,' I say, and I feel like I'm handing over the keys to my own heartbreak. My voice comes out dry and weird. 'In this instance I'd imagine it was whether or not one of us had feelings about being ... you know. Together.' I let my words hang there, between us, in the silence that follows. I can't look at him. 'I'm sorry, I – I can't –'

'No. No, Tim, I – I'm ...' He takes a breath. Shakes himself. 'I'm sorry. And I'm going to go and have a shower. Be alone for a bit.'

'Of course.'

And he leaves, without even looking at me, and my heart hurts. I can feel it like a physical force in my chest, pressing. Squeezing until I think it'll break me in two.

I don't sleep easily that night. Even though we've gone to bed officially OK with each other, something still feels off, like we haven't said all there is to say – because, of course, we haven't. I haven't told him that when he touches me, I can't think anymore. That every time we're alone together, all I want to do is crawl inside him and live there. I want to meld with him so I don't have to say things out loud, and all my stupid, messed-up feelings can be safe, away from where anyone can hear them. I haven't told him I trust him, that I think he won't make fun of me if I say, out loud, that I love him, just a bit. I haven't said *anything*, because I don't want him to just call it all off if I do. I'd rather be repressed and have him than let it all out and lose him. He'd have every right to walk away – it's the complete opposite of what we agreed to and I can imagine what he'd say. *'For goodness sake, Te Maro, can't you control your feelings?'*

Obviously, I can't. After Dad left I was miserable for months, and then my girlfriend dumped me for someone I hate and I couldn't decide whether to cry or hit something. But when Elliott showed up, and wedged himself into my life, he was like a calm spot in the storm. I only had simple feelings about him, mostly loathing, and that was a perfect distraction from the sadness. But then my feelings changed, and now every day we're together, every time he calls me *darling*, I get sucked back towards the edge of sadness, waiting for it to all go wrong. One day I'll stand there on the precipice with nothing left to lose and I'll shout into the void, all my feelings pouring out of me like blood, and I don't know what I'll do if he just walks away.

I dream as much. Of black holes and clifftops, and jumping over rocks and spiky ravines. Vivid images of the wild nothing of the South Island offer a brutal backdrop to all my emotional brambles. Images of the bush flick in and out. A river, a stretch of glacier. I imagine almost drowning, almost falling, almost burning under a black sun. My heart is thumping and my throat hurts and I jolt awake, right as I slide off the side of a twisting path, down a rocky bank and into the icy water of an unnamed creek. My skin is damp with sweat and the air is cold and I can barely breathe.

He stirs beside me in the dark, the rustle of sheets a beacon in the darkness, bringing me back to reality. A hand on my arm, a tether to the comforting, safe horror of my actual life. His voice is low.

'Tim,' is all he says.

'Bad dream,' I say, needlessly, because I'm sitting up, panting, and it's the middle of the night. 'Sorry.'

'Stop being sorry for things that aren't your fault,' he says. 'Come here.' And he pulls me over so I'm draped across his chest, still tense and awkward from my violent return to consciousness. His touch is too much of a comfort to resist for long, though, and I snuggle into his side. Maybe I'm relying a lot on his polite empathy, playing the nightmare card just to feel him next to me, but I don't care. I run my fingers along his collarbone and pretend like we're OK for real.

'It won't be too hard, will it, being secretly married to me for a few more days?' I say, and I feel like it might be the bravest thing I've ever said.

He sighs and pats my hair. 'I'm sure I'll cope.'

'Fortunately, I have no other suitors. You won't be forced to duel anyone.'

'See, that's the part of courtship I was actually looking forward to.'

'Sorry to disappoint you, I'm just not that popular.'

'Can I be mean to your ex-girlfriend, at least?'

'Yes,' I smile. 'I will allow you to smote her.'

'Excellent. A task for tomorrow,' he says, and kisses me on the head, like I'm his.

My smile drops away and I feel my tattered emotions swing the other way. I practise holding it all in, though; it's the least I can do.

CHAPTER 31

QUIET GIRL

Over the course of a single Tuesday, our three remaining rival eggs all die. Buttercup's the first to go, right before breakfast, and Nikau is devastated. He blames himself, and there are tears in his eyes when Hana walks into the lounge. We see her melt a little, right before she stalks up to him and kisses him in front of everyone. She, all five-foot-six of her, with her tippy toes and her peppered kisses, soothing this six-foot-two softie who was so terrified he'd disappointed her.

Fabergé is next, and we never hear the details, but there's a suspicious dent in the door of one of the girls' bathrooms and the rumours flying around at morning tea suggest that the egg-mum was in there with another guy while the egg-dad was left at home with the baby. No-one close to the couple will confirm or deny, but Ana whispers the name of the accused and everyone stares at the poor girl so much she bursts into tears. In a telling lack of solidarity, the other girls sitting at the same table don't move in to comfort her.

Right after classes are over for the day, Lizzie and Blake have a very public break-up in the main atrium outside the dining hall, attracting a sizable crowd of seniors and juniors alike. It ends with a theatrical shoving of baby Agatha into Blake's arms, which of course he fumbles, and the golden egg drops to the concrete floor with a crack and a gasp from the crowd. Lizzie doesn't flinch, just whips her hair around and stalks off towards the lounge, leaving him to deal with it. Elliott makes a quiet joke about Blake being a bit useless with his hands in general, and his voice in my ear is like … something I need, desperately. Close, and always combined with the tickle of his breath and the heat of his shoulder pressed against me. But every time an egg drops we lose time in this arrangement – and this was the last one. And I still haven't figured out how to stop loving him.

After a moment, someone else does the same maths I did as soon as I heard Liz shouting, and yells out that we've won. Elliott and I are congratulated with far more enthusiasm than it warrants. Someone pulls out their phone and yells something about photos for the yearbook and we're shoved together, Meggan peeking out of Elliott's jacket and me with two backpacks over my shoulder, straps tangled and my jumper pulled askew. We aren't ready for the first flash, but we have ourselves mostly arranged for the second. I'm not expecting a third, and I can only assume Elliott isn't either, because he pulls me closer, long fingers wrapping around my neck, and kisses me hard on the side of the head. My eyes must be bug-wide when the flash goes because there's a moment when I can't see properly, and just hear a chorus of titillated jeers and whoops and one very familiar voice yelling 'get a room'.

'That seems a weird way to end this, but OK,' I say, quietly, because the general populace has seen enough for one day and I don't need anyone asking what's ending.

Elliott gives me an odd look, but holds his tongue until we're alone and heading back home. 'Who says I'm ending it?'

'Wasn't that the agreement – for the duration of the assignment?' I say. My voice comes out surprisingly calm considering I'm pretty sure I'm falling apart on the inside.

'It's *our* agreement,' he says. 'And the assignment's not over. I said that it would be for the duration of our living arrangements, and we still live together, and Meggan is still alive, so it seems a little callous of you to be trying to wiggle out of it the second you might see an out. I know we didn't mean to end up *stuck* together, but I thought –'

'I'm not looking for an out!'

'Then what the hell are you doing?'

'I thought that was the plan, OK?' I say, my temper rising at the hideous irony of his words. 'I was under the impression you were doing all of this because it was a convenient way to get off, annoy Blake, and get through the assignment.'

'You think I was hooking up with you because of an egg?' he hisses at me, and Meggan starts to whimper.

'No, I –' Why is this so *difficult?* 'This isn't coming out right. I just – I have no idea what's going on and I'm sick of feeling like I'm on the back foot with you.'

'I can't help it if you're confused by simple things.'

'This was simple two weeks ago. It's a bloody mess now.' I've lost any hope of remaining calm; all my feelings are spilling out onto the floor. 'Can we talk about this later, when we're feeling less on edge?'

'What do you know about how I'm feeling?' he snaps and, well, I guess we're doing this now then, right here in the corridor.

'Nothing. I literally don't know how you feel,' I throw back at him. 'All I know is that you came into this with an out clause and a history of hating me,' I point out. 'And then you make me partner you in the world's stupidest assignment, and suddenly we're living together, and sleeping together and then –'

'You hated me too,' he says. 'And the out clause was for both of us. And I didn't make you partner me, or live with me, or sleep with me. I just offered, so stop blaming me if you're having regrets, because it isn't my fault.'

'I don't have regrets.'

'Neither do I, just in case you can't tell.'

'I honestly can't. I can't even tell if we're breaking up or not.'

'Do you want to be?' he asks, his eyes on mine, boring holes into me. Meggan starts to cry.

I'm about to tell him no, or at least try to, when a voice comes over the tannoy: *'Tim Te Maro and Elliott Parker, please report to B4'*. Van Mill. How did she find out already? *'Tim and Elliott to B4.'*

'I don't know,' I say instead, because I can't think. I don't even know if you can break up with someone you're bonded to. Will the magic let us? What happens if we're apart for too long? Are we going to die in our sleep? It's too much to process and my heart is fluttering for too many different reasons and I just *need a minute.*

'Well, fuck you, Tim,' Elliott says, and he sounds sad and annoyed. 'Let me know when you figure it out.'

He leaves without the expected fanfare. No stomping, no shoulder-checking me, nothing. Not a thing that would help me hold on to my residual anger and ignore the tell-tale shine in his eyes. He just turns on the spot and starts heading towards Van Mill.

I fall into step behind him, Meggan's cries subduing only slightly as he murmurs to her, his soft voice calming her and making me feel inexplicably worse.

Van Mill is far too perky when we get to her, and seems determined to ignore the tension radiating off the two of us. Meggan is still grizzly and unhappy when Elliott hands her over. He twitches as if to snatch her back when Van Mill strips her of her little blanket and plonks her unceremoniously in the cold-looking brass bowl on her weird, gadgety set of scales. She picks up a little silver thing in her left hand and swishes her right hand over the fake baby that's kept us up at night and side by side. A sad sort of regret comes over me. Elliott's gone very quiet too, and I want to reach out for him as she ignores our baby's cries and keeps running her diagnostics, clucking curiously at whatever they're telling her.

'You've done well, boys,' she says, and that tone of surprise is still grating. 'I bet everyone's a bit shocked.'

'Not really,' Elliott says. 'We're both quite capable of caring for someone.'

'Elliott, dear, it's an enchanted egg, not a person.' Van Mill gives him a look like he might be delusional, and I want to hurt her.

'She has a personality,' Elliott says, his gaze still locked on Meggan.

'I'm sure she does,' Van Mill says, off-hand and back to focusing on her diagnostics already. 'All right, you end with a …' She swishes her hand one more time and straightens up. 'Goodness, ninety-four per cent for the practical. I hope your book work is this good.'

'And we won,' I point out, because she's still acting like we're completely incompetent and this is some sort of miracle.

'It's not about winning, Tim,' she says, and I wish that was true, because I feel like I'm losing right now.

At least with her being such a cold bitch about the whole thing, I can feel my sense of loyalty fizzing to life. It's almost comforting that no matter how much of a mess Elliott and I are in, I'm prepared to tell her exactly what I think of her and get myself expelled just to please him. If I care that much, I might actually manage to be his friend after this. The thought makes me brave and I reach out for his hand, hoping he's not too angry with me.

She sees the movement and her mouth twitches as our fingers lace together, and I want her to say something horrendous so I can punch her in her the face and tell Mum she provoked me.

'Right, then, you two are done here – you're dismissed,' she says.

She turns back to her desk just as Elliott asks, 'But what happens to –'

And before he can finish, she waves her hand and the sad wail of our baby, who just needed a hug after being poked and prodded and put in a cold hard basin, just … cuts off. Dead. Silent.

His fingers crush mine, and I let them. I let the pain ground me, and I let his grip hold me still, and when he tugs at my arm, seconds or minutes later, I let him drag me away. The echo of our child's silenced cry replays over and over again, and when I try to pin it down so I can stare it in the face, it dissolves into mist and haunts me again from out of sight.

'Elliott,' I say, my voice shaky and cold.

'I know,' he says, 'but you can't.'

'But how could she –' I cut myself off. Did she kill her if she wasn't really alive? Does that matter when I feel like I've lost something anyway – when I feel like it's been ripped from my gut and thrown in the corner?

We make it halfway down the corridor before he drags me into an alcove and shoves me up against the wall, covering my mouth with his own and never once letting go of my hand. He's unforgiving and constant and my breath is all but gone by the time he pulls away.

'Your dad's rooms,' he says and I nod, because I haven't remembered how to speak yet. And then he leans in and whispers in my ear, low and desperate, *I need to feel something else,* and I have to close my eyes.

CHAPTER 32

TEEN HEAT

My hand is still in his, both our bags still slung over my shoulder, as we zigzag our way to the staff wing, trying not to draw too much attention. We reach Dad's rooms, slip unseen through the door and I flick on the lights and set our bags on the couch. Elliott locks the door behind us.

'Are you OK?' he asks, and his voice is quiet and I don't know what to tell him because I'm not OK, for so many reasons.

It seems pointless to lie, though, and even if I tried I don't think he'd believe me. 'Not really, no,' I say. 'No, I'm not.'

'Me neither,' he whispers, like he's afraid talking about it will make it more real.

He's looking at me like I'm the one who was taken from him, and there's a ferocity in his gaze that pokes at all the feelings I'm hiding. I could so easily imagine he's thinking about how much he needs me in his life forever. How he hopes I'll stay even though our daughter, our only legitimate connection, is gone. How maybe it's enough that she brought us together; that even though her time here was short, we'll never forget her because she made us what we are. I imagine he's thinking that what we are isn't fragile, and temporary, and merely the cracked shell of a relationship that has nothing inside but sadness.

It makes my feelings for him feel even bigger, thick and spongy and expanding silently into the warm, citrus-and-wool-scented space between us. I imagine them as vapour hanging over us, billowing out of my chest until we're standing in a cloud of my embarrassing lack of self-control. My failure to compartmentalise, to stick to a simple agreement, to keep from falling, stupid and in love, into the arms of someone who has already made it quite clear that we're destined to be parted, even if it's not as soon as I expected.

'Do you think everyone felt like this when their eggs died?' he says.

'How could they?' I say, and hold out my arms to him. He says nothing, just steps in close, his own arms coming up around my shoulders and holding me tight. 'It's different for us,' I whisper against his skin. 'There was more than just Meggan. It was – us. We got all mixed up with it and

I didn't realise how much we'd become like –' I pause, knowing it's such a melodramatic thing to say. So typical of a child of divorce, feeling all abandoned and seeing things that aren't there.

'Like family?' he says, and I nod.

'Is that weird?'

He sighs and presses his lips against my temple. 'No, Tim, it's not.'

We stand there for a minute, arms around each other, desperate at first, clinging, then softer, more like it was before. Before the fight and the rings and the stupid. It feels dangerous – easily misinterpreted.

'Are we OK?' I ask, leaning back to look at him.

He nods, slowly, almost like he's trying to save this image of me. Like all of what he's said about it being *our* agreement and *our* choice is a lie, and he knows that this is it, the last time we'll get to be together.

Puts the whole thing in a different light, really. Makes me feel sort of reckless.

'I guess we don't have to worry about accidentally making the bond stronger anymore,' I say.

'Interesting change of subject.'

I nod, and my ears go hot. Maybe he wasn't thinking what I was thinking. 'Sorry.'

'Sorry for making me keep my hands to myself this whole time for nothing?' His arms tighten around my back.

'We had to. And technically we aren't actually a hundred per cent sure, but –' I don't know how to explain that since

I feel so bad already, making a bigger mess isn't going to make much of a difference. I also know that I, personally, don't mind being stuck with him – but I can't make that decision for the both of us. I lean in so I don't have to look at his expression, and speak to his shoulder. 'I would be OK with risking it if you ...'

There's a pause.

'If I needed you?' he says softly against my temple.

'Yeah.'

He moves – mouth hot on my skin and hands skimming down my back, under my jumper, my shirt, pulling them up and over my head, letting them drop to the floor. He leans in for another kiss, grappling with the front of my trousers, and nudges me towards the bedroom door. He shifts his attention to my neck, kissing and nibbling and sucking on my skin, everything just a little too hard, too sharp. I let him push at me until I realise that if this is truly the last time, I should be taking proper advantage of it, building another vault in my wank bank at least, making another memory for when I'm alone. I push his hands away and tug at his jumper, pulling it off and fluffing up his hair in the process. I want to slide my fingers into it but I want his shirt off more, so I yank it out of his trousers and start on his buttons, pulling him against me as my back hits the bedroom door.

'How do you want to do it?' he asks, his breath in my ear as he reaches down next to my hip and turns the handle.

We stumble through. Elliott looks up and freezes, his gaze fixed on a point over my shoulder, hands suddenly off me and eyes wide.

I turn around.

Oh ... shit.

'*Dad.*'

CHAPTER 33

HOME AGAIN

My father is here, in his pyjamas, and armed – there's a taiaha in his hands and it's pointed right at us.

'Tim.' He relaxes his stance, lowering the point of the spear to the floor. Mostly. 'And Elliott Parker?'

'Hello, Sir.'

'You're back,' I say.

The softness of my voice annoys me. Like I'm so bloody happy to see him that I've forgotten the fact he *left* us. That I've been miserable for the months since. That I've needed him and he wasn't here.

'Yeah,' he says. 'Sorry I haven't been in touch recently. We've been out of cell service areas for a few weeks.'

'We?' Who the hell has he been off with?

'I've been with your uncle. We, um … spent some time in the bush.'

'Right.' I'm not sure if I believe him. That doesn't sound like Uncle Eddie – Taika was the outdoorsy one, but he died on a mountaintop and I doubt Dad was off tramping with his ghost.

'I probably don't need to ask what you're doing here.' He looks pointedly at my bare chest, then at Elliott's rumpled shirt with half the buttons undone.

'Mum gave me the key.'

'For this?' He points at Elliott.

'No. She –' This isn't what I want to talk about – it's not important right now. 'Why are you back?'

'Your birthday's soon. I had a few days off work. I wanted to see you.'

'And you picked *right now?*'

'No, Tim.' He smirks, gestures to the fact that I'm standing in the doorway of *his* bedroom. '*You* picked right now.'

'Should I go?' Elliott says, and if he thinks he's wriggling out of this, he's wrong.

'No,' I say, and grab his wrist. 'Stay. We still don't know how to fix any of this and Dad might be able to help us.'

'Are you two OK?' Dad asks, and his posture shifts.

He's a big guy: fit, strong. He can be menacing without trying, but he also has a softness to him when it comes to protecting things. He's hand-raised orphaned birds, he used to carry our old cat around like a baby, and he sang me to sleep when I was sad. I've missed him like someone ripped out my actual heart and I don't have it in me to be mad anymore. I need him. *We* need him.

'We –' I try to think of where to start. 'Something weird happened.'

'OK,' he says. 'Shall we sit and have a cup of tea?'

We move into the living room, and Elliott and I put all our clothes back on while Dad's in the kitchen.

'Tell me the worst thing first,' he says, slipping into pastoral mode as he pulls his desk chair over to the couch and sits down facing us. 'That way it can only get better.'

I take a breath. 'We kind of got married. A bit. Maybe. Accidentally.'

He stares at me for a long moment, flicks his eyes to Elliott, then comes back to me. 'You got married?'

'We –' I hesitate, but this is what I imagined – joking with him about my own stupidity. 'We got a bit drunk, and we don't actually remember what happened. But we came home with rings on, and we can't take them off.'

'Why can't you?'

'Feels like wanting to die,' Elliott says. I wasn't expecting him to talk, and his voice is quiet, like he wasn't either. He clears his throat. 'We tried swapping back, but that didn't work either.'

Dad nods and blows across his tea. 'Was there a ceremony? A priest? Did you sign anything?'

'We don't remember,' I say. 'It's all a bit blurry.'

'I remember a little,' Elliott says, shooting me a quick look before focusing on Dad. 'But I don't know what relevance it has. There was an old guy there wearing all black, and there was lots of singing.'

'I don't remember those things,' I say, a kernel of something turning over in my gut.

Elliott turns back to me. 'You were utterly bladdered, I'm not surprised.'

'But weren't you?' I flick an awkward glance over at my dad. 'Drunk, I mean? I thought we were both –'

'Tim, you made me drink moonshine out of a bucket. I was very definitely drunk.'

'But you *remember*?' I don't know how we've got this far without him telling me any of this yet.

'Some things, sure.'

'Do you remember us *getting married*?'

'*No*. I –' His eyes go wide, worried. 'I remember standing in the garden, and I remember wearing a blanket over my head, and you lifting it up and kissing me. That's all.'

'I remember the blanket.' I hold his gaze and he doesn't look away, as if he's willing me to believe him. I can't think of any reason he'd have to lie.

'OK,' Dad says. 'Where did the rings come from?'

Shit.

'Um. This was Elliott's,' I say, holding up my left hand. 'And, um, you left your wedding ring lying on the vanity and I found it, so I was wearing it that night ... and, yeah.'

273

The corner of his mouth quirks up and I notice how long his stubble is. He hasn't shaved for days. 'I wondered where that had got to.'

'Sorry.'

'I'm sure Elliott will look after it.'

The two most important men in my life right now are staring at each other, and it's weird. The situation is obviously horribly uncomfortable – my dad caught me half-naked with a boy – but it's also a relief to be here, telling an actual adult who might be able to help us.

'I can assure you I won't be taking it off,' Elliott says, and my father gives him a grim smile.

'But you *do* want to, I hope?' he asks. 'Seventeen is young to be married. I can imagine this is putting quite a bit of pressure on you two.' He looks at me then, and I know he's thinking of all the times I was sullen and grumpy and swamped with school assessments. He usually ended up helping me out with them as well. I'm no good under pressure.

'We don't know how to reverse it,' I say. 'We were hoping you would.'

He nods and takes a sip of his tea. 'Depends on if it's actually a marriage or something else.'

'We couldn't think of anyone who would want to curse both of us, or who'd actually be capable, so some sort of bonding was the only answer we could come up with,' I say. 'The research we did into marital bonds fits the best.'

'OK, well, if it *is* just a simple marital bond, I can help you, but you're going to have to be sure of a few things.'

I've never been more thankful to have parents.

'Like what?'

'Where this happened. When. And you'll have to be sure you both want it to end; the magic knows your intent, and if you both, evidently, wanted to be married when you did it ...' He leaves the implication hanging and I'm too embarrassed to look at Elliott until the words sink in.

Both wanted to be married.

Both.

Could Elliott have the same intentions as I do? Are we *both* sitting here, stupidly in love and afraid to say anything? I can believe he likes me, but ... My hope lasts about three seconds.

'I want this ring off my finger,' Elliott says. 'No offense.'

'None taken,' my dad says. 'I wouldn't mind having it back.'

We talk logistics, then. All the elements of a successful divorce (which are similar to all the elements we must've had for a successful marriage). Whens, wheres, links to our magical lineage and how we're going to sneak out of the school in the middle of the night. Even what we'll eat in place of the traditional feast. Dad doesn't seem too worried about the school rules, or taking someone else's son off school grounds after curfew, but I guess he's not a teacher anymore, he's just my dad, and I suppose taking your teenage son and his husband to get a magical divorce isn't so weird.

I hug him before we leave, and he holds me for a long

time before standing me out in front of him, his giant hands grasping my shoulders. 'You look good, son,' he says.

'I don't feel it right now.'

He lets me go and pats me on the shoulder. 'You'll be fine.'

'Yeah.'

'Though,' his voice drops lower, 'what happened to Lizzie?'

'Dumped me for Blake Hutton.'

'That's a bit of a downgrade. Seems to have worked out for you, though,' he says, and nods over towards the door where Elliott is waiting.

It occurs to me that my dad probably taught Elliott before he left, and might actually know him just as well as I do – though in less intimate detail, obviously. I wonder if he likes the idea of having him for a son-in-law. Elliott's smart enough for him; they'd probably get on fine. Shame it's not going to happen.

'It's not like that,' I say.

He tilts his head to the side and gives me a look. 'It looked a lot like that.' He wiggles his eyebrows.

'*Dad.*'

'You can tell me about it later,' he says, and I absolutely won't. Not ever.

'Good*bye*,' I say.

'See you in ten hours. I'll message you.'

Once we're in the corridor, I ask Elliott what he wants to do next, and we end up sitting in the empty dining hall.

We eat as soon as the servery opens, then go for a walk outside while we wait for dessert. We don't say much. We return just in time to score the remains of a huge dish of apple crumble, which is way more than the normal serving, so I feel fat and strangely content as we make our way to the senior lounge.

A group's sitting around the fireplace there, talking about having drinks tonight after Lorraine has done her check-in and left us alone. Elliott and I have what's left from a couple of weeks ago, but we aren't meant to have alcohol on school grounds, so when he shoots me a questioning look I shrug. I don't want to get in trouble, but I also don't mind him giving away the port.

The collective enthusiasm for alcohol sets the tone and it doesn't take long for someone to suggest spin the bottle, or for Nikau to quirk a wholesome eyebrow and wonder aloud what the point is if half of us are coupled up already.

I have to counter his point with my own – it's probably time I stopped thinking of myself as part of a couple, since I have plans to get divorced later tonight. 'Maybe that's the fun? Doesn't have to mean anything.' I don't know what it says about me that I want to kiss all my friends to avoid having feelings about never kissing Elliott again.

'If we're all going to be making out, I'm going to need a proper drink.' Elliott sighs and stretches. 'Anyone else got anything stashed away, or are we stuck with Tim's shitty rum and a meagre splash of port?'

'I have peach schnapps,' Manaia announces, and everyone turns to her. 'What?' she says. 'I'm allowed to like girly shit, you know. There aren't *rules*.'

'I have quite a lot of vodka?' Hana says, and Nikau's jaw drops.

'You do?' he asks, and it's clear her angelic exterior might be hiding far more than Nikau was expecting.

'It's in my room, come help me find it,' she says with a grin, and Ana rolls her eyes.

'Manaia's schnapps is in my desk drawer, can you grab it?' she calls after them as they disappear down the girls' corridor. They don't reply. 'They're never going to come back, are they?' She sighs. 'I should've got it myself.'

'We can tide you over,' I say, and ask Elliott if he wants me to get his fancy whiskey as well, which, of course, he does. So I do.

As I walk down the boys' corridor I hear a comment I probably wasn't meant to, about our domesticity and how cute it is. Contrary to what it would've done a few days ago, it leaves me feeling shitty, and the solace of drinking takes on a different sort of promise.

CHAPTER 34

MIDNIGHT MARAUDERS

The game is put off until after Lorraine has been and gone, and once the door clicks behind her people pull out their stashes from under cushions and jumpers. We start with some standard binge-drinking warm-ups to soften the mood and dispel any awkwardness. Elliott and I share a look that says 'let's take it easy this time', since we should probably be relatively sober when we meet up with my dad so he can undo the thing we did *last time* we drank.

We start with an impressively large collection of chocolate, chips and drinks. Cups are scavenged, beverages are poured and we're all comfortably capable of both consent and spontaneous fits of giggles when Ana declares it 'time to play'.

She lays out some house rules and gathers us into a circle, having each of us space ourselves out evenly and keep our hands visible. 'It eliminates sneaky behaviour,' she says. Presumably because no-one can slide a hand into their pocket and nudge the bottle into a favourable position with magic. She's a bit wrong, of course, because all the Elementals who are here – plus Elliott, apparently – could absolutely move an almost empty bottle with nothing but air, but it seems confrontational to mention it.

The first few rounds are pretty safe. Ana's first spin points to Matt, who looks startled despite the entire purpose of the game and quickly video chats his girlfriend back home for permission to play. He gets the all-clear – he can do anything he'd be OK with her doing back in Taranaki. It's declared a decent overall rule for couples, and all affected parties agree to it. In a telling turn of events, Manaia, Sam and Silvia all look discreetly over at us when we don't volunteer our immediate agreement as well. I ignore them. Elliott and I might be sharing a couch, but we aren't actually touching. You could fit a whole other person between us.

The turn moves around the circle to the left and Manaia kisses Corey. On her left, Silvia kisses Hana, Sam kisses Hana, Hana kisses Matt, then Nikau gets to spin and ends up kissing Hana, who swears she isn't doing this on purpose. Elliott stretches his legs out and burrows his feet under my arse while a clutch of Elementals I don't really know that well take their turns.

It goes past us with no major embarrassments and all the

way back around the circle. At some point Elliott tugs his foot free and impishly slides it behind my back, his fluffy socks tickling my skin. The only way I can stop him is to pull his feet onto my lap and hold them there while he wriggles. Nikau spins again and kisses Manaia before he hands over to his left again, to Corey. I'm too busy thinking about it being my turn soon to realise when his spin has landed on me and I have to do something *now*.

'Tim?' Corey asks. He's kneeling, facing me, and I hope he doesn't take my confusion for horror. 'Sorry?' he says.

'No, it's fine, I was –' What do I say? I was distracted by my impending divorce? 'Nothing.'

I close my eyes and Corey must think I do it for him and not because I'm embarrassed, because he leans in then, quickly, and there's a girlish 'whoop' from the circle after a couple of seconds pass and he's still on me. Even then, I've barely recovered from the surprise before he pulls away, flushed and incapable of looking me in the eye. I force myself to wonder if there's anything in it – if he's actually into guys – because objectively, he's not a bad option for when all this shit with Elliott falls apart. Clever enough, decent looking, and not too much taller than me. I'm half hoping I'll land on him with my spin because his lips were soft and he seems pretty normal and maybe it'll make me feel better to have a foot out the door already.

What I wasn't hoping for, after pushing Elliott's feet away and leaning out of my seat to swipe at the bottle, was for it to land on *him*. But it does.

I don't know how to kiss him without it being obvious we've done it before, and the thought of people thinking we're together when we're on the cusp of being separated is too depressing. I can't tell what Elliott's expecting by the look on his face when I manage to get back onto the couch. Maybe he's thinking *'inelegant as ever there, Te Maro'*. Or maybe, if Dad's right, and he loves me, he's waiting to see if I'm happy to kiss him in front of all of my friends.

So I stalk towards him on all fours, knees sinking into the couch cushions as my hands find the armrest behind his head. His expression goes neutral, which probably means he's freaking out and doesn't want anyone to know. He's surrounded: I'm hovering above him with my thighs either side of his legs and my wrists almost touching his shoulders. He's trapped. If he protests, then we'll look more suspicious. And if he calls my bluff and tries to sex it up, I might just do it.

So all I do at first is say, 'Hi,' and lean a little closer.

And then I kiss him.

Properly.

Like I would if we were alone, except we aren't; we're in a room full of people and they're all watching.

Silently. Waiting. Wondering, maybe, if there was more to it than an egg-baby. But they can't be expecting the softest kiss I've ever delivered, or for Elliott's eyelids to flutter shut, or for his hand to drift to my jaw, holding me there as he opens his mouth under mine and rises up in his seat. I know they can't, because I didn't, and I've kissed him before.

I don't know how long it lasts, but I feel his tongue against mine and a gasp from the circle and the distinct sound of the lounge door closing before I bring my lips together and pull back. His pupils are blown wide and he looks … startled.

'I'm never going to get my room back, am I?' comes a voice from the entryway, and we turn simultaneously, our bodies frozen in position, to see Blake standing there with Lizzie's dance-group friend. She has her hand wrapped around his arm and I reckon ex-friend is probably more accurate at this stage.

I retreat to my corner of the couch, Manaia staring at us still. I look over at Elliott and he seems … I don't know. Maybe annoyed. I can't tell if he's plotting revenge or plotting what he'll do once he can kiss me again. Maybe they're the same thing.

Too dazed to contribute, the conversation about room-swapping happens without our input. This is the last night as we are; tomorrow everything goes back to normal. Eventually the hubbub settles, Blake and his new friend sit down and we all get back to it, though Manaia declares a switch to truth or dare. At one o'clock Hana dares everyone to go to bed, and we all grumble and mutter and crawl out of our seats with the finesse of pensioners.

We clear up the bottles and chip packets, and Ana and Silvia try to clean all the mugs with magic, despite being a little tipsy. Manaia hands me a pile of floor cushions and gathers a pile of her own, shoving me towards the storage cupboard in the corner. We've never put them back in there before and I wonder what her real objective is. She doesn't beat around the bush with it.

'Tim,' she says, her voice low as she flings the cupboard door open, hiding us from the room. 'If you hurt Elliott, I will kill you.'

'What?' The irony hits me like a brick. If anyone's at risk of being hurt, it's definitely me.

'Don't "what" me. You're not an idiot,' she snaps, loading her cushions in. 'Not really. But if you don't want him, and you lead him on, I will hex you until you have the brain capacity of a lopsided pavlova.'

'OK …?'

'I mean it,' she says, taking my cushions and jamming them into the cupboard. 'I will end you. I will make you sorry you ever touched him. I will make your dick cry fat, bloody tears.'

'All right, all right.'

'He's waited long enough and he's been through enough shit with Blake – I don't need you adding to it.' She snaps the door closed and smiles to cover up our secret chat. 'Goodnight, Tim.'

'Yeah. Night then,' I say to her back as she flounces away, dragging Ana off towards the girls' corridor.

'You all right?' Nikau says from my elbow.

When I turn, he's right next to me, looking down with an expression of mild concern. I nod, not convinced but not wanting him to worry.

'See you at breakfast,' I say and give him a hug, because I bloody well need one. Bless him, he pats me firmly on the back and doesn't say another word.

The next hour before Elliott and I have to meet Dad is weird. The game, that kiss, and what Manaia said are all hanging over me, but Elliott's fallen asleep so I have nothing to distract me. Everything is quiet and it makes Meggan's absence all the more obvious. Her little purple cot is still there, empty except for my T-shirts still rolled up in the bottom. It wasn't long ago that I put them in there, and yet here I am. In bed with the guy I've been sleeping with, and marrying, and tonight I'll be divorcing him. Add to that, his best friend thinks I'm trying to lead him on. It's not surprising I can't sleep.

He's curled against my side, his breath ghosting across my neck. His hair is tickling my ear and my arm is going to sleep under his head, but I don't care. If this is the last night I get to hold him, then I'd put up with worse. We have no excuse to keep this up anymore. No Meggan, no more room sharing and, in a couple of hours, no magical approximation of marriage. Which means no more of *this*. And we'll go back to being ... what? Rivals? Or will we stay friends and I'll spend the rest of the year pining, never far enough away to get over it?

I look down at him, peaceful in sleep, and wonder how I ever hated him. I try to think of anything he's done to me directly, anything that wasn't seventy per cent his stupid friends' fault, anything I can cling to to push away the feeling building in my throat. Because if I don't get to live with him, or be with him, maybe I want to at least stay married to him. And if I let myself want that, then I'm going to get it, because the magic isn't as stupid as I am, and it's going to know, and the reversal isn't going to work.

I could tell him how I feel and hope he rejects me so viciously I can't keep loving him. Or maybe I should ask him how *he* feels – maybe his indifference will hurt me enough that divorce will seem like a respite. Should I try now, before Dad's around to overhear? Should I wait and let the undoing fail, then use the disappointment on my shackled husband's face to change my mind?

There's too much that might go wrong and no easy way out of any of it, so I'm almost glad when my phone beeps and my options diminish. Dad's message says for us to meet him at the shuttle, so I roll out of bed and start pulling my boots on. I could say something now, but Elliott seems less than impressed that he has to be awake, and my most indulgent brain cells ignore all my uncertainty and pretend it's because he's sad we're about to be unmarried. I'm my own worst enemy.

CHAPTER 35

THE UNKNOWN AND THE INFINITE

We've layered up, but it's still cold in the corridor, and I want to reach out for Elliott's arm and pull him close. I don't. Even if I can't control my feelings, I should at least control my hands.

There are lights on in the shuttle bay, and we see the Camry waiting for us, Dad loading things into the boot.

'Morning,' he says, looking far too OK with the ungodly hour.

'Hey, Dad.'

'Morning, Mr Te Maro.'

'Elliott, as my son-in-law for the next hour, you can probably call me Henry.'

'OK.'

It's still weird hearing them talk to each other, let alone having Elliott call my dad by his first name. I should get used to it – they're both going to have a lot to say when I inevitably screw this up.

'Need a hand?' I ask.

'All good, son. I just needed to make sure we had a blanket and our feast for afterwards – gotta make sure we do this thing right. We're ready now. Unless you remembered anything else?'

'No, nothing.'

'I see you've got your taonga,' he says, pointing at the pounamu mere around my neck. 'Were those the clothes you were wearing that night?'

'Yeah, mostly.'

'You were mostly wearing clothes that night?' He wiggles his eyebrows and I *die*.

'*Dad*.' I give up and get in the car. I don't know if this is worse than him being icked out or mad at us for violating his room, but it's not fun.

Elliott gets in the back beside me and I make sure to keep my distance. There's no point fuelling Dad's sense of humour.

It's been ages since I was driven all the way out of here in a normal car, so it's interesting enough to keep me staring out the window the whole time. We cruise past the pedestrian exit where the shuttle bus drops us off to walk in through the woods, and it's annoying how little time it takes to get to town from there. I get the need for secrecy and the increased risk of being seen if we drive the same van in and out multiple times a day, but I also resent the hour-long walk between the shuttle and the shops.

It's a similarly short trip between the hidden on-ramp and the pub, and we find the old house easily. Dad pulls alongside and parks and Elliott asks how we're going to do this without getting caught. Dad points out that if the locals had wanted to avoid a front-row seat to a divorce then maybe they shouldn't have let two seventeen-year-olds get married. He also promises to be quiet and stick to the garden, though, so it might not be too bad.

Elliott picks the spot that feels the most familiar and dons his blanket, and I wish I could remember any part of our wedding so I had something to offer. He looks cute with the blanket draped over his head, though, a pale puff of curls poking out from underneath it, so at least I've probably remembered how I felt at the time.

Dad flicks through a notebook, pen between his teeth, an amorphous, blueish light hovering over his shoulder.

'You kids ready?' he mumbles around the pen.

It's happening too fast and I still have no idea what to do. 'Yeah.'

'OK, so, Tim, you have your heirloom your pounamu, Elliott, you said you were carrying something of your nan's that night, did you bring it?'

'No, it was –' His eyes flick up to mine and then down to my left hand and my heart implodes a little. 'The ring Tim is wearing was hers.'

I had assumed it was one of those expensive fashiony rings and that Elliott was just being edgy. The black stone and the angular setting seemed modern, masculine. Looking down at it now, though, I see something else: hints of Art Deco, as if the entire town of Napier had manifested in a piece of jewellery. I feel guilty for having taken it away from him and for being responsible for having something engraved in it so he won't be able to forget any of this. Even if he has my dad's ring on his hand, that's only special because it's Dad's, and now that he's back I don't need it to remember him by.

'OK, well, good that it's with us. That'll help ground your ancestral power here, where you stand.'

'OK.' Somehow Elliott looks more forlorn with the blanket on and I want to hug him, to make him feel better, even though it's probably my fault he's here and he's sad. He's going to be sadder soon, and that's going to be my fault too.

Dad slips the notebook and pen into his pocket and gestures at us to give him our hands, then clasps each ring between thumb and forefinger. I curl my fist slightly so I don't feel like it might slip off. He whispers a long incantation, and I don't understand all of it, but the general gist of it seems to be 'hey, Earth, please channel the power of a thousand generations of magic users so that I can fix my only son's stupidity'.

But then he says 'tēnā koe' in a deep, reverent voice, and the feel of old magic permeates me, and I know we're no longer just three men standing in someone else's garden at stupid o'clock in the morning. Elliott feels it too and his face sort of crumples under the weight of it, so I reach out and take his other hand without even thinking. His fingers close around mine and he feels cold and his grip is too tight, but I squeeze back for a second before letting go, telling him I'm here too.

'Are you ready?' Dad asks, looking at each of us in turn.

Elliott nods, and I mimic him, because it's too late now and I'm just going to have to let it fail. The whole thing seems so unfair, and I was an idiot to think I could ever be his friend after this. It feels like something is dying.

'I'm going to recite the first part, and then each of you, in turn, need to declare that you no longer wish to be married. You'll have to focus on why, and you'll have to mean it, otherwise it won't work, so ...' He shrugs. 'Be sure.'

I'd give my entire savings and every single one of my NCEA credits to be living with a different type of magic – one that just did what you told it instead of constantly questioning the validity of your request based on how much you really mean it.

Neither of us says anything, and Dad seems to take that as assent. 'Join hands,' he says, and I take Elliott's hand again. For the last time. Except it won't be, because we're going to have to do this again once I've found a way to get over him.

Dad starts speaking, low and quick, and he says our names and his own, and I catch the words that basically mean 'let them be gone from each other's lives and live happily apart' and I feel like I might cry. To be honest, Elliott doesn't look totally happy either, even though he probably doesn't understand enough of what's being said about his future and how I'm not going to be a part of it. I close my eyes and try to squeeze everything back in.

Dad finishes and nods at us both to say our bit. We look at each other and I bet Elliott can see the shine in my eyes and I bet he knows what it means.

He opens his mouth to speak, and there's a pause, a tiny one, just enough, before he manages to say, 'I –'

So I cut him off.

I just look at him and stop thinking, stop worrying. I let my sleep-deprived brain have a rest and instead I speak with my stupid, idealistic heart.

CHAPTER 36

THE LOVE CLUB

'I love you.'

Dad turns his head. Elliott is frozen with his mouth half open and his eyes wide. I keep talking.

'I know you didn't mean for any of this to mean anything, and I know we had an agreement, and yeah, I know it's our agreement and we can change it, but –' I take a breath. 'I don't want to just keep hooking up with you and have it mean nothing.'

'Oh ...' Elliott says.

'But if that's all you want –' I take a breath. 'Or, if you don't like me like that, then OK, but I don't want to lose you completely.' I have to look away from him, and my eyes fix on our joined hands instead. 'I'd really miss you.

So … I want to stay married to you. And since I want to stay married then I don't think this ritual is going to work. And I wanted to tell you before it didn't.'

'You want to stay married because you're afraid I don't like you?'

'It sounds stupid when you say it like that.'

'It sounded stupid when you said it, too. Could we not just actually go out, so I can get this bloody nightmare thing off my finger?'

'What do you mean?'

'It's giving me anxiety, Tim. What if something happens and I lose it and I have to spend the rest of my life crippled by sadness because you were an idiot and thought I didn't like you?'

'No, I mean – you wanna go out with me?'

'How is that not *painfully* obvious?' he says. 'I thought you didn't like *me*.'

'But you –' I'm so confused. 'If you liked me, why would you suggest – why give it an end date?'

'Because when I asked you to kiss me, you looked at me like I was *mould*,' he says, and for a second I don't know what he's talking about. 'And then you came back to me the next day and you were like, yeah, let's fool around, so I told you, sure, wh–' he stops suddenly and shoots a quick look at my dad like he's just remembered he's here.

Oh.

'Whatever you want?' I say, and he nods.

'What the hell did you think I meant?'

I had assumed that had been more about the *physical* aspect. That I was only good for one thing. That he was offering me his body and not his heart. I still thought it up until a second ago – even after days of affection, and care, and ending up married to him.

'Doesn't matter,' I say, because now it doesn't. Hopefully. Because if he wanted me back then ... 'Does it still stand?'

'You're such an idiot.' He sighs. 'Yes, Tim. Please be my boyfriend.'

'And not your husband?'

'Yes.'

A smile bubbles out of me as the weight of blame lifts off my shoulders. 'OK.' It's the opposite of taking off the ring – my heart is light and skittering and I feel happy for the first time in a while. Loved. Like the world is mine. 'Boyfriend.'

The moment doesn't last. 'Are you two done? I'm too old to be standing out in the cold like this.'

'Sorry,' I say, mindful that if ever Dad needs something more to tease me about, this'll probably last until I'm fifty.

'Sorry, Sir.'

'Henry.'

'Sorry, Henry.'

'You have to say the words now,' he reminds us.

'I don't want to be married to you,' Elliott says, and squeezes my hand, pulling me a fraction closer.

'I don't want to be married to you,' I say. And I mean it. I do, because this is better. Way better, even if it had to happen in front of my dad.

He continues his recitation and I tune him out, lost in the idea that I get to keep Elliott, that he likes me, and that he likes me enough to think I'm an idiot for asking. That seems like a good sign. His hand stays clamped around mine, keeping me close, his eyes fixed on me for the most part, until the final incantation. Our fingers tingle slightly under the rings, the magic leaving them as they were before. Then he leans in and kisses me.

Dad clears his throat. 'Unconventional for a divorce, but OK. I'll wait by the car.'

I barely hear him.

The ride home is weird. It's really, really good, but that in itself is weird after so many months of things being not-quite-right with Dad gone, and worse without Lizzie, and then a bit shit with Elliott slowly breaking my heart on top of it all. Except he wasn't. And I'm an idiot.

He's holding my hand in the back of the car as I finish up our 'feast' of Whittaker's chocolate and a box of raisins, his thumb tracing lazy lines across my knuckles. He has his head back, eyes closed, knee pulled up on the seat to press against my thigh. He looks amazing, even at this hideous hour of the night. I squeeze his hand and he lifts an eyebrow at me, peering out from under his eyelashes.

'Tired?' I ask.

'Mmm. This is officially the most exhausting relationship I've even been in.'

That word again, falling so easily from his lips. I don't get time to think about it; we're back too quickly and Dad is gesturing at us to get out so he can put the car away, telling us to get some sleep and to not wake our roommates. I decide this is no time to admit we *are* roommates, at least for tonight.

'You still going to be here tomorrow?' I ask him through the car window, and he looks devastated that I need to ask, which pretty accurately sums up how I feel about it too.

'Yes, of course. We'll talk tomorrow – about everything, promise.'

'Night, Dad.' I reach in and squeeze his shoulder and he puts his hand over mine, holding it there for a moment before letting me go.

'You two OK?' Elliott asks as the Camry pulls away.

'We will be.'

'And are we OK?' He smirks, and I'm guessing he knows we are but wants to hear me say it.

'Yeah.' I try to hold my smile in but I can't, and it would be embarrassing but Elliott looks just as sappy about it.

He laces his fingers with mine and pulls me towards our room. It all seems a bit surreal. Half an hour ago I was married and everything was terrible. Now it's all fine and I have an actual, legit boyfriend.

We get back to the senior lounge and he closes the door behind us before I crowd him against it, one hand on his chest, and kiss him. He pulls me closer, hands spreading slowly across my lower back. There's a new hesitance in it, something that wasn't there before. A vulnerability. We used to do this because it felt good and we wanted to, all our feelings safely tucked away out of sight. Now, they're right here, out in the open. He's holding me close because he likes me; I'm kissing him because he's pretty and I want to and he's letting me. The heat in my belly is growing because I'm stupidly in love with him and he's OK with that, and he said *whatever you want* so I can just –

'Maybe not in the lounge,' he says, pulling back. 'We do have a bed.'

It's weird how much weight that word holds now. *Bed.* There's another layer of something on top of the knowledge that we've done everything already and it was awesome and now there's no time limit, no near-future cut-off point. The enormity of possibility is laid out before us. There's something else, though, too – a second chance to start something real. It seems to come with a strong sense of not wanting to rush in and screw it up.

'Shall we go, then?' I ask. I step back out of his grip and take his hand.

It's a short walk that takes us longer than it should. I can't keep my hands off him, and he's the same with me. We take turns pinning each other to anything solid: the sideboard, the wall, another wall, and eventually our own door. We could be making out in the safety and comfort of our room, but somehow this seems right. That new beginning, baby steps. A play at innocence before things get ... less innocent.

Once we're in our room it sort of stops, and we fall into our domestic routines and end up pyjamaed and socked and cuddled up in the middle of the bed, talking and dropping chaste kisses on anything we can reach. It's comfortable and sweet, and so quiet without Meggan's soft snores. It's amazing to think of all the things that've happened just today, let alone over the previous weeks.

'I can't believe this all happened so fast.'

'For you maybe.'

'What do you mean?'

'Manaia didn't give me away?' His eyes dart up to mine and away again.

'What?'

'She messaged to apologise earlier for maybe going a bit too far with what she said to you. Said she might've been less than helpful.'

'*That's* what she was saying? That you liked me?'

'Yeah. And ... that I might've done for a while.'

'But you and I never even talked to each other.'

'You do have qualities other than your scintillating conversation skills.'

'We spent no time together, though,' I frown. 'How could you like me?'

'You're not invisible, Tim. I could still *see* you. And I liked the look of you lately.'

'You liked the miserable fatherless bastard look?'

'Not *lately* lately, just … lately. The last couple of years you kind of …' He blushes, and it gives his words a whole new depth. 'I don't know.'

'The last couple of *years?*'

'Shut up,' he says and pokes me in the chest. 'Honestly, I don't see how it's worse than you thinking you love me after only four weeks of us actually spending time together.'

I cringe a little on the inside, but he's being honest and so should I. 'Three weeks.'

'What?'

'It was after three weeks of hanging out with you. I realised the night we got married.' I reach out and touch the gold ring that's still on his finger. We haven't swapped back yet. Now that the rings can't hurt us the impetus is gone, and honestly, I kind of like wearing something of his. 'It's one of the only things I remember from that whole night: lying there and realising I loved you, and then realising how utterly buggered I was.'

'Well. In a way you utterly *were*, but not on that couch.' His hand slides down to my hip, tugging me closer to him. 'We haven't done that in a while.'

'Romantic, thanks. I tell you I love you and you complain about the lack of sex.'

'It's been *ages*.'

'Well, stop talking then.'

The awkwardness dissolves as he nudges me onto my back and covers my mouth with his. I've missed it, being this close to him, and my entire body tingles with anticipation, knowing we don't have to hold back anymore. Time falls away. He's a bit different, maybe, or I am. Both of us. Knowing we're in this together. Holding each other tighter, and closer, and I don't want to take my lips off him for even a second. He keeps muttering things in my ear and half of them make my face heat even if we're in the middle of doing them already. I keep waiting to get tired, to want to stop and sleep, but all I need is more of him.

We're awake until it's properly morning, the alarm on his phone going off just as I am. He pulls me close and whispers in my ear, his lips brushing over my skin, 'Good morning, darling.'

SOMETHING GOOD

'Tim, what is this?'

'It's a present.'

'Why isn't it wrapped properly? You can't gift someone something in an old cardboard box.'

'Elliott,' I say. 'Open the damn thing.'

He steps closer to Sam's bed, which is still usually empty, even though we've technically all moved back to our old rooms. He pokes the carton and it makes a sound.

'What is it?' he asks.

'It's a *present*. I'm not telling you what it is, you have to open it.'

He glares a little and I smile and he gives up and turns back to the box.

'Will it hurt me?'

'I guess it might. Maybe initially by accident, but eventually ...' I think back to the last thing we took care of together and I can't bring myself to lie to him. 'Yeah. It'll hurt. But hopefully not for about sixteen years or so.'

'What have you done?'

'Open the box.'

He does. Lifts the flaps one at a time and stands back, waiting. There's a small scratching sound and a pathetic mewl.

He leans forward and peeks inside and I watch his face change. His dubious expression softens, and his mouth opens slightly. He looks over at me, sitting on our bed.

'You bought me a kitten.'

'I bought *us* a kitten.'

'Is it safe to pick it up?'

'Of course. She's twelve weeks old, she's litter-trained, and she likes people. Scared of butterflies, though.'

Elliott reaches into the box and pulls out a fluffy black explosion of fur and toes and panic. He pulls her close and bundles her against his chest and she clings to him, eyes wide. 'She's so fluffy,' he breathes. 'Where did she come from?'

'There was a, um, night-time visitation at the cattery up in Greymouth. A rather determined tomcat got into things he shouldn't have. So she's half-Siamese and half-Norwegian Forest cat, and an embarrassment to her pedigree parents. She'll be pretty big and very chatty.'

She chirps as if to prove her worth, and Elliott beams at

her. 'Is that where you went with your dad this weekend? Greymouth? Is that where we're working next year?'

'Near there. The place is hidden, obviously, so I don't know exactly where it is. Dad was obliged to blindfold me since you and I haven't been officially sworn in. From the inside it's just another underground compound with a bunch of surveillance equipment.'

'So what happens to the cat when we go off to work with him next year?' Elliott says, his brow furrowed in worry. It's ridiculous that it took me so long to realise what we had – *have* – when he falls in love so obviously. 'We can't just have her for a few months and then leave her behind.'

'Norwegian *Forest* cat. She comes with us. Dad said a lot of what we'll be doing is remote surveillance work – apparently once the cameras and mics are installed it's mostly sitting around watching them and hoping nothing happens. Dad figured it'd be nice for you and I to have a little friend to keep us company,' I say, and he seems to like that, knowing the three of us won't be separated after school ends. 'Though obviously we need to train her to ignore birds.'

'Of course.' He smiles. 'I don't think we can be part of a conservation team like that if our cat is part of the problem.'

'I think there are more threatening things in the forest than a cat, Elliott. That's kind of the point of the team existing.'

'Whatever. It's my turn to choose the first name,' he says.

'OK. I've been calling her Mog, though. If you like that.'

'Oh.' He looks over at me and I can see him melting from the inside. 'After the cat in the book.'

'Yeah.'

'It'd be nice to have something to remember our first daughter by,' he says. 'I'm happy with Mog. But I'm going to choose the middle name.'

'Agreed.'

And that's how our cat ends up being called Mog Maleficent Parker-Te Maro. She sleeps on our bed, and she follows Elliott around, and she squeaks every time we pick her up. She also wakes us up in the morning because she's hungry and bored and sometimes we have to get up in the night because she's tried to do something silly and got stuck somewhere. But she's ours, and she's real, and no-one can take her away.

ACKNOWLEDGEMENTS

The first shout-out goes to Luna, the editor of my dreams, who has been delightfully fun to work with, and my Beta Prime, Christina, who yells at my characters in the most gratifying way.

To my family, thank you for acting super smug when you told random strangers about this, that was also gratifying. My mother has told literally everyone in my home town and I'm so glad I finally gave her something new to be excited about. Thank you to James, my supportive, patient partner and Chief Male-Anatomy Consultant, who put up with several bouts of me not doing my share of the housework so I could write. Thanks also to Uncle Lawyer who helped with the contract, and Uncle Accountant who will hide my millions of author dollars from the IRD.

To all the baby gays out there (hello LC Skittles!), and all the Kiwi kids who've not seen themselves represented in a book before, and all the librarians and booksellers who cringed apologetically when I asked 'do you have any NZ YA from the last five years', this is for you.

To Emma, Sonia and Marie, thanks for being there when I got life-changing emails, love yous. Kia ora to Carol,

Jenn and Frances, for the te reo help. To Tayyibah and Min, Kiara and Riya, and all my other favourite students, thank you for your earnest and ongoing enthusiasm. To my students in general, thanks for not throwing things at me every time I said, 'As a published author …'

To my collection of writing people: The Pingwings, The Pirates, The Tired Owls, Maggie, Sacha, and Kate – weird shit is possible, take heart, keep writing the good write.

A big, wide, emoji hug to Astolat, AO3, fandom in general, and all my Discord and Tumblr peeps. :ta-da:

One thousand kudos to Julia, who designed the cover and made me look cool (and my boys look hot). Thanks to Penny, who always brought good news, to Pat for the flawless typesetting, to Jane for the flawless contract, to Ella for proofing and loving Taylor Swift, to Lauren, who did a bunch of smart marketing stuff I probably only know a small fraction of, and to Kate, who made strangers look in my general direction and coerced me into filming myself, for which I will never forgive her :P To everyone else at HGCP whose name I don't know, but who knows Tim's name, thanks for your enthusiasm and hard work. Team Te Maro!

Many :sob: and :heart: emojis to the first ARC readers, especially Hannah, Tobias and Liz (who is drinking port somewhere while I write this).

And lastly, thanks to Marisa, the most enthusiastic publisher ever, whose pathological fear of missing out led me to put her thank you at the very end, just to mess with her. XX

ABOUT THE AUTHOR

H.S. Valley grew up on the Waitematā Harbour in Auckland, at the foot of Takarunga. She was raised by her fabulous mum, her deeply Scottish grandmother, and her quietly Canadian stepdad. She met her father years later in a cafe and has been learning about her whakapapa through his endless stories ever since. Usually over coffee and cake that neither of them should be eating.

She now lives with her partner and an unreasonable number of plants, many of which haven't died yet. She likes unicorns, rainbows, flannel shirts and her Subaru. No-one, other than herself, has ever been surprised to find out she's bi.

This is the first original novel she's finished, but it won't be the last.

the ampersand prize

Making writers authors

H.S. Valley's debut novel, *Tim Te Maro and the Subterranean Heartsick Blues*, won the 2020 Ampersand Prize, the premier award in Australia and New Zealand for first-time authors.

Since it was established in 2011, the Ampersand Prize has launched the careers of some amazing writers, including Erin Gough (*The Flywheel, Amelia Westlake*), Melissa Keil (*Life in Outer Space, The Incredible Adventures of Cinnamon Girl, The Secret Science of Magic*), Cally Black (*In the Dark Spaces*), Rhiannon Williams (*Ottilie Colter and the Narroway Hunt, Ottilie Colter and the Master of Monsters, Ottilie Colter and the Withering World*), Lisa Siberry (*The Brilliant Ideas of Lily Green, Plum and Woo: The Puzzling Pearls*), and Frances Chapman (*Stars Like Us*). Their books have won awards and been published all around the world.

For more information on the Ampersand Prize, including how to submit your manuscript, follow us at @AmpersandYA or visit our website: https://www.hardiegrant.com/au/hardie-grant-childrens-publishing/ampersand-prize